THE MASKED RIDER ARCHIVES
VOLUME 4

MASKED RIDER

ARCHIVES VOLUME 4

FEATURING
THE FORTUNE HUNTERS OF CHAVO
BY GEORGE C. SHEDD
AND
WIDE OPEN TOWN
BY JACK DRUMMOND

ILLUSTRATIONS BY
MONROE EISENBERG

ALTUS PRESS • 2025

PUBLISHING HISTORY

"The Fortune Hunters of Chavo" originally appeared in the May 1936 issue of *The Masked Rider Western Magazine* (Volume 3, Number 2).

"Wide Open Town" originally appeared in the June 1936 issue of *The Masked Rider Western Magazine* (Volume 3, Number 3).

TABLE OF

CONTENTS

THE FORTUNE
HUNTERS OF
CHAVO
BY GEORGE C. SHEDD

CHAPTER I

STRANGE HAPPENINGS ON A ROAD

SILENT, MOTIONLESS, TWO men peered intently through a mask of bushes on a wooded slope. The men themselves were not masked; they depended entirely on the screen furnished them by nature at this point, some sixty feet above a road that wound at the base of their hill. One of the men wore the sombrero and dress of a *vaquero*, but the arresting contours of his face stamped him at once as not of a common variety. The pride of ancestry flowed in his blood and spoke in his features. He was the Mexican Indian, Yaqui in heritage, Blue Hawk. The other, garbed in black, was the most famous outlaw in the country. But for this moment he was not The Masked Rider—he was Wayne Morgan, alert, cautious, secure, but inquisitive.

At the base of the hill, and crowding the road close, was a mountain creek. Ordinarily only fetlock deep at this ford, where the wagon trail forked with one branch crossing the water course, it was this morning running and boiling wild and swift, fed by a heavy rain somewhere far back in the forest-blanketed chain of peaks. Between its borders of underbrush it tossed and rushed with a low roar, with sinister flashes, with a seeming purpose that was intent and malevolent. At places it lapped the very edge of the road.

But the lone rider approaching down this road did not so much as glance at the flooded stream. A thick-set cowman

of about sixty years, he rode chin on breast, unheeding, unseeing. A long, gray mustache dipped below the line of his jaws. His weather-beaten face sagged in folds and his lips twitched and jerked. Directly beneath the watchers, where lay the hidden ford, his horse stopped, snorted, and looked around at its rider, which roused the man from his preoccupation.

He stared at the racing current as if in surprise and then cast his gaze uncertainly about. His countenance showed worn and haggard, his eyes bloodshot. Suddenly a fierce satisfaction appeared on his face, he gripped the reins and plunged spurs into his mount, at which the beast bounded into the water and plunged into the brown current. The cowman kicked his feet from the stirrups and let go the lines, spreading his arms wide and raising his face, crying, "Take me, drown me! And God have mercy on my guilty soul!"

But as swift and strong as was the creek, it was narrow and the horse so determined that two desperate lunges bore it and its master through. It scrambled up the farther bank in a final effort, there to stand streaming water and

blowing moisture from its nostrils. Raising right hand, the cowman clenched fist and shook it at the water. "You wouldn't, curse you!" he shouted, savagely. "I begged it, but you wouldn't! And now you're chucklin' and leerin' at me and mockin' me, leavin' me to live on, damned and double-damned!"

His face became distorted in anguish, his uplifted fist slowly sank, and his chin again fell upon his breast. After a moment the horse stepped off of its own volition on the trail that led northward along the foothills, until beast and man passed out of sight over a rise.

Wayne Morgan and his bronze-skinned companion regarded each other with questioning brows. Among the rough men of the wild Southwest whom they encountered violent passions were not uncommon, but this sudden revelation of bleak despair, of the naked, tormented soul of a chance passer-by, left them startled.

"*Por Dios,* that one rides with *un diablo* on his back!" Blue Hawk exclaimed, at last.

"With a devil is right," Wayne Morgan agreed.

"Perhaps he will put a gun to his ear and a bullet in his head, *señor.*"

"No; he wants to die, but he draws the line at killing himself, that's plain. We all draw certain lines we won't cross; taking one's own life is the last one for everybody who is sane. But he is in bad trouble."

BLUE HAWK GRINNED contemptuously, and said, "It is nothing to us, this trouble of another."

"Well forget it," was the answer. "For once trouble rode right past us on horseback, and kept right on going. Our camp up there in the timber is well hidden. Our horses have good grazing and will get the rest they need. We'll rest too and keep away from everyone until tomorrow night, then we'll slip down near that town we see yonder in the south, you can buy some supplies there, and we'll push on."

Wayne Morgan's dark, stern though youthful face relaxed, as his gaze, keen and penetrative, slowly swept the wooded flanks of the mountain range extending north and south, the open, tawny, broken land in front, and the solitary phantom peaks in the east.

The wagon trail below them wound up the creek canyon to a basin where lay several small ranches, "nesters," by the look of them, whence a horse trail ascended to a high pass. The two men had come over the pass, circling the grassy basin to escape notice. One could surmise that the road forking northward led to other ranches, in any case, to the ranch of the cowman just gone. Visible in the south, five or six miles distant, was a cluster of dots by the creek that flowed thither, at the base of a mountain: a settlement, like most in remote regions of Arizona, half native Mexican village and half American cowtown.

"Yes, we'll keep away from everybody," Wayne Morgan repeated, "and all I ask is that everybody keep away from us."

A note of grimness sounded in his last utterance, almost like a challenge. For Fate had a way of mocking his desires and intentions, this man whom the law had proscribed, on whose head was much prize money, whom it pursued relentlessly, and who even to his faithful companion, Blue Hawk, was animated by strange purposes and actions, fraught with peril, as a result of accidental situations. It seemed, in truth, as if Fate deliberately spun for him webs of danger from events.

As all unknown to him, it was doing now!

Two hours wore away. Another traveler appeared on the road from the town, driving a team pulling a light mountain wagon painted red and yellow that contained painted wooden cases. The watchers grew more and more curious as the outfit drew near. Wayne Morgan distinguished painted lettering on both wagon and trunks.

"Of all things to see in this back country!" he said, with a chuckle.

"What is it, *señor?*"

"A quack doctor with his medicine wagon. But look, what's the matter with the man? He's waving and talking."

The team was plodding forward at a slow footpace, the lines hung loose and at the moment slipped to the ground over the dashboard. The driver, a small pursy individual wearing a long black coat and a plaid vest, check trousers stuffed in boots, white collar and bow tie, and a battered silk hat, was gesticulating and gabbling steadily.

"Drunk," said Blue Hawk.

"Doesn't act as if he were drunk," Morgan replied. "More as if he were crazy."

"He eat of the loco, mebbe," the Yaqui remarked.

The team and wagon arrived below them, where one of the horses chanced to tread on a dragging line, which caused both animals to stop. The driver rose to his feet, but there was no break in his movement of hands or racing talk, in the turning of his face now this way and now that, in the feverish medicine sale "spiel" being delivered to some imaginary crowd.

Suddenly the words died. The little quack doctor swayed, put a hand to his eyes, and collapsed where he was like an empty sack.

"Come," Wayne Morgan said, quickly.

"No, no, *señor.*"

"The man's sick, delirious."

"Was it not agreed we would keep away from everybody, *amigo?*"

"We can't let the man die!"

"Bah, what is this one to us! You did not ask him to come."

"He came, just the same."

"Always so, always so you say you will do one thing and you do another, *señor,*" the Mexican Indian grimly intoned. "Always so you risk the head in business what is not your own."

A faint, shadowy smile showed on Morgan's lips at this accusation; beckoning, he moved through the undergrowth down the slope, and with a shrug Blue Hawk followed. On reaching the road both men scrutinized the trail in both directions before emerging from cover.

Morgan swiftly climbed into the wagon, examined the unconscious doctor and spoke to his companion.

"Skin burning and mottled, pulse weak and fast. At a guess, I'd say he has mountain fever. Bit by a tick, likely. Can't leave him. May die anyway. Dip up some water in your hat and I'll cool his face and hands. Step lively. We'll drive up to the first ravine and take him to camp."

"To our camp, *señor?*" Blue Hawk cried, incredulously.

"Yes. Nothing else to do. Move him somewhere into other hands tonight. Now the water. Then lead the team up the trail."

"This one is loco, you are the same to do this, and me, I will be loco too," was the ironical answer. "For, is it not said God guards the mad?" And with his hat he dipped water from the creek.

AN HOUR LATER the wagon was in camp and the unconscious stranger lying on a blanket. Morgan had given him a big dose of quinine, which he found in a search of the trunks, and bathed his body to reduce the fever.

"Nothing more we can do," the young man said. "He'll have to make his own fight. You covered our tracks where we turned off the trail?"

"*Si, señor.*"

For a moment Morgan studied the sick man's face, listened to his hurried breathing, and turned to the team. When the horses were unharnessed and staked out to graze, he and the Indian set to work to move their effects and mounts to a new spot higher in the mountains, for caution warned them that they ran a double risk in remaining where so conspicuous an object as the brightly painted wagon stood. That change made, they returned through the woods to their place of concealment above the road. Their first watch over the road had been but idle observation, this one now would be alert, wary, and purposeful. Danger had a way of flowering for them from even commonplace happenings.

Hardly had they halted at their post when Blue Hawk thrust his head forward, sniffing.

"Smoke of tobacco," he whispered, to Wayne Morgan. "Very little, but I smell it. Cigarette smoke." He remained leaning forward with nostrils expanding, then he darted pointing forefinger toward the road below in a snake-stroke. "In the trail, see! Cigarette! Still burning!"

"I see it," Morgan said.

"One has just passed, throwing it down there."

"Probably one of the ranchers living up in the basin."

Yet a sense of uneasiness pervaded both men, in part

because they were "hunted" and because in part they felt it an unnatural circumstance for travelers to be so frequent on a lone wagon trail. The sun stood not yet overhead, and already three persons had come.

"And here comes a fourth!" Morgan breathed.

"*Valgame Dios!* Is this a city street?" the Yaqui muttered.

This visitor was again a horseman, his mount advancing at the mile-eating easy lope of a cowhand horse, which dropped to a shuffling canter and then to a walk as the road ascent increased at the mouth of the canyons. The rider was a townsman, as the pair on the slope perceived, a thin middle-aged man with a reddish moustache and bony frame. He was examining the flooded creek with interest and, as he passed below, reined his horse closer to the water, bent a little sidewise for a better view.

A rifle shot *pommed* in the canyon. And the horseman, who had leaned over to gaze at the water, leaned farther and farther over, until his horse, shying suddenly, he pitched headforemost into the stream and was swept behind the nearer border of bushes and out of sight.

"Ambushed, by heavens!" Morgan hissed. "After that killer, Blue Hawk! Grab him, if you can; get a look at him, in any case. I'll follow the other down and drag out his body if it lodges. Of all the cowardly murders!"

The Indian vanished noiselessly, his moccasined feet bearing him swiftly on his vengeance hunt. As for Wayne Morgan, he raced southward on the slope, weaving through the undergrowth parallel to the creek and striving to catch a glimpse of its grisly flotsam. He dipped down into a gully and, while ripping a passage through a dense growth of mountain maple, heard a roll of hoofbeats as a horse raced down the road.

The killer! Morgan swung sidewise and plunged fiercely to extricate himself from the thicket, to reach the mouth of the draw so that he might catch a look at the rider. But when he broke out beside the wagon-trail the fellow was two hundred yards away, and he and his mount at the instant disappearing around the shoulder of a hill. Of all infernal luck!

A HALF-OBSCURED, HALF-SUBMERGED mass which lay pressed against a bush of the creek's border attracted Wayne Morgan's look. Leaping across the road, he gripped a sapling, stepped into the swirling water and seized by the coat collar the snagged form of the ambusher's victim. A heave and the man came free, a strong pull and Morgan had him half out the stream. He was turning the dripping figure face downward to allow water to dribble from the mouth when the horse which had borne the man hither came galloping down the trail, reins knotted over the pommel and stirrups swinging. It shied off from the spot where Morgan knelt, but thundered on. Then Blue Hawk came running along.

"*Señor*, I was too late," he stated, when he arrived. "He rode away before I saw him, that one of evil. But I found where his horse stood hidden and where the man waited. Though I saw neither man nor horse, their tracks remained; I shall know those tracks when I see them again."

"Yes."

"Seeing you here, I came, after tying the lines of this one's horse and starting it off with a slap. All that is left to do is to bury this body."

"He's not dead," Morgan replied.

"No?"

"See here." The speaker pointed at a crimson gash in the

prostrate man's scalp just above the left ear. "The bullet only creased him. Evidently his act of bending over to look at the water as that killer fired was what saved him."

"*Bueno.*"

"But the scoundrel imagines he's dead, shot through the brain and his body carried away by the creek. Well, it's a bad joke on him, or will be."

"And now, *señor?*"

"We'll add this one to the other. Can't leave him here in this condition, any more than the other. Looks like we're making a collection of sick or wounded men, Blue Hawk."

"Always, always, you—"

"Don't say that again," Morgan interrupted. "Throw him over your shoulder and start with him for camp; he's a light weight. It may be some time before he comes to. Never can tell with a skull crease."

"We get more loco all the time. But, *señor*, I will take him as you wish. And then do we come back for more?"

"This probably ends our run of luck. Things run in threes, it's said, so we should be done for today."

"Yes, we have seen a man wanting to die, a man selling medicine to spirits, and a man shot off his horse. It is enough. It is very *malo*. Tonight we will leave these men at a ranch and go from this place before a worse thing happens." He hoisted the insensible man to his shoulder and with Morgan behind him began the ascent of the slope. "Will it not be so, *amigo?* Will we not play safe?"

Wayne Morgan was examining some letters, wet but with writing still decipherable on the envelopes, which he had taken from the man's coat pocket.

"By this I see he is an editor of a newspaper. These are

addressed to him. The man's name is Edward Grantly, and the town yonder is Chavo."

"But we will ride away tonight, *señor?*"

"We ride to town."

"No."

"Yes. I have this affair to look into."

"Always you—"

"Don't repeat it, Blue Hawk. This is a grave matter and we're involved in it in spite of ourselves."

"Very *malo*, but am I not your *amigo?*" was the response, given in a brisker tone. "We'll go to town and look into this thing, as you say. Do we not laugh at Sheriffs and others who seek you?"

A smile crossed Wayne Morgan's lips, but his eyes remained cold. There was truth in Blue Hawk's words, and it may have been that which caused his lips to unbend—or perhaps Fate—

CHAPTER II

A SECRET SEARCH

THE MASKED RIDER sat his black stallion in the
gloom of giant, gnarled cottonwoods in a bend of
the creek behind the little town of Chavo. The night was
moonless and the starlight did not penetrate the inky darkness under the leafy boughs. The powerful ebon steed and
his rider, hatted and hooded and enveloped in a voluminous cloak, all black, would have been invisible to one passing two paces from the huge tree trunk where they waited.

A stone's throw in front of the cottonwoods lay the town,
two straggling rows of flat-roofed 'dobe structures facing
each other across a street that was no more than a widened
section of a road. The shapes of the squat buildings were
vaguely outlined in the starlight, in several of which lamp-
lighted windows and open doorways formed yellow panels.
From one such came the muted sounds of men's voices,
burst of laughter, or the musical tinkle and thump of a
piano: a saloon's clamor on a lively night.

To the hooded horseman there was nothing new in the
scene. He had known many such towns, native villages
little changed by the addition of rough, aggressive Americans who came in with the settlement of the Southwest.
His interest in it lay only in the fact that here was centered
some malignant spirit engaged in devilish schemes; and
though he was himself a breaker of certain laws, his nature

revolted at sheer wickedness and flamed into active opposition.

From a little way off came the chirp of a sleepy bird. He answered with a like signal. A moment later Blue Hawk spoke low at his knee.

"*Señor*, I have the food, and the cartridges."

"Good. No one grew curious?"

"No one was in the store but a Mexican clerk. Him I told that I was a man from the north hastening south to a dying man, not stopping even to sleep."

"Did you find the newspaper office?"

"*Si, si.* I said I had a message for one named Grantly and the clerk told me he lived behind his office. It is the third building south of the saloon."

"Very well. Stay here, until I come back. Get the sack tied behind your saddle."

"Be careful, *señor.* A man went into the place."

"What more?"

"Nothing. He broke the lock of the door at the back, where I followed him, and went in. I waited and watched. But he struck no light and I did not hear him move about after entering. Yet he stayed there. So at last I came away. What do you make of that one?"

"He's there for a reason, which I'll try to learn. Perhaps he is the fellow who shot Grantly. In any case, I suspect he knows of the shooting, or he wouldn't have risked breaking into the place. It's a lead, anyway."

With that The Masked Rider swung down from his saddle and moved rapidly off toward the south end of the street, keeping near the trees. Ten minutes later he stood at a rear corner of the long low structure which Blue Hawk had designated. His approach through the greasewood clumps spotting the open ground behind had been slow, vigilant, and soundless. For now a light moved inside the building.

HE CREPT TO a window, whose lower sash was raised a few inches. He flashed a glance within and then crouched to listen. What he had seen was the interior of the newspaper editor's bedroom, a plainly furnished chamber in the disorder resulting from a fierce rapid search being made by two men, one a big Mexican, with heavy eyebrows and a huge sweeping moustache, from whose vest hung a massive gold watch chain, the other a slim, smooth-shaven, hatchet-faced American, whose mouth was but a thin hard line under his hawklike nose.

"See, we find nothing," the Mexican was saying, turning from the mattress which he had slashed open with a knife to examine. "Neither in the office nor in these rooms."

"We're not done yet," the other snapped.

"Perhaps Grantly lied when he told you he had a written and signed confession of where the money went from that miserable wretch of a bookkeeper who lost his nerve and skipped out."

"No, Grantly didn't lie," was the reply. "He wouldn't bluff, he wouldn't have dared threaten me unless he had the confession, Valdez. If I had that yellow cur Simmons here, I'd cut his throat for letting slip to Grantly while he was drunk what he did, so that Grantly was able to scare him into writing and signing the story. I thought I had the young fool firmly under my hand."

"A bad mistake, Pete, a bad mistake. Perhaps Grantly carried it with him, that paper."

"If I knew that for sure, I wouldn't worry. It would be gone along with his body."

"Ah! Since we do not find it, it must be gone."

"We'll keep looking until we're sure. It certainly isn't hidden here in his bedroom, for we haven't missed a place. We'll hunt in the office again."

"No, Pete. Already someone may have seen a light and become curious. Let us go; we can come back after midnight when we will not be seen."

"Anyone seeing a light will think that Grantly is here."

"Not if he chanced to glance in a window and saw us with this mess."

"Mebbe you're right."

"We'll go to your office in the Court House, Pete, and talk things over. Me, I am not much anxious about this paper, I believe it is gone with Grantly. Ha, it was lucky that you saw and recognized him as he stole away when you looked out of the door last night during that business with Underwood! Otherwise he would have had even more than this confession to use against us. Now he can't interfere with our using the deed Underwood gave us after—ha, ha, ha!—he killed his friend. We are very kind and good to that cowman in agreeing, for a little consideration between old friends, not to tell he shot Bill Lawson and so saving him from being hanged, eh, Pete?"

"We've only begun operations," was the sardonic response. "Yesterday morning things looked bad, but by this morning we held all the aces."

"And that young cowboy in jail?"

"We want a man to fill the role of killer of Bill Lawson, don't we? Need one to make the story good. I figgered it out this evening that Les Bridges would fill the bill perfectly. He's hotheaded and rash, as everybody knows; he was drinking some last night and put up a hard scrap at daylight when Joe pulled him in; and in the hearing of three or four men quarreled with Lawson about midnight. Lawson was found in the middle of the street shot dead. Who killed him? Why, this young puncher." The speaker paused, then continued. "And with him out of the way—"

"Go on, Pete."

"Nothing."

"With him out of the way, why, Pete Brill will grab that pretty Betty Underwood, eh?"

"You repeat that to anyone and you'll have me to deal with," the other grated.

"Now, now, Pete; I was only joking. What you do or don't do there is nothing to me. I will not remember it, what I said. Look, what's that? *Dios,* I saw a black shadow at the edge of the window! If someone is there! Quick, your gun!"

WHEN, HOWEVER, THE two men burst out the rear door and ran around the corner to the window, and then around the whole building, and finally hunted about over the ground on all sides, they found no one. Warned by the Mexican's exclamation, The Masked Rider had flitted away as silently as a bat. He heard from his place in the grease-wood the hurried search made by the pair, their guarded utterances, and final words agreeing that Valdez must have been deceived in thinking he saw something.

The light was put out in the building and the two men departed, moving northward in the starlight behind the row of structures on that side of the street.

Like a shadow The Masked Rider trailed them. Already he had learned more than he had anticipated, and with luck he might gain still new facts. Of one thing he was convinced, this pair of scoundrels were the prime actors in some diabolical conspiracy being perpetrated on the community. They were prepared to go to any depth of treachery or infamy.

He was led to a square, two-story stone building at the upper end of the street that stood a hundred yards back from the roadway and an equal distance apart from the nearest house. Rows of young leafy trees surrounded it, while in the rear was a low adobe jail, as The Masked Rider discovered on making a circuit of the main building, a court house.

Suddenly he checked his step when a few paces from the jail. A taunting voice was speaking.

"I been waitin' for the chance to wring some of the smartness outa you, Les Bridges," it said. "And it's come. You'll learn what a real tough *hombre* can do when I set to work on you tomorrow. I don't like your face, I don't like your talk, I don't like your smart alec ways, nor anything about you. I'm comin' in tomorrow mornin' and beat you numb, just to satisfy my feelin's. And don't imagine the Sheriff will prevent it, because he's at the other end of the County huntin' a horse thief. And don't figger any of your friends are goin' to help you, because they won't be let."

"Put your face closer to the bars of this window, fella," came a reply, from within the jail.

"You must think me easy, cowboy."

"I don't have to think; I know what you are—a sneak and a crook and a snake in the grass. Your head's shaped like a snake's and if you come in here and try to beat me I'll crush it under my heel as I would a rattler's."

"Just for that I'll gun-whip you good tomorrow. And how I'm goin' to laugh, afterwards, when I see you swing for murderin' Bill Lawson."

"Bill Lawson? Me killed him?"

"Sure. You was seen."

"You're a liar!"

"Cuss away. Won't do you no good."

"I know who's behind all this," the prisoner exclaimed, angrily. "It's Pete Brill—and you're only his hound dog! I have always been suspicious of him ever since I saw him stackin' a deck in a poker game; but I learned for sure when Ed Grantly told me last night that—well, something."

"So you learned something, did you?"

"You're danged right I did."

"Well, I'll see Pete about it right away. For once you've talked yourself into a hole. Mebbe we'll have to stage a little accident to shut your mouth."

In the man's tone was a hard, sinister note. That this creature was a Deputy-Sheriff, that he was the Joe referred to in the talk between Valdez and Pete Brill in the editor's bedroom, and that his remark carried a deadly menace for the young cowboy, The Masked Rider realized. In such a situation, to see a menace to an innocent person was for him to act.

As the Deputy turned away from the window and moved off toward the Court House, The Masked Rider glided swiftly after him, his hand drawing his six-gun. A panther could not have been more silent, more intent. In ten seconds he was at the heels of the unsuspecting Joe, the gun swept up and down in a single movement and the gun barrel thudded dully on the hatted head. Without so much as a grunt the man buckled at the knees and went down in a heap.

The outlaw's fingers expertly searched his pockets and drew forth a ring of keys. Wheeling, he strode to the jail where after harkening for a moment toward the Court

House, he pressed against the jail wall by the door and felt for the keyhole. Finding it, he inserted one key after another in trial for the right one.

"Keep away, you skunk!" the prisoner shouted.

A KEY TURNED the bolt. The Masked Rider withdrew it and sought the barred window where the Deputy had stood to hurl his taunts.

"Bridges," he spoke.

"Who's there? Don't sound like Joe Mallett."

"It's not, but another man, never mind who. I knocked him out and took his keys and unlocked the door. You can walk out. Get out and make tracks for a hiding place where you'll be safe until you can stack up with friends. You're in danger. Get going and going fast."

"Say, who're you givin' me orders?" the youth demanded, resentfully. "This looks like a trick to me."

"Don't be a fool."

"And I don't intend to be fooled, either," was the retort. "Even if you ain't one of 'em, I ain't goin' to run like a coyote at the first yell. I ain't done nothin' and I ain't afraid. What's more, I'm goin' into the Court House and get the gun they took off me. I ain't leavin' town without that. If this bunch wants trouble with me, they sure can have it."

"You'll play right into their hands, boy. Use sense. A murder charge is being framed against you and your enemies will stop at nothing. Leave town, I tell you, until your friends can act for you."

"I never killed Bill Lawson."

"They'll fake evidence you did."

"And who'd believe 'em? Everybody knows I wouldn't lift a finger 'gainst Bill. People would laugh at a charge of

THE FORTUNE HUNTERS OF CHAVO

murder laid on me. I ain't goin' to be driven by them, or you, or anybody. I'm free, white, and twenty-one. I'll go and come as I please, and to hell with any gent who tries to stop me! And I ain't goin' without my gun, you can swear by that." He paused, and concluded, "Now, Mister, tell me who you are."

There was no answer. He had seen no one, peer as he would. Puzzled, he presently moved to the door and tried it to see whether or not it was unlocked; it swung open and he bent low and dashed out. Well, the unknown visitor had told the truth; he had unlocked the door. After casting a look about, the puncher struck off for the Court House, his gaze fixed on two lighted windows in a room on the second floor which he knew to be the County Treasurer's office.

He had not seen the prone form of the unconscious Deputy, nor did he see now the shape of The Masked Rider lurking in darkness a score of yards off along the wall. The window was too high from the ground for the young fellow to look in, though he heard voices through the opening. So he set off running around the building to the front, where a main entrance led into a hallway, off which various official chambers opened.

Without warning he burst in upon Pete Brill and the Mexican, Valdez, who sat at a table discussing matters relating to a document spread before them. This paper Brill quickly folded and thrust into an envelope and laid aside on the board, facing around to confront the hatless, disheveled, angry young puncher.

"Who let you out, Bridges?" the official questioned, with sharp wrath.

"Just walked out when the door was unlocked," the boy barked, "and that's enough for you. Now I want my gun.

It was took off me in here by your polecat Joe Mallett and put in a drawer of your desk, which shows the Sheriff had nothin' to do with my arrest. I want it, and I'm going to have it." With which he made a spring forward to clutch Brill's hand that had dropped toward a drawer.

Brill sprang up, crying to Valdez to seize the cowboy. Instantly the three men became involved in a furious struggle, swaying, staggering to and fro over the floor, a contorted group, until foaming and cursing Bridges was dragged to the doorway and out into the hall. There, however, he suddenly jerked his arms free as he realized he was being hauled back to the jail, wriggled his body loose and leaped out into the night.

"Got away!" Valdez growled, his lips curled back in rage. "He struck me in the stomach!"

"Not escaped for good, though. Joe will round him up again," Pete Brill snarled, fingering his bruised mouth. "The young fool shall pay for these blows."

"Well, let us go back; a drink will do us good."

THEY ENTERED AN instant after the hooded and cloaked figure of The Masked Rider passed through the open window. On the table was the long envelope, in all appearance untouched and with its contents the same as before. Brill picked it up, ran the flap along his tongue, sealed it, and put it away in his safe.

"When shall we record this deed of Underwood's ranch?" Valdez inquired.

"Not until everything is cleared up."

"How he looked when he was signing it! As if he were handing over his heart! Well, my friend, such is life. Men of courage and brains take what they will and keep what they have. That little paper in the safe means at least one hundred thousand dollars to us."

Outside under the window The Masked Rider smiled under his hood. That little paper in the safe meant exactly nothing to anybody, for it was only a folded blank sheet. The deed rested in the outlaw's pocket.

CHAPTER III

A COMEDY OF MASKS

NOT AT ONCE did the hooded outlaw leave his vantage point. Too much was yet obscure for him to perceive the main threads of the plotters' web. What he had heard at the newspaper man's house and here had convinced him that the rancher Underwood was the chief victim of these crooks' machinations, as the murder of his foreman Bill Lawson was the center knot of the mesh. Brill and Valdez had blackmailed the cowman out of his property because of the killing; the cowman believed he had committed murder, or he would not have submitted to their threats; and yet Valdez' reference to the fact that Grantly had been a witness of the affair and would have been able to use it against them if he had not been taken care of had stirred a suspicion in The Masked Rider's mind that the whole business was a trick.

He stood pondering possibilities. Had the cowman not actually slain his foreman? How could that be and the man still imagine he had? How could he have been deluded so completely? What happening had occurred that enabled these two wretches to seize upon the circumstance, bend it to their advantage, terrify the cattleman, and step in a few hours from a bad financial condition up to one assured and strong. For, by Pete Brill's own statement in answer to Valdez during the colloquy in Grantly's bedroom, that was what had occurred.

Underwood! The Masked Rider had already divined his identity. Who other could he be than that haggard-faced, despairing horseman who, at the creek ford below the northern hill, had that morning unwittingly revealed to the unseen watchers such profound remorse, such self-loathing of soul, such desperate desire for death? And at the thought the jaws of the hooded outlaw closed hard and his hands clenched.

Inside the office he heard the clink of bottle on glasses. Then talk was resumed, and he strained to hear.

"An idea has come to me," Valdez spoke. "It is to advertise this ranch in the East and sell it quick for cash, even if we get but half its value. That would be fifty thousand dollars. The cows, which we'll take from Underwood, too, will bring as much even if sold now out of season. Then we'll have enough for you to pay back what you borrowed from the County, keep our mine working, and have some for ourselves, too. As you know, I have used every penny I could scrape up, and I haven't a dollar to buy goods for my store, where the shelves already are becoming bare. Who would have guessed that damned mine would have hid its gold so deep? But it is there. We are close to it now, surely. We can't stop. To sell the ranch and the herd for cash quickly is necessary."

"I don't put another cent into that mine," Pete Brill snapped. "It would be to throw away more money in the hole; we've got nothing and there is no prospect of getting any gold in paying quantities, by all the signs, and so we'll just pocket our loss and quit. Only a fool keeps on with a losing proposition."

"But I tell you, Pete, it is there, the gold!"

"Nonsense."

"If we keep on with it, we'll be rich. You're mad to think of stopping. Why, you took this forty thousand of the county money to put in it, and I put in even more, selling all my cows and my ranch and throwing in all the money I had! And now you talk of pocketing the loss!"

A prolonged silence followed, until Brill replied, "All right, *amigo*, we'll go on with it. I won't let you down."

IN THE RESPONSE there was a peculiar note, which to The Masked Rider made the words ring false. Some thought, some subtle consideration, had caused the County Treasurer to make a pretense of yielding to the indignant protest of his partner, though in reality he purposed doing what he had stated. Evidently the big, robust Mexican missed the undertone of insincerity, for he said:

"*Buen', buen'!* I knew when you took second thought, Pete, that you would see the foolishness of stopping development when we are at the point of success. And it is agreed that we sell the ranch and cows?"

"No. That is not necessary."

"But this shortage of County funds? How will you pay it back?"

"I shall not pay it back."

"But—"

"That money is to be stolen."

"Stolen? When it is already gone?"

"Exactly. And the rest that is in the safe, and the bonds there, too, will go with it. A thief is going to take it all, some convenient thief. And I shall rave loudest of all for his capture. Nobody except us knows that forty thousand is gone—us and that damned clerk who knows too much to come back and that dead editor. You must think me simple-minded to pay back the money when a little hold-up will make it unnecessary, and put the rest of the funds in my hands, in addition."

"Ah-h-h-h!" came from Valdez' lips, in profound admiration. "Long as I've known you, Pete, I never realised until now how good are your brains!"

"You don't yet know how good they are, for that matter," Brill retorted, with a trace of sarcasm. "You've still more to learn about 'em. Well, you'll get a slice of the plunder, too. You see, I'm a generous man."

"Never had one so generous a friend as I. But I too have been open-handed and loyal. Now this hold-up? Will it be soon? In the next few days?"

"Tonight," said Brill, calmly.

"What? This night?"

"This night, yes. In fact, immediately. When luck is running one's way, the thing to do is to play it for all it's worth. It's ten o'clock now; before eleven this safe will have been robbed by a bandit. And who do you think that bandit is going to be?"

"Joe?"

"No. Joe is useful, but it's wise to keep him from knowing our real secrets; he's a good tool for rough work, but no more."

"You will act the bandit?"

"Oh, no. For it is necessary for me to be away when the safe is robbed, and with a lot of witnesses who will prove that the County Treasurer had nothing to do with the stealing. I shall be in the saloon. And when presently I send that drunken old Jim, the swamper, here to get my reading glasses, which I'll have left here on the table, he'll run into—you!"

"Me?"

"You'll be the bandit."

"No, no, no! Do you think to catch me in a trap?"

"Trap? Don't be silly. You haven't anything to fear from that boozy old fool, for you'll be masked. Listen, haven't you heard of The Masked Rider, who is the most marvelous bandit and outlaw in the country?"

"Who has not? But he has never been in this region."

"He is going to be tonight," Pete Brill asserted. "This job has to be cleverly done, and since Joe tells me there are whispers going around about something queer with the County funds it has to be done now. Just an ordinary hold-up might look suspicious in view of these damnable rumors. But with Jim scared to death and seeing The Masked Rider, who has a fashion of appearing and disappearing like a crafty devil, there won't be any such suspicions of a fake.

"THE MORE FANTASTIC a thing is, the more readily it is accepted by the general run of fools. People know The Masked Rider does things impossible for most men as if they were commonplace, so they'll believe at once that he was here. They'll swallow Jim's yarn whole. See? All you have to do is get from your store a black sombrero, a black silk handkerchief for a mask, a pair of woman's black gloves, and a black mantilla to wrap about your body. Then you'll be The Masked Rider. The safe will be locked, but I'll write out the combination so that you can open it. I'm not removing the cash box and the bonds because it is essential that Jim see you actually taking them. You will be in here in half an hour from now, at which time I'll have the swamper arrive. He will come with my keys, open the door, light a match and then you will stick a gun into his ribs and have him light the lamp. The old soak won't move after you've backed him into a corner away from the door. You'll rob the safe, let him see you taking out the stuff, and tell him The Masked Rider helps himself where he will, disguising your voice. Then you'll slip out and remove your black garb and return to your store, where you'll hide the plunder. And old Jim will do the rest."

"As you tell it, it sounds easy," Valdez said, hesitating.

"Doesn't even take nerve. It'll go off smooth as oil. Not a soul will be around except you and Jim. And, man, think of the thousands we'll have to develop the mine!"

"That's so."

"Then it's settled."

"*Por Dios,* I'll do it even if there is danger! That much money, I'd almost rob a train for that!"

"All right, come along. Here are the reading glasses. As it happens, fortunately, I sent Jim for them in the same way only a week ago when I needed them to look over a newspaper in Mike's place. So that part will seem natural. Half an hour should be sufficient for you to get ready and be back here; I know the clerk has closed your store and gone to bed by now. There won't be a hitch. A fine Masked Rider you'll make with your big body, Valdez. Ha, ha!"

The lighted window went dark as the lamp was extinguished and diminishing footfalls marked the men's departure.

Thought The Masked Rider, "So that fat fool Valdez thinks to clown in my clothes and character! So be it! They may shuffle the deck to suit them, but I'll deal the cards!"

A faint groan from the spot where the Deputy Sheriff lay caused the outlaw to speed thither. The fellow was recovering consciousness and might, on regaining his senses, create a disastrous complication in the prospective fake robbery. Catching the inert figure under the arms, The Masked Rider dragged him to the jail, heaved him inside, and locked the door. Thereupon the hooded man went to the front of the Court House, where he posted himself not far from the steps and waited in the darkness of the wall.

At length a black shadow materialized, scarcely to be distinguished in the night even when close, but betrayed by the soft scrape of boot soles in advancing. The Masked Rider's double had come. He went up the steps and in. Again silence fell about the building, which after some five minutes was broken by new sounds of approach, this time by unsteady, scuffling footfalls and hoarse breathing. The second actor in the burlesque robbery to be played in the County Treasurer's office had entered the scene, the boozy saloon-sweep, Jim. On the steps he stumbled, mumbled curses, groped upward and also disappeared inside. Shortly there came from within a yelp of fright, answered by a sharp command.

THE MOMENT HAD come for the third and unexpected player to move upon the stage. Stealthily The Masked Rider slipped into the hallway; at the inner doorway of the office he glimpsed a grimy, bearded, scared little old man, with arms uplifted and eyes glassily fixed, gazing at a figure invested in black from hat peak to heels, who knelt searching the interior of the office safe. The outlaw crossed the doorway into the deeper shadow beyond.

"What The Masked Rider wants he seizes," sounded in deep tones. "Do you know who I am?"

"N-n-n-no."

"I am The Masked Rider. Now you know."

"O-O-Oh, gosh!"

"See, I have the money, the papers, everything. They are now mine. Now I shall vanish as I came, in darkness. And like darkness, none can catch me, none can trail me, none can know me, any more than they can catch or trail or know a shadow."

Grimly the real Masked Rider listened to this fulsome self-praise. Valdez appeared to enjoy himself very much in his fictitious part. But he was too shrewd to forget that he should not invite possible discovery by delay.

"We will go," he said. "Remember my pistol is at your back while you walk out. One shout from you and I shoot. Keep your arms up until you are down the steps, then without turning to look, run."

To the lurking outlaw, it appeared as if the thin, trembling old man had not—in his terror of his big black-masked, black-robed captor—strength enough to reach the outer air. Nevertheless, he went tottering forward and down the steps and then, with a squeal, disappeared in the gloom.

A low laugh broke from Valdez, as with money box and packet of bonds he stood for a moment in the doorway looking after the swamper.

"The Masked Rider takes what he wants," he said mockingly, and laughed once more.

A hard object was pressed against his back. He felt his gun being removed.

"The Masked Rider takes what he wants," came in mimic tones. "Turn slowly. Now hand over the stuff."

Incredulously, the startled eyes of Valdez beheld his own counterpart, perceived gleaming eyes gazing through slits of a hood into his own, and felt his heart turn cold at this uncanny materialization, as if from shadows of the unknown. By the faint light reflected from the lighted inner doorway, the pair of Masked Riders glared at each other. And as if under a spell the masquerading outlaw put packet and steel cash box in the hands of his adversary.

Then the real Masked Rider tapped with forefinger the breast of the false one, who was still too dumbfounded to move.

"Laugh at this jest if you can, you ass clothed in a lion's skin!" he said, in a voice of ice.

Whereupon he made a leap through the door, landed lightly on the ground, and vanished from before the steps into the darkness of the wall.

CHAPTER IV

FANG NULLY GETS A SURPRISE

T HE OWNER OF the Big 9 Saloon, a squat, barrel-shaped man, with close-set eyes, a long upper lip, shaven head, great muscular arms, and a surface manner of geniality, apparently was little interested in anything except his business. He had shown up in Chavo a year previous, when he had bought the saloon. He had speedily learned the name, identity, rating, and reputed character of every individual living in the town and region, and by calculated liberality and joviality with Americans and natives alike had increased the patronage of his drinking place and gained a common opinion of being a fair, good-natured, substantial citizen who conducted his affairs better than average.

The Sheriff himself said so. For Mike Grogan, though he did not mind noise and men having a good time, was quick as a cat to dissolve quarrels, break up fights, and eject trouble-makers with the remark that "most everything goes in the old Big Nine, but at raisin' hell we draw the line." This policy won him a general good will. Moreover, he shrewdly aligned himself with the political leaders of the town and county, and without seeking favors or special privileges gave them his support.

But all this was but crafty camouflage on his part to conceal a secret design he had in mind from the first. At heart he was avaricious and lawless, as in mind he was cunning and persevering. By instinct he sensed crooks, and his suspicions had been early aroused as to Pete Brill, whom he considered the cleverest of the County officials. The County Clerk was a mere cipher; the County Assessor a weakling under Brill's thumb; the County Attorney a drunkard; and the County Judge a red-nosed old soak with little legal training, a befuddled mind, and a foul tongue.

Alone of all the officers, the Sheriff was a straight and able man; and he was handicapped by having two poor Deputies, forced upon him by political considerations, one, Joe Mallett, who was ignorant, vicious, and disloyal, and the other Mart Jones who was lazy and stupid and faithful. So Mike Grogan, suspecting that Pete Brill was engaged in somehow skinning the County and convinced that the occasion was ripe to start his own secret operations, had sent for a certain man to come to Chavo, a former partner in rustling cows in New Mexico.

The man had ridden in that night after darkness, signalled the saloonkeeper from the back door, and been hidden in the stable behind the saloon. Later Mike should join him to discuss their business.

But Fang Nully, as the newcomer was called, had got tired of the pentness of the small adobe stable. The sounds from the saloon, the upraised voices, piano banging, laughter, all the conviviality, made him restless. He finished off the last swallow of whisky in the half-pint bottle Mike had slipped him and stepped outside. He was a small, chunky, bow-legged individual, past his youth, with his upper lip lifted on the left side in a perpetual sneer because of a protruding yellow fang. Hence his designation.

The hour he knew to be about eleven o'clock. Mike had told him it would be one o'clock before the crowd in the saloon thinned down to where he could leave the place in charge of the night barkeeper and come to the stable—a long wait yet. It would do no harm to stretch his legs and get a notion of the town, as long as he kept back of buildings.

He moved slowly northward, now pausing, now advancing. After a time he came even with the last structure facing the street and perceived the dim outline of the Court House behind saplings, in which light showed at two windows in the lower story. He noted the fact, but without interest, moved forward until he was in front of the grounds.

THEN HE HEARD a sound and stood still, ready to slip away. To his surprise a man passed him in the starlight some ten paces off, running as if chased by the Devil, giving vent to gurgling moans, and holding his arms above his shoulders full length. Fang watched after him, his curiosity stirred; had he but known it, it was the swamper Jim he saw in desperate flight to the street and the saloon.

Another footfall. He swung about toward the Court House and just in time to see a vague, black-shrouded form with a black head, hatted but without face, stop and confront him almost within reach. Hardened as he was, Fang felt a cold shudder ripple over his skin at sight of the dark faceless figure. He had a flash of comprehension that this ominous visitant was what had sent the runner flying by, and that it was actually the Devil. And with a gasp, a recoil, he instinctively swung his right fist in a defensive blow. The shadowy shape swerved and whirled and disappeared in the darkness of the young trees.

"Hell's Hinges, what was that?" Fang ejaculated.

For three minutes he stood frozen and staring and

incredulous. All at once he laughed ironically. For he recalled that his fist in its stroke had brushed draping cloth, and if he had felt a garment, why, then the unknown had not been an apparition. Not the Devil, but only a disguised human. But what was the game going on here?

Again hurried footsteps. Fang quickly crouched to earth. To his amazement, and to his satisfaction too, for he was burning with curiosity now, he saw the same dark shape— the same he believed it to be, at any rate, though in this he was mistaken—that had appeared before. Now it was a dozen paces distant. It loomed even larger in the starlight, and whereas it had come on him previously almost without sound or warning now it strode past hurriedly and heavy-footed.

Fang was after the cloaked man like a coyote on scent. He was too old a hand at such work to betray his pursuit to the ears of the other and he came to pause only when the quarry turned in at the rear of a long, broad, low building. The black-garbed, masked man quietly entered, at which Fang Nully marked the location of the store by its placement in relation to the saloon and, grinning to himself, went back to the stable. He knew where Chavo's devil dwelt.

An uproar in the saloon drew him to the open rear door, where he glanced within and leaned ear near the door frame to catch a notion of what the disturbance was about. A knowledge of the cause of it was quickly given him. A crowd was milling about a little rat of an old man in excitement, shouting questions, yelling about a robbery of the County Treasurer's safe, crying for an officer and a posse, demanding that The Masked Rider be caught and swung and the tax-money got back. Safe cleaned out... over a hundred thousand dollars in cash and bonds stolen... the

County left bankrupt unless the thief were captured… The Masked Rider!

Emitting a deep breath of interest, Fang Nully squatted on his heels to consider the amazing matter. So there had been a robbery! That explained the queer happening of a few minutes before. The old man with a wispy beard in the saloon must be the scared runner who had fled from the Court House, while the cloaked and masked man whom Fang had encountered and followed could be no other than the robber.

Fang had heard innumerable tales of the mysterious outlaw called The Masked Rider who had acquired a wide notoriety in western regions. With them went a confusion of opinions. According to some accounts he was a desperate scoundrel, and to others a wronged man; he was a diabolical criminal, and he was one driven by harsh injustice to make reprisals; he was a ruthless wolf, and he was defender of the weak and hapless against human vultures. In any case, he was a bold unknown whose identity was a mystery—a law-breaker, a hunted man with many a golden price upon his head, a horseman riding a powerful black steed and never appearing, so far as reported, except attired in black sombrero, black hood with eyeholes, black gloves, black clothes and boots, and a black enveloping cape—a figure inspiring dread, with a fox's ingenuity, lightning fast in action, deadly when crowded hard, and famed for marvelous triumphs and escapes.

COULD THIS LEGENDARY *caballero* be, after all, merely a Chavo man? Fang shook his head. It did not somehow fit with The Masked Rider's record of wide roving. This fellow whom Fang had trailed to the store must be an imitator, an impostor.

Therefore, what now?

Fang licked his lips and his eyes narrowed. He had, by luck. seen the thief getting away. He knew where he dwelt. He realized where the contents of the County Treasurer's safe had been taken. To him alone, except the perpetrator, was vouchsafed the all important secret. He grinned mirthlessly.

"And more'n a hundred thousand, too!" he whispered. "Right in that buildin', right there. Him believin' likewise nobody knows and figgerin' everything is hotsy-totsy. Well, there ain't no need of changin' plans 'bout rustlin', but what now will be rustled won't be *cows*."

He heard someone approaching in the darkness, wormed himself back into denser gloom. Into the dim lamplight falling through the doorway came a man—a big-bodied Mexican with a huge crow-wing moustache across his swarthy cheeks. He halted for a moment to peer within, then entered to join, unnoticed, the clamoring throng.

As Nully regarded the Mexican pass in he was puzzled by a haunting familiarity in the big shape, which all at once resolved itself into identification. He exultingly slapped thigh with palm. That was it! The same fellow! The man had stripped off his black garb and now had come in his ordinary character of a townsman.

Smart trick, thought Fang. In the excitement none would remember whether this one had been there or not, and he could assert that he had been, when the scared bearer of the news burst into the place. Well, well, there were all kinda of laughs in this business.

The babel of high-pitched talk diminished, some agreement had been reached, and with a shout the crowd poured through the front door into the street bent apparently to start a hunt for The Masked Rider. In the saloon Grogan and his barkeeper alone were left.

To find The Masked Rider! Again Fang Nully chuckled.

Grogan removed his apron, spoke to his attendant, and came to the rear door, stepped forth.

"I'm right here, Mike," Nully greeted him.

"Oh, all right, Fang. Been having a little excitement. County Treasurer's safe just been robbed."

"By a Masked Rider, yeah."

"You heard?"

"I knew it before that; I saw the gent. But, wait; tell me who's the owner of the store three doors up on this side."

"Three doors up? Why, that's Valdez' place."

"Has a big black moustache as thick as two fingers, eh?"

"Yes."

"That's him, your Masked Rider."

"What!"

"Yeah. Him."

"How d'you know?"

"I saw him comin' away from the Court House. I got tired of stayin' in the stable and so I strolls out and up that way for fresh air and a look around. No more had I reached them small trees growin' 'round the Court House when a little fella run past me from the place like a bat outa hell. Next a big gent all in black and masked nearly bumps into me and give me a scare, I admits, but when he sees me he ducks back outa sight among the trees. Howsomever, he comes out again almost immediate, goes past, and bein' curious, I trails him. He comes along down behind buildin's to that store three doors up, uses a key and goes in."

"No mistake in this, Fang?" Grogan demanded, sharply.

"Nary a mistake. He never gets outa my view once after I picks him up the second time. And, I repeats, he was all in black—black hat, black mask, black cloak. Big, too. Yeah, he disappears right in that store."

"Valdez! Well, by God!"

"Then he comes 'long here not two minutes ago, after peelin' off them black duds, and walks in and becomes one of the crowd just before it leaves you. I knew him, I knew him by his size. That gent is The Masked Rider, but not the real one, Mike, as you'll agree after thinking it over. The genuwine Masked Rider is something diff'rent from this Greaser, or I ain't heard right."

GROGAN'S HAND CLOSED on Fang's arm in a fierce grip.

"Then he has the stuff!" he exclaimed, low.

"Sure."

"And it's hid somewhere in his house!"

"Of course."

"So it was only Valdez!" And the saloonman's voice revealed the surprise that still affected him. "Valdez! Which means that Pete Brill is in the steal, too. Pete is the Treasurer, Fang, and he was in there a moment ago yelling loudest for the bunch to get after the thief. Valdez is Pete's mining partner and political henchman among the Mexicans. The slick crooks! They sure pulled a fast one in this trick, but what we're going to slip over them is going to be a lot faster. Listen, Fang, that money is coming to us."

"You ain't tellin' me nothin' new, Mike," Nully replied.

"It's as good as in our hands this minute. A hundred thousand and more in cash and bonds that them wolves figger to share between 'em! But they won't; we'll grab that plunder. And nothing under heaven or above hell, Fang, is going to prevent us getting it!"

" 'Zactly my feelin's," Nully stated.

"This is going to be the smoothest haul ever made in the Southwest," said Grogan. "Wait here. I'll get a bottle of whisky. Then we'll go back in the sagebrush behind the stable far enough off to be certain we can't be overheard, and talk. Taking this stuff away from Pete Brill and Valdez just strikes me on the funny-bone!"

CHAPTER V

A FUGITIVE

I F EVER THERE was a wrathful youth, he was Les
Bridges as he rode home that night from Chavo. His
being jailed, Joe Mallett's taunts, the attempt of Brill and
Valdez to return him to the *calabozo,* the outrageous charge
against him of murder, the realization that he actually
was in danger of his life, all filled him with rage. His first
impulse was to make war by defying his enemies and stir-
ring up such a row that the town would take notice, but this
feeling was succeeded by one of anxiety on recalling that he
was, after all, a nonentity while the County Treasurer and
the town's chief merchant were men of powerful influence.

So he had got his horse from the livery stable and headed
for Agate Creek Basin without loss of time. From time to
time as he galloped northward for the canyon, his anger
blazed anew, boiling over in curses. The whole business
was a dirty trick. The reason was because he had once told
Pete Brill to stop annoying Betty Underwood with his
attentions. That was at the bottom of it. The worst of the
situation was that the skunk would send the snake-headed
Deputy Sheriff, Joe Mallett, after him on the morrow to
take him back to jail.

Back to jail? Not on your life. Joe Mallet would have to
catch him first, Les determined, and the Deputy would
have a swell chance of doing that with all the mountains for

one to play tag in. It looked as if he, Les, would be driven to adopting the course advised by the man, whoever he was, a friendly puncher no doubt, probably a Box U rider, who had released him from the jail. Yes, he would have to duck into the woods first thing at dawn, where he must stay while friends worked for his safety. Best not even to sleep in the cabin tonight in case Joe Mallett and a bunch fogged after him at once.

Therefore it was that the young fellow staked his horse in the grassy mouth of a hollow a hundred yards back of his cabin and took his rifle, bridle and saddle, a sack of food, and his blankets, to a spot by some bushes near his corral.

"This is outsmartin' 'em, I reckon," he grunted, as seated on his blanket he pulled off his boots.

The wisdom of his precaution was disclosed when he was awakened by some sound. He sat up, listened. From a window of his house came lamplight and he heard voices, the stamp of a horse. Snatching his gun belt and fastening it about him as he ran, he circled until he was in front of his log dwelling. Now he could see five horses standing near the open doorway and heard and saw their riders inside moving about. He crept closer. Joe Mallett appeared in view for a moment, then Valdez, then the others, three Chavo men, as they moved about the table which held a lighted lamp.

Presently the Deputy Sheriff stalked out, followed by the three of Chavo.

"Ain't been here, by the looks of the place," Mallett growled. "Still in town, prob'ly. Don't waste no more time, Valdez."

A sudden shout from the room caused Mallett and his companions to wheel about.

"Look!" the big Mexican exclaimed. "You think he has not been here? Behold what I find rolled in a bearskin in this corner! A black sombrero, a black mantilla, a black handkerchief mask!"

"Here, let me see," the Deputy cried.

"So it is this young renegade who robbed Brill's safe!" Valdez continued, and Les could see him holding high by the lamp the articles he had named. "Not satisfied with killing Bill Lawson, he steals the County's money."

"Because he had murdered him, prob'ly," spoke a man, "figgerin' that since he was due to swing anyway he might as well go the limit."

"Ha! That's it," the Mexican said. "And I was right in suspecting him and wanting to come here. Didn't a man, undoubtedly one of the nesters here on this creek, knock you in the head, Joe, let him loose, and lock you in the jail? These nesters all stick together; they've all been rustling; they're all crooks. We ought to run them out of the country. And this coyote of a Les Bridges is the worst of them all. He kills, he robs the safe in the Court House of more than a hundred thousand dollars in cash and bonds. This disguise is the proof. We must look for the money, and if we don't find it we'll stay here until he comes back and walks into our hands."

ALL THE WHILE, Les Bridges had stood mystified and dumbfounded. What was this about a robbery? Who had got a hundred thousand dollars? How had the sombrero, cloak, and mask, come to be there in his cabin?

"Mebbe Bridges is on his way outa the country," one suggested.

"Not him," Joe Mallett replied. "The young fool won't leave, because he's stuck on that Underwood gal. I'll grab him—don't make any mistake about that—and get back the money if I have to put a red-hot wagon rod to the soles of his feet. I expect we might as well hide close here somewheres on the chance that he may come back, which will let us catch some sleep while we're waiting. Only one man at a time need be on watch. Well, Valdez, the County can thank you and your hunch about Bridges for savin' its money."

"You betcha!" another exclaimed.

"Take charge of these things, Joe," the merchant said. "They're the proof that he was The Masked Rider; I'll feel easier with them in the hands of a law officer."

Valdez was relieved in mind at the successful outcome of the matter, for a more important reason than that. Despite his bulk and usually deliberate manner, he was not slow of wits. Indeed, in his way, he was shrewd and calculating; and the instant he had recovered from the shock of being robbed by the real Masked Rider, he realized that he was in a dangerous trap. The loss of the money and bonds was a terrific blow, but that was not the worst of it, for Pete Brill knew that he had got the money from the safe and would never believe for a second a story of the plunder being taken by another black-garbed robber, actually the notorious Masked Rider. The story *was* fantastic, incredible. Pete was ruthless. He would be convinced that Valdez was double crossing him—and the Mexican sweated in cold fear at the prospect of dealing with Brill.

If Jim the swamper had only seen the other hooded man! But he had not. Somehow evidence to support Valdez' story must be found or created to make it credible to Pete and to allay his murderous mood when told the money and bonds were gone. How could such evidence be most convincingly provided? His mind flashed back over the successive incidents of the night. Ah, that young rancher,

Les Bridges! He had threatened Pete. He had a grievance. He had already been arrested for murder. He was a plausible, the most plausible, culprit for the part.

This far the Mexican had got in his contriving when he entered the rear door of the saloon. Fortunately the aroused crowd rushed out into the street as he joined it, so that Pete Brill, who was its leader, failed to note his presence. Valdez followed to the Court House, though keeping back out of sight; and when the other finally organized a posse of a dozen riders and headed with it southward, the merchant's satisfaction was great. The explanation was postponed for hours, which gave him time to develop his plan.

A number of men still hung about the Court House, speculating upon and arguing the chances of catching The Masked Rider. Then someone remembered Joe Mallett's non-appearance and this was discussed. At last several boys, aroused from sleep with other townspeople by the hubbub, and questing about, discovered Joe Mallett shouting through the jail window. A duplicate key was turned up in the Sheriff's desk and he was released.

After awhile when his story had been told and debated, Valdez drew him aside. The latter insisted that Les Bridges must be the robber, which to the Deputy Sheriff's inflamed mind was a natural conclusion; whereupon they called three other men and went for horses to ride to Bridges' cabin.

AFTER HE HAD saddled his mount, Valdez slipped into his store, bundled up the sombrero, mantilla, and handkerchief mask he had concealed after use, and fastened them securely at his cantle. The single risk he would undergo would be in transferring the articles from his horse to the interior of the cabin.

This he reduced to nothing by having the bundle free and ready when the little party pulled rein before the house. First to dismount, he strode forward and pushing open the unlocked door crossed the dark room, while bidding Joe Mallett seize Bridges. The Deputy ordered the young fellow to surrender and warned him not to resist on penalty of being shot. As there was no response, no sound, Joe at length struck a match and found the cabin untenanted. Meanwhile, the wily merchant had on groping about found a box by the cook stove and under it thrust the incriminating garb. Now there remained nothing for him to do but share in a momentary search and to make a pretended discovery of the damning proof.

Little wonder Les Bridges had been mystified and astounded at the scene enacted before him. When, however, he gathered the meaning of it, his anger swallowed up all caution.

"You sneakin', lyin' hounds!" he yelled. "Framin' me for something I never done! Lay a finger on me, Joe Mallett, and I'll blow a hole bigger'n that door through you!"

"Grab him!" Valdez bellowed.

"Keep off; I've a gun!"

"I'll drop him," the Deputy snarled.

His right hand darted to holster and his gun was half-drawn when from a corner of the cabin a shot crashed, the six-shooter was knocked from the gripping fingers at the impact of a heavy bullet, and Joe Mallett stood stunned by the unexpected happening. So too his companions.

Nor, for that matter, was Les Bridges less startled by the flash and boom of the shot. Who had fired it? As he still marveled, a hand caught him by the arm and a voice hissed in his ear.

"Get going, you fool, while the going's good!"

Over his shoulder he glimpsed a dim shape, a black-cloaked and masked human form, whose eyes gleamed through openings in the mask. Next instant he was whirled aside by the hand and barely saved himself from falling. Regaining his balance he looked where he had been, saw no one, nothing, whereat he took to his heels. He found the place where he had slept.

"My Golly, who was that?" he gasped, with an involuntary shiver. "I reckon that black ghost was right, at that!"

At the house the men were running about, calling to each other, searching for him. Once one fired at the darkness.

The youth rapidly rolled up his blankets, pulled on his boots, set hat on head, and adding sack, bridle and saddle, and rifle to his load, made for the place where his horse grazed. It was still two hours until dawn, but he was fleeing. The gravity of his position had at last fully saturated his mind. He was being hunted in earnest as a robber and murderer, false and fabricated though the charges were, and it would be folly to face them. For the time, he was a fugitive from the law.

"I've gotta see Betty as soon as possible," he muttered, as he led his saddled pony up a wooded hillside. "They'll be tryin' to make her believe I killed Bill Lawson and robbed the County, damn 'em, so I gotta tell her my story first. But I better leave out 'bout this fella in black; she'd think I was nutty."

CHAPTER VI

AT THE BOX U RANCH

DAYLIGHT WAS DISPELLING the last shadows in a forested ravine when Les came down a ridge into it. He had not gone far from his cabin, only a quarter of a mile or so, for amid the darkness of the pines he could make only a groping advance; in the place he reached, he again unsaddled and flung himself down for a short period of sleep. With first light he was up, ate a cold breakfast and pushed on along the mountain side, not daring to risk a passage of the swollen ford in the dark, or to go too close to the road leading to the Underwood ranch.

He came down into the ravine and around a heavy growth of underbrush stumbled upon something that caused him to draw rein. The something was a gaily painted wagon filled with letter-painted wooden cases. A medicine wagon it was. And here, of all places!

"Say, this is the last straw," he exclaimed, "comin' on top of everything that's happened, I reckon I'm goin' bughouse and have just been 'maginin' things the last couple of days!" He rubbed nose with forefinger, and went on, "Why, the last time I seen this outfit was only evenin' before last up by the Court House, the doctor makin' camp there! Something myster'ous in this!"

He rode around the wagon, peering at it and all about the ravine. A little way off, hidden hitherto by bushes, he saw two men, each prone on a blanket and well-wrapped up in others apparently asleep. A white bandage encased the skull of one. Kneeing his pony closer to the figures, he leaned forward to scrutinize their faces; and something in their stillness struck him as strange. He peered at them a second time.

"One sure is that little quack doctor," he ruminated aloud, "who I talked with by the wagon there in Chavo the afternoon before yesterday and who said he was feelin' sick. How'd he come high up here in the timber, I'd like to know, him and his wagon? The other looks like—By Golly, it *is* Ed Grantly! With his head tied up! I saw him in town, too, night before last. What's he doin' here?"

"Getting good care," a voice spoke from behind him.

Bridges turned his head sharply and saw a tall young man in dark clothes, whose firmly featured, tanned face wore an expression of composure.

"When nature helps a doctor, the chances are all for the patient," the speaker continued. "Dr. Chessington has mountain fever, and Mr. Grantly is suffering from a head wound. I am a believer in the value of rest, fresh air, and simple herbs in the treatment of sick folks. Chessington's fever is down, and Grantly's wound is healing. Luckily I ran across them both when medical care, except my own, wasn't available. I was passing through the country, but stopped to give them attention. Couldn't do anything else, of course. My name is Wayne Morgan."

"Well, Doctor, I reckon they're in good hands."

"They have improved since yesterday, at any rate."

"Funny you should have them up here in the timber."

"Think so?" the other queried. "Would they get well quicker in some stuffy 'dobe house?"

"Sure not. You're right, come to think it over. But what happened to Ed Grantly's head, Doc?"

"Got creased by a bullet. Someone ambushed him on the road by the ford down yonder, and I happened to see it happen. Found he was only creased, so I brought him up here to be with Chessington, whom I'd earlier run across in delirium. Slight concussion of the brain in Grantly's case, but he may pop out of it any moment."

"Didn't see who ambushed him, did you?"

"Saw the man afterwards when riding off, but he was too far off for me to recognize him if we met again."

"Well, I gotta hunch who's behind the shootin'," Les announced, darkly. "Grantly is after some crooks in town and told me only night before last he had the goods on 'em. They done it."

"Then you don't want to tell anyone he's here, or they will try to do a better job of it with him."

A LAUGH CAME from Les Bridges. "Me tell anybody? Listen, Doc, those same crooks are after me to frame me for a killin' and a Court House robbery, neither of which I done. They had me in jail up to last night, when I got out. They come to my cabin early this mornin' and tried to grab me once more, but didn't make it. So I'm on the run; they're seekin' me. You're lookin' at a outlaw, that's what. Which is why I gotta be mighty careful who I talk to or be seen by. Don't fear none I'll be relatin' to anybody 'bout Ed Grantly, and if I was you I'd move your sick gents higher up yet, for a posse might stumble on you here while seekin' me. Now I must be ridin' 'long; got a friend to see before I fades deeper into the mountains. Good luck, Doc,—and don't let them town skunks get scent of Ed."

He was no more than gone from sight when Blue Hawk

came from the direction of the canyon. The five men at the cabin in the basin were still in hiding about it, he reported, though so poorly hidden that the Mexican Indian had had no trouble in locating their position. Except for one who kept watch, they slept.

"We'll hitch up the team and drive it farther back," Wayne Morgan said. "Then we'll move these men too on a stretcher. This spot is too close to that cabin for safety."

"*Señor*, the wagon can't be taken far because of rough ground."

"I want to put it in those breaks; less chance there of it being discovered."

An hour later the vehicle was concealed half a mile away in a space between a dense clump of jack pines and a cliff where—to a casual glance—the trees seemed to grow close against the rocky wall. Thither too the sick men were carried. The spot was at the end of a box canyon, whose stone bottom left no trace of hoofs or wheels.

Over a small fire breakfast was cooked and eaten, the ashes covered cunningly, and the patients given a last examination. Much as Wayne Morgan wanted to be present when the wounded newspaper editor regained consciousness, it was necessary to risk missing the moment, because the desperate situation in which the owner of the most important ranch stood demanded urgent action.

"You take with you the money and papers you got last night, *señor*?" Blue Hawk inquired. "It is a great pity not to keep and use them. We could go to Mexico and live at ease for a long time." He spoke with a sardonic grin that proved he was in a kidding mood.

"We may be outlaws, Blue Hawk, but we are not yet

brigands," Morgan responded. "Now let's be going. How is the water in the creeks?"

"Dropping fast. We can cross anywhere without difficulty."

They rode out of the box canyon and mounting upon a ridge turned their horses westward so as to circle high above the basin on their northward course.

The buildings of the Underwood ranch lay before the mouth of a canyon ten miles north of the Agate Creek ford, whence a stream flowed forth some distance into the desert and then bending southward joined Agate Creek below Chavo. There was a long, low, thick-walled adobe ranch house comprising seven rooms, four of them bedrooms; a mess house, where a bald profane range cook ruled; a bunk house for the half-dozen cowpunchers employed; a granary; a blacksmith shop; a large corral and a small one; and a quarter of a mile downstream three houses where lived—with their families—Mexicans who tended the irrigated alfalfa and grain fields.

TOWARD NOON OF this day Betty Underwood came out of the house and walked to the small corral where a grizzled cowboy sat on the ground fitting a new *latigo* to a saddle. He had been a Box U hand since the girl was a small child; he had seen her grow into the slender, lithe, brown-eyed, brown-haired girl—the prettiest girl in Arizona, he swore—whose countenance was now so filled with concern.

"Lafe, Dad is taking Bill's death awfully hard," she stated, dropping to a seat at his side. "All day yesterday and ever since he came home he has acted as if he had received a mortal blow, not eating, hardly uttering a word, scarcely moving, only sitting in his chair in the living room and staring out the window. I don't understand it. Bill was our oldest hand and our foreman, of course, and I loved him and was terribly shocked when Father said he had been shot by somebody; but it doesn't seem natural for Dad, much as he thought of him, to be so mute and helpless.

"Can't make nothin' of it myself, either, Betty."

"It's so unlike him. Why, before this he would have been leading everyone of you out to learn the killer and then get him! He's always been such a hell-roarer when it came to anything or anybody harming you boys. I know you and the others wanted to hit for town as soon as he said Bill had been shot down, but he stopped you."

"Yeah."

"He's just the same today as yesterday, and he looks ten years older than when he went to Chavo."

"Don't you worry, girl; he'll be himself tomorrow," Lafe said, loyally. "I reckon it's just been too much of a shock. He ain't as young as he used to be, and he thought the world of Bill."

"As did we all." She furtively wiped her eyes. "I suppose the boys don't understand his doing nothing, any more than we do."

"Well, they was kinda surprised and set back on their heels at not bein' 'lowed to hunt the skunk that killed Bill, I admit. But they ain't said much, not 'round me, anyway."

"Who do you think could have done it!"

"Must've been some saloon loafer or mebbe some drifter who thought Bill had a roll on him. Can't make no other explanation seem reasonable, for Bill was a peaceable fella and had no enemies I know of, and I would know. I sure would like to meet up with the yella snake what done it!"

"I hope you do, Lafe," she exclaimed, "for it was cold-blooded murder if there ever was such, by the little Dad could tell. They found Bill in the street dead. Nobody saw him slain, or even heard the shot, apparently."

"Somebody knows and ain't talkin', you can bet your sweet life on that," he replied, grimly. "Men don't get killed thataway, even at night, without some pair of eyes witnessin' the murder. If the Old Man would let me do some inquirin' 'round in Chavo—" He broke off, staring downstream. "Riders comin'. Bunch of 'em headin' up the trail. Mebbe something's been learned 'bout Bill's shootin'."

The visitors turned out to be a posse of half a score of men, led by Sheriff Colton, a bony faced, gray-moustached, little man, whose bleached blue eyes had a penetrating quality that belied his drawling speech. With him was his other Deputy, Mart Jones. They had arrived in Chavo at daybreak after an all-night ride, been told of the Court House robbery, and after a meal and a few hours of sleep had sworn in the men with them and ridden north to pick up any possible trace of the mysterious Masked Rider.

Of the party was Pete Brill, who with others had gone south in search of the outlaw, only to discover nothing and to return to town while the Sheriff was making up his posse. Brill joined it. Must he not exhibit himself as a distraught Treasurer whom neither fatigue nor loss of sleep could divert from his duty?

BETTY AND LAFE rose to their feet to greet the riders when the company of horsemen came to the corral. The Sheriff imparted his grave news and inquired if anyone at the ranch had seen or heard a stranger pass in the night or during the morning. After further talk, he announced that they would ride on to other ranches.

"Wouldn't this Masked Rider have headed into the mountains?" Lafe questioned.

"Probably. Likely he's over the range by now, too. He had cover of darkness to help him and the timber for a screen. We're just sweepin' these trails on the chance he mightn't have struck into the hills. Well, it looks like this is one more feather for this outlaw to stick in his cap. In cleaning out the County funds he sure hit us a hard jolt." He turned to Pete Brill, who was dismounting. "Stayin'?"

"Yes. Reached the limit," was the answer. "I'll rest here for a little and then get back to town. Been twelve hours in the saddle."

Condon nodded. "You've done all you could, I reckon."

"To have this happen while I'm in office!" Pete groaned.

"Your conscience oughta be clear, at any rate," came drily from the Sheriff. "There's some low-lived folks who would be mean enough to say you was The Masked Rider, Pete, because of one thing and another, but your bein' in the Big Nine at the time of the robbery sure makes it easy to show 'em you're innocent as a little babe. Now, now, don't get sore! My jokes ain't got no sting."

Without awaiting a rejoiner from the angered man on the ground, Condon swung his horse and beckoning his posse-men trotted off. In Brill's face the smoldering wrath gradually died and his features, hardened and sharpened by weariness, assumed an expression of pleasure when he directed his gaze at Betty.

"Ain't you goin' to give me a welcomin' smile, girl!" he asked in an ingratiating tone.

"You're welcome. As for smiling, smiles don't come easily so soon after Bill Lawson's death."

"Oh, I forgot about that, so much has been happening.

Too bad about Bill. But though young Bridges slipped out of jail last night, we'll catch him again and swing him for murdering your foreman, be sure of that."

"What's that you're saying?" Betty cried. "You're accusing Les of being Bill's murderer?"

"He's guilty."

"I'll never believe it!"

"Too bad, Betty. He done it, men saw him, the proof's overwhelming. The boy quarreled with Bill and threatened him and finally murdered him without giving your fore-man even a chance to draw in defence. If ever there was a lawless, good-for-nothing young scoundrel, it's Bridges."

"The hell you say!" Lafe sneered. "Fine business, a cheap politician like you lyin' 'bout a puncher, and one who worked here one time, behind his back."

A wave of murky crimson flooded Brill's face, while his eyes flashed dangerously. A cool and calculating man ordinarily, loss of sleep and exhaustion had reduced his self-control to a minimum; the other's sneer rasped his vanity; and the girl's quick championship of Bridges exas-perated him still further.

"Be careful what you say," he snapped at Lafe, "or you'll be out of a job before you know it."

"And when did you start hirin' and firin' on the Box U?" the grizzled puncher drawled.

The contempt in the voice bit like acid into Pete Brill's egotism and inflamed to the limit his already aroused temper.

"Today, now! If I feel like doing it!"

"So?"

"Yes, that's so, and you may as well know it."

"You're crazy!" Betty cried.

"Crazy am I?" he snarled. "You'll be quick enough to change your tune when you learn the truth, and to come fawning to me for favors. You won't be so haughty, you'll be glad to beg for my good will."

"Never, never!"

"You won't, eh? Why, you pretty little fool, you and your father are sitting in *my* house now! I own this ranch, I own these buildings and corrals, I own the very bed you sleep in! Now think that over while I go in and finish my business with your Old Man. Didn't he tell you? Ha, ha, I imagine he has put off doing that! He wasn't very lucky at poker in the game we had when he was in town night before last and so the ownership of this ranch passed to me, land and cattle. Yes, I have the deed and am going in to get a bill of sale for the live stock. The Box U and everything on it is mine, young lady, and so you'd best begin to make up to me if you don't want to wear calico instead of silk." And with a snap of finger and thumb he went to the dwelling.

"Oh, no; oh no! It can't be true!" the girl gasped, to Lafe.

"He's lyin'," he said huskily. "Yet the way your dad has been actin'—"

"The Box U gone, lost! Oh, I can't believe Dad would ever have done this! Though he liked to sit in a game, he never gambled heavily; we know that. And to bet away the ranch and herd, he wouldn't do that—no, oh, no! His very life is centered in it! Tell me, Lafe, that that dreadful man was only mocking us!"

THE PUNCHER TOOK and patted one of her hands awkwardly.

"Stay here, Betty, till I come back," said he. "I'm going in to ask the Old Man outright 'bout it; and if that skunk Brill *is* lyin' I'll sure beat him within a inch of his life."

He rocked away on his high heels and disappeared within the house. He was absent only a moment. When he came out, his step was slow and bearing despondent; at sight of him Betty's heart grew sick.

"It's true?"

"Yes."

"Lafe, Lafe, it can't be!" She gazed incredulously about her at buildings, corrals, fields, lands and mountains. "No more ours! No longer home to us! I can't bear the thought of it!"

Whirling suddenly she ran from the corral past the house and up a path by the creek, winding amid clumps of underbrush and upthrust boulders, until she was in the canyon. There at a certain ledge she climbed a slope until she was on a tree-clad ridge, where she sat down on a flat slab of stone. Since a child, she had come here when desiring privacy: to solve perplexities, to make plans, to endure disappointments, to hug joys, to evoke dreams. And instinctively she had run hither for perhaps—who knew?—the last time, to steel herself to face this terrific blow.

How long she sat suffering and thinking she did not know. Noon was far past, and the rays of the sun were slanting more and more through the trees, when she at last became aware of the passage of time.

"How could such a thing have happened?" she burst out, as she felt anew the disaster. "How could Dad have been so mad as to gamble everything away? He *must* have been mad to do it!"

A voice answered:

"Or deceived into doing it."

Startled, she sprang up and faced about. A man wearing a black sombrero, a black hood with eyeholes, a black full cloak, black gloves, stood motionless before her; an ominous figure that caused her blood to chill. Too, she saw below him a short distance among the trees in a hollow, the head of a horse, unquestionably the strange visitor's mount.

"You need fear no harm from me, Miss Underwood," the speaker continued. "As I remarked, your father must have been deceived into parting with his property, deceived and coerced. I am here to help you."

"But you—you are The Masked Rider!" she cried.

"So you have heard of me. And has all that you've heard of me been bad?"

"Not all, sir. My Dad in telling of you said he believed you were as much sinned against as sinning, that you had been known to have done kind acts and brave deeds."

"All men aren't so fair-minded, Miss," said he, grimly. "Most of them believe me black in mind and heart as well as in clothing."

"I don't know what to think," she remarked, doubtfully. "I don't know that I should even be talking here with you, an outlaw. Why, the Sheriff and a posse were at the ranch just before noon hunting you! They said—they said that you had robbed the—" Her voice faltered and ceased.

"The County Treasurer's office?"

"Yes."

She perceived his eyes gleaming through the eyeholes and a tremor of fear caused her to shrink farther back. When at last he spoke his words were cryptic:

"What was in a false hand fell into a true. What was stolen was saved."

CHAPTER VII

DEEP WATERS

"**B**UT THAT IS not what I am here to talk about," he continued, after a pause. "It's this business of your father, who's bogged to the neck in trouble."

"Why should that interest you!" she questioned, forlornly. "It's nothing to do with you."

"Strange as it may seem, I can't pass a man or beast caught in a bog without throwing out a rope to pull him back to solid ground. Your father—"

"It's too late in his case."

"Don't be so sure, girl. It happens I know more about this matter than you do, or even he, and while I haven't got to the bottom of it yet I'm certain that he can be hauled out to safety. I'm sure of this much, he's the victim of a trick and if the trick can be exposed he will be free of trouble and hold his ranch."

"How could he have been tricked! He lost the ranch in a poker game. Were the cards marked against him?"

"The cards *were* stacked against him in my opinion, at any rate," said he, enigmatically. "There's more in this than just a poker game. Deeper water is running in this business than he has any idea of; it not only is sucking your father down, but has cost your foreman his life and is sweeping your young friend, Les Bridges, to destruction, too. Your father must be saved, and the boy must be rescued. Will you help?"

"Help? Of course I will help!" she exclaimed.

"I thought you would."

"But is there really a chance to do this, sir? Tell me. Is it really possible? It makes me tremble to think there may be, but how, how?"

"First, by persuading your father to tell you everything that occurred that night while he was in town, so that you can tell me. His story should throw more light on the trick played on him and of which he suspects nothing. Keep probing at him until you have every fact and incident, whether it appears important or not."

"Is that all?"

"No. What kind of a man is your Sheriff?"

"He's the one square officer of all those at the County Seat," Betty stated. "And a friend of ours."

"So much the better. Tomorrow morning early you will come up here and tell me all you've learned from your father and then go see the Sheriff to inform him too of everything and to get him to pry into the mess."

"Pete Brill, the County Treasurer, is the man I suspect in all this," she exclaimed, bitterly. "I've always distrusted him, and now I hate him. He's down in the house now talking to Dad. He got mad by the corral at something one of our boys said and snapped out that he now owned the ranch and that Dad and I were here only on sufferance."

"There *now*, is he?"

"Yes."

"Putting the screws on your father again, I reckon. Well, if I could trust you—"

The girl's face flushed.

"Why then propose my helping if you don't trust me?" she answered.

"Experience has made me distrustful of most folks; so many of them lose their scruples when they think they have a chance to collect the gold on my head. I'm an outlaw, I'm fair prey. Scanning your face, though, I see no greed there. What I meant was more this: can I trust you not to betray me unintentionally, or when questioned hard?"

"I can keep my mouth closed when I wish, and I've a will of my own."

"A heedless word or a yielding to fear might cost me my life," he stated, sternly. "Bear that in mind always."

"I shall."

"Not only my life is at stake, but Les Bridges' too, and possibly even your father's if his enemies become desperate. I'm telling you plainly, hell is loose on this range."

BETTY SHIVERED. "OH, then what are we to do?" she beseeched.

"What I told you. Get from your father his story and stir him to make a fight, then go to the Sheriff with what you know. Now here is something to use with your father." Thrusting a hand into his bosom under his robe, he produced a folded document which he handed to her. "It's the deed he gave Brill and Valdez making them owners of the Box U Ranch. Show it to him; the sight of it and your having it should jar him out of his despair. But retain it, keep it safe."

"The deed! How in the world did you come by it?"

"Never mind how. The Masked Rider has ways of his own of getting things he wants. Brill and Valdez aren't aware yet, I imagine, that it is no longer in their possession."

"Ah, I understand. You found it when you robbed the Court House."

"No. Nor did I rob the Treasurer's safe."

"You make everything so strange and mysterious," she said. "Of course, it makes me only the more curious, but I'll ask no questions about that. This letter, now. Father will demand to know how I got it."

"Sure, he will. Let me consider what to say."

The Masked Rider stood in thought. Hidden as his face was by its black hood, Betty could nevertheless divine his concentration of mind as he wrestled with the problem. Once he turned his head as if gazing through the mask's eyeholes all about him in search for an answer; and once he slowly clenched gloved hand.

"Nothing else for it, I reckon," he remarked, at last. "You'll have to mention me, after all, or he won't be satisfied. You'll have to tell the Sheriff of me likewise. But first you must swear them both to secrecy as to my part in the business before you speak. Yes, when you've got from your father what he knows, take him to the Sheriff and relate everything and enlist his aid. I see no other course."

"Won't the Sheriff want to capture you?"

"That's my risk. But I'm counting on you to talk so fast and hard about what he must do for your father that he'll be busy for a day or two with that job. By then I hope to learn everything. And what you'll have to tell about your father's mix-up ought to give him plenty to investigate."

"But there's only Dad's losing the ranch in a poker game."

"He didn't lose it gambling."

"What!"

The Masked Rider dismissed the card game with a gesture of gloved hand.

"There's far more in this affair than you dream," said he, gently. "I don't like to tell you more, for it will shake you to your very soul. Yet I must tell you if your father and the Sheriff are to he handled right. Remember this, though, that however black things may look, they're not as dark as they seem, because in the whole occurrence there is something unexplained, deceiving, false and devilish."

The girl paled at these words, at the man's hard, fierce tone at the end.

"You terrify me," she whispered.

"Well, you have to hear. As I read you, you've good stuff in you, you're no weakling and coward, girl though you are. You have fighting spirit, too. Call upon that spirit now. Take your courage in your hands and face this business bravely. Ready? All right, listen. Your father didn't deed over the Box U to Brill and Valdez because he lost it at cards, no. He handed it over because those two scoundrels, those false friends, caught him in a trap and wrung from him the property under threat of prosecution for murder."

"Murder!" Betty gasped, in horror.

"Yes. Murder of Bill Lawson. And I reckon he only gave in to them because he dreaded the disgrace and shame for you."

"But murder! It can't be!"

"That's what Brill and Valdez are holding over your father's head, anyway."

"It's preposterous!" she cried, flaming suddenly into passion. "Dad kill Bill? Why, it's the craziest thing I ever heard of! Don't you see? Bill wasn't just our foreman, he was like one of our family, dear to us. He'd worked and lived here for years, and once had saved Dad's life, and used to take me riding before him on his saddle when I could hardly more than toddle. He and Dad were like brothers. Dad trusted him, had no secrets from him, respected him, loved him. He would listen and heed Bill as he would no other man, and if Dad were lingering a bit too long over drinks with friends or sitting too late in a poker game Bill had but to smile and say, 'Reckon it's time we were gettin' 'long home, Clem,' and Dad would start at once. No, Dad never killed Bill, never! It's absurd!"

"Unless he was blind drunk and didn't know what he was doing."

"PUT THAT STRAIGHT out of your mind. Dad took a glass now and then, just as he enjoyed a little game of poker, but he never got blind drunk, nor drunk at all, not even a bit tipsy."

"All the more reason for suspecting something crooked in the business. We'll dig into it."

"Who says Dad murdered Bill?"

"Brill and Valdez."

"They're lying."

"Exactly what I suspect. Yet if he did not, how comes it that your father is convinced that he did? The trick they worked must have been smooth to deceive him in such a vital matter. I say 'trick' because I'm sure that's what it was, for I overheard a few words passed between Valdez and Brill in town that made me sceptical about your father's guilt. Somehow they fooled him. That is what we're going to find out, the how of it. Once you get from your father the story he has to relate, every incident and every action even the most unimportant, we'll put our finger on the solution and expose the trickery."

"Yes, yes; we shall."

"With what you now know and with the deed, you should be able to make your father talk."

"Believe me, sir, he will," she exclaimed. "Poor Dad! I understand now why he has been in such a terrible state of mind since coming home. To believe he killed his truest friend! To have that held over his head! What an awful secret! A woman's intuition tells me that that wicked Pete Brill had a hand in Bill's death. The instant the man is gone from the ranch I'll talk with Dad."

"I'll be here early in the morning to meet you."

"Count on my coming."

"Then you and your father can go to Chavo to see the Sheriff."

"What if he should feel it his duty to arrest father when he has heard our account?"

"Make him hold off until he can dig up the real facts in the case," The Masked Rider replied. "Your father's going to him voluntarily, their friendship, the doubts and suspicions you must raise in his mind, should cause him to smell crooked work under it all and to leave your father free until he learns the truth."

"If Pete Brill discovers the deed is missing, he'll try to get another."

"Your father must refuse to give it."

"They will then accuse him of the murder."

A sardonic laugh came from The Masked Rider.

"Not when they've thought about it twice," he rejoined. "They don't realize the fact yet, but they won't dare. They would be shown up as accessories. They've shielded him, blackmailed him, and openly asserted they had proof that *Les Bridges* committed the murder. They're caught in their own net. They can't go into court against your father, because they would be liable to imprisonment for their own breaches of law. Point that all out to your father to stiffen his nerve, and to the Sheriff to rouse his wrath."

"I will."

"As a matter of fact, I figure Brill and Valdez never intended to accuse your father of the murder under any circumstance. That would be too dangerous for them, in a lot of ways. Besides, it's their game to keep the matter secret to make their blackmailing effective. They don't want your father dead, at least not until they have completely skinned him of his wealth and—and Brill has married you, which is his plan."

"The beast!"

"That's the reason he is falsely accusing Les Bridges of the crime. To get rid of the favored rival, if you don't mind my saying it."

"Why should I mind? I love Les."

"You'll therefore be working to save both your father and your lover."

Springing forward a step, Betty spread her arms wide before the other, while her eyes glowed and her lip trembled with emotion.

"You may be an outlaw," she exclaimed, "you can be The Masked Rider with a price on your head, you may have robbed the Treasurer's office, you may be accused of a hundred crimes and lawless deeds, but I shall never believe anything of you except what is good!"

"Ah, girl, to hear you say that—" he began.

At a cry from among trees higher on the ridge, the deep

snarl of a mountain lion, he broke off abruptly in his utterance to listen. It was Blue Hawk's signal of warning.

"I must go, there's danger for me," he said, quickly. "Remember we meet early tomorrow. I'm depending on you for much. Don't fail."

Jerking his black sombrero lower over his masked face, he ran with cloak billowing about his form down to his horse, swung up into the saddle, for an instant waved gloved hand back at her, and disappeared as his stallion with a plunging bound galloped behind screening underbrush and trees up the hollow.

Betty went down her dim trail into the canyon. She had not yet come to its bottom when a man on a pony raced past below, making for the ranch.

"Les, Les!" she called.

But he did not hear, vanished around a bend. Then she became aware of another clatter of hoofs. Riders came in view—five, with Valdez and Joe Mallett in the lead, hard in pursuit.

Time seemed to stand still and the distance all too long as Betty hurried to the ranch. The revelations of The Masked Rider brought a host of new angles to what originally seemed a simple although knotty problem.

CHAPTER VIII

IN AND OUT AND ALL
ABOUT

THE SAME IMPISH destiny that had been giving Les
Bridges a runaround for two nights and days still had
him hopping about on the hot griddle.

When he left Wayne Morgan's camp he rode westward
fully intending to get to the Box U Ranch without loss of
time. Coming to the head of the basin, he swung down a
hillside to an opening in the pine wood where he might
have a look over the little mountain "park" to see what was
doing at his cabin a mile distant. He could see it plainly in
the clear air, but was unable to distinguish the forms of any
of the party he knew to be lurking there. Nearer were two
other cabins, one of them half a mile away in the middle
of the basin and the other almost below him, the domiciles
of neighbors.

It occurred to him that his friends should be warned of
the presence of the posse and of their hostile feeling. So
he sent his pony down the hillside and to the first house,
where he found the small rancher and his family at breakfast.

"Hey, Burney, you may have visitors," he said, walking
in. "Hell's been poppin' in town. Bill Lawson, of the Box
U, was murdered night before last in Chavo, and the safe
of Pete Brill's office robbed last night. They're tryin' to
frame me for both jobs, damn 'em! They had me in jail for

the killin', but I got out and home. A posse headed by that coyote Joe Mallett come to my place early this mornin' to catch me, but I was sleepin' outside and they didn't succeed. I didn't know 'bout the robbery till I heard 'em talkin' about it and me bein' guilty while they was searchin' my house. They're hidin' 'round there still, thinkin' I'll come back for the stolen money and bonds, which of course ain't there, me never havin' took 'em. Well, I stopped to tell you I'm on the run. Takin' to the woods. May need some chuck later, so if you hear a tappin' on your window of nights you'll know who it is. Me. More, I want you to go to the Sheriff and tell 'em it's all a lie 'bout me what they're claimin' and then stir up folks you know. They're talkin' of runnin' us all outa here, us bein' nesters and rustlers, something they never dared do openly before."

The other, a stocky bearded man, got to his feet.

"Let 'em try runnin' us out," he answered. "I ain't surprised at what you're tellin' me, with them fellas in control of the county. Rustlers! We'll rustle them if they try to grab our ranches!"

"Well, that's all for now, Gus," Les concluded. "Don't want any of that bunch yonder knowin' I'm here."

Burney followed him outside. They gazed eastward across the basin to where Bridges' cabin stood.

"I see 'em," the man remarked. "Looks like they're ridin' this way."

"Jumpin' Mavericks! That's what they're doin'. Comin' fast, too. Must've seen me when I stopped in that open place on the hill to look before comin' down here. Figgered they couldn't or wouldn't, but as it's turned out that was kinda imbecile figgerin'. I'm leavin' pronto. Don't let 'em browbeat you none, Gus."

"I'll talk to 'em through a winder with my rifle cocked. Good luck, cowboy."

Les did not force his pony as it climbed the ridge. Through carelessness he was in for a chase now, probably a long chase, and impetuous though he was he was too sensible to jump his horse into a run where the going was hard. There were five of them and they would scatter out to come round him on both flanks, but as against that he had the cover of the forest, an intimate knowledge of the ravines and ridges about the basin, and a rifle if they got too close.

BY MIDMORNING HE had led them several miles back into the mountains. At noon he thought he had lost them; and was doubling back. It was the middle of the afternoon when he slipped down through the trees behind his own place and after a careful scrutiny advanced toward his house. He guessed that in the haste of setting off after him, the posse had left the black garments planted in his cabin as incriminating evidence, and he purposed grabbing them.

"That will leave 'em with an empty bag," he told himself, grinning.

There in the house were the sombrero, mantilla, and mask, sure enough. He examined them with curiosity, tried them on with a chuckle, and finally carried them out and placed them in the sack at his cantle. So busy was he with this that he was oblivious to the fact that the five horsemen who had pursued him and who had abandoned the hunt were coming toward him not two hundred yards up the creek. It chanced that his house intervened. When he rode off, he and the members of the posse sighted each other simultaneously; a yell burst from Joe Mallett, and at once Les jumped his pony into a run to head down the creek trail.

Thus the chase began anew. He galloped for the ford, dashed through it and northward, until he turned up a ravine two miles before the Box U Ranch buildings were reached. The horses of all were jaded by now, and in consequence the young fellow was able to make no faster pace than the men after him. They kept him in sight most of the time, now and again sent bullets at him, and thrice were able to prevent him from working deeper into the hills, finally heading him as the sun sank low down into the creek canyon where Betty Underwood saw him and his pursuers racing past.

Flying down the trail too, she followed. When she gained the ranch house, she discovered that the hunt was over and Les a prisoner. His pony had staggered to a stop by the corral, where he had made an appeal for a fresh mount to Lafe and three other Box U punchers who had just come off the range. Before the men grasped his urgent need and could rope a horse, the posse arrived too on their exhausted beasts.

A hot dispute was in progress as Betty joined the group.

"He's a liar," Les was shouting. "You know I'd never shoot Bill. As for robbing the Court House, that's rot."

"We're takin' you in to stand trial for murder and robbery, and you can do your talkin' in court," Joe Mallett growled. "If you get too smart with me, you may not even get to town."

"You can talk all you want to me right now, Les," Lafe stated. "I'm kinda interested in hearin' your side."

"He's a prisoner, you don't talk none to him."

"Listen, fella, you may think you're bad," Lafe said, with

his grey eyes growing flinty, "but if he wants to talk, he talks."

"I certainly intend to hear what Les has to say," Betty burst out.

"And my gun is backin' you," the grizzled puncher stated. "How 'bout it, boys!"

"Yeah," the three other cowboys chorused. "Nobody's interferin', either."

A murky flush darkened the Deputy Sheriff's face, and a scowl rested on his low brow. However, he hesitated to force the issue, for he was none too sure of the staunchness of his men in front of these cowpunchers who had a reputation as fighters. It was the big Mexican, hitherto silent, who came to his aid by a surprise move.

"Wait," said he, with a tight smile and forefinger pointing at an end of black cloth protruding from the tied neck of Les' sack of provisions. "What is this?"

His nimble fingers swiftly unknotted the cord and drew forth the black sombrero, black mantilla, and black mask. He held them up for everyone to see, his smile now broad and malicious; and an exclamation of dismay escaped Bridges.

"And he says he didn't rob Brill's safe!" Valdez said. "Yet here in a sack on his saddle we find his disguise worn while engaged in the crime. Bah, he hasn't a leg left to stand on!"

THE YOUTH GAZED wildly from face to face, his gaze settling to rest at last on Betty's with a desperate, pleading look.

"How do you explain this, boy?" Lafe asked, curtly.

"They planted it in my cabin, they came there last night. They've been chasin' me in the hills all day and when I doubled back I found these things in my house and took them."

"Sounds pretty thin, Les."

"Still, it's the truth. I know it looks damned bad, but—"

"Come, fella," the Deputy ordered, with an evil grin. "The boys here 'pear to have heard enough of what you have to say. What 'bout usin' the blacksmith shop, Lafe, to keep him in after he's hog-tied, until we can get a bite for ourselves and a feed for our horses!"

Lafe nodded and turned away.

"It's all a lie, a frame-up, I tell you!" Les shouted.

"I know it," said Betty.

"Tut, tut, girl," spoke Pete Brill, who had come unperceived from the house. "You know nothing about it at all. In time you'll learn what a rattler he is."

She opened her lips to make a hot retort, then closed them tight without speaking. With a scornful glance at him she left the spot. On reaching the door of the kitchen her self-control failed and she rushed inside and on into the living room, where her father still sat in his home-made cowhide chair staring haggardly at nothing.

"Dad," she said, clutching his shoulder. "They've just arrested Les for killing Bill!"

His head lifted, he half-rose, but sank back once more, wordless. She shook him a second time, and more vigorously.

"Are you a coward?" she cried. "Are you going to sit there without raising a finger in defense because those rogues, Pete Brill and Carlos Valdez, have fooled you into thinking you murdered Bill Lawson? Have you lost all your fight? Are you going to let—"

Her father was on his feet glaring at her.

"You know?" he demanded, hoarsely.

"I know you didn't kill Bill."

"I did, I did."

"You were deceived, hoodwinked."

"No, no, lass! It's all like a hideous nightmare, and the shooting part is foggy, but I killed him. When I came to myself, I was standing over him with my gun in my hand and Bill dead at my feet and the sound of the shot still ringing in my ears."

"Where did it happen?"

"In Brill's office. We had been playing poker. We had had a couple of drinks, but the last drink didn't set well with me and my head began to swim, and then Bill came in—and I killed him."

"Who else was there?"

"Brill and Valdez."

"So they were the only witnesses."

"Oh, God, Betty! I feel as if I were going mad!"

"Buck up, Dad," she said, catching his hands. "You never shot Bill, it was Pete; they tricked you."

Slowly, as if a ray of light were beginning to make its way into his mind, his eyes lost their glazed look and came alive. His fingers tightened on hers.

"If that were only true!" he muttered.

"It is true, and we'll get the proof. We're going to fight them and whip them, Dad, and if you'll but stand firm and refuse to believe their lies we'll win. You've suffered, but you're going to suffer no more. You've endured agonies of remorse, and all because you were deluded. You gave those ruffians the Box U to save yourself from arrest and me from shame, and it was a hollow sacrifice. But we still have the ranch."

"No; that is gone."

"It is not gone. I have it, the deed you surrendered."

"You?" Her father stared. "That's impossible, girl."

"Well, see." She drew out the paper and unfolded it to his gaze. "But Pete Brill and Carlos Valdez do not yet know they have lost it, and we must not let them or anyone know, except the Sheriff, whom we'll go and see and tell everything first thing in the morning. Now I'm hiding it again. Oh, Dad, everything is going to come out right!"

"At least you give me hope," he said, in a new voice. "How do you know so much, and how did you get that paper?"

BETTY LAUGHED SOFTLY. She had shocked him out of his despair and kindled his old-time courage and spirit.

"After supper I'll tell you all," said she. "But the sun has gone down and it's growing dark, and I must start supper. For two days you've not touched food; now you will eat. The teeth of the trap we're in don't hold us quite so fast. What did Brill want here today?"

"A bill of sale for the Box U herd."

"Did you give it to him?"

"No. I told him I would after supper, but now—"

"You won't."

He regarded her with a shadow of fear reappearing on his visage. "If he should carry out his threat?"

"And reveal that he covered you, and so too is guilty?"

"By God, you're right!" he exclaimed. "I'll refuse, and fight it out!"

"Ah, but you must not show your hand, Dad; you must go on pretending to be in their power but evade and postpone doing what they want." She ceased, lifting hand for quiet. "What's happened?"

From the direction of the blacksmith shop came an outburst of yells, shouts, and the report of shots. Together Underwood and his daughter ran through the living room into the open. Night was falling. They could not distinguish at the distance the cries and calls came from what was occurring, nor make out the forms moving there.

Betty darted ahead of her father to the building.

"What's happened?" she asked, on meeting Lafe running thither too from the bunkhouse with the rest of the punchers.

"Les must have made a break," he panted.

"Pray that he wasn't shot!"

No bullet had struck the youth who was so hard to hold. An enraged Joe Mallett was cursing furiously when they pulled up before the door, while his men were making excuses.

"I tell you I got a knock on the head when I stepped outside for a moment," one protested, with a whine, "and it laid me out. I just glimpsed a fella in a black hat and mask and robe, and then the lights went out for me."

"Bridges had dressed up while you wasn't lookin', I suppose," the Deputy Sheriff sneered. "The only trouble with that story is that I've the hat and mask and mantilla what was in his sack. Fix up a better lie next time."

"I ain't lyin'," was the surly answer.

"And where were you other two fools? Takin' a nap?"

"Takin' a smoke at the end of the buildin'. We figgered with Zeke inside watchin', the young fella was safe." Then he added, "Must've been one of these Box U cowboys."

"Of course," the Deputy growled.

"Wasn't you talkin' to us at the bunkhouse, Mallett, when the alarm was raised?" Lafe inquired, sarcastically. "To all *four* of us? Use your head. Les Bridges slipped outa the ropes and away while your guards loafed outside, that's all there is to it."

The Deputy turned on his men with a fresh stream of curses, at which they sullenly announced they were quitting as possemen. It was at this point that the Sheriff and his party came on the scene at a pounding gallop.

"What's all this rowin' about?" he demanded. "And the shootin' we heard?"

"Only your Deputy grindin' his teeth," Lafe replied.

CHAPTER IX

A FLYING KNIFE

IGNORING THIS FLYER, Joe Mallett gave his superior a rapid account of events as they involved Les Bridges.

"Let me look at them articles," Condon said, dismounting. "Turn our horses into a corral, men; Underwood will feed us, I reckon, before we push on to Chavo. Eh, Clem?"

"Sure, Amos. You yourself will eat with Betty and me."

"All right. Now, this disguise."

"Come 'long to the mess house, where I left 'em," said the Deputy.

They went to that building, followed by Pete Brill and Carlos Valdez, as Condon became aware when the two entered a moment later. The bald cook, who was tending pots and kettles on a stove at the far end of the room, rolled eyes upon the visitors and when informed that he had nearly a dozen more mouths to feed swore lustily.

Mallett unrolled the black cloak from about hat and mask and passed them to Condon for inspection. Under a lamp the Sheriff gave each a close examination. He was puzzled. What he knew of the young, impetuous, fiery puncher who had started a small ranch in Agate Creek Basin did not fit with the role of a cunning robber pretending to be the notorious Masked Rider asserted by the Deputy.

"He must've bought these things from you, Valdez," he addressed the Mexican merchant."

"No, no; not from me. That would give him away. So he must have got them from a store distant from Chavo."

The Sheriff made no further comment, but rolled up the articles and with a word to Mallett to take charge of them led his Deputy out. He was not loquacious at any time, and he had a "poker face." Neither by word nor look did he reveal a discovery he had made, namely, a distinctive red grilled price tag fastened to the hem of the mantilla, the price tag invariably used by Valdez for his merchandise.

The mantilla had come from the Mexican's stock, no question of that. So too probably had come the sombrero and the black silk handkerchief in which had been cut eyeholes. Yet Valdez had quickly denied the goods; if anything, a little too hastily. Why? The Sheriff's suspicions stirred. Valdez' denial did not accord with the evidence of the price tag, while Les Bridges' ascribed crimes did not conform with his character. Something fishy in all this.

He had noted moreover as he left the room, a fleeting smile of derision on Pete Brill's face. Long before, he had divined Pete's crafty nature and ruthless spirit, as he was convinced of Valdez' equivocal mind and greedy soul. For months the pair had been thick as thieves. Had they manufactured this evidence for some sinister purpose to make Les out a criminal? For what purpose? He, Condon, would like to hear the boy's side of the tale.

Pete Brill's smile had, after the two officers' departure, expanded into a grin of enjoyment. He pulled Valdez outside and gripping his arm led him apart, slapped the Mexican on the shoulder and indulged in a low laugh.

"Didn't know you was so smart, Carlos," he exclaimed, in

a whisper. "Puttin' those Masked Rider things where they would throw suspicion on that fool, Bridges, was clever. Makes the story of the robbery even better than to have it done by the mysterious outlaw himself. And we both have played the part of outraged citizens and sacrificing posse-men so well that not a soul will ever suspect it was us who got the stuff in the safe."

"You don't know all that happened, Pete," the Mexican answered, anxiously. "My riding to catch The Masked Rider wasn't tomfoolery."

"Sure not," Brill chuckled, "you were in dead earnest, and so was I."

"Mia Madre, won't you listen? I'm telling you that that thief, young Bridges, was there at the Court House too last night. He wore that black hat, black mask, black mantilla; I did not put them in his house as a trick. What I wore is again in my store. His were not mine. *Por Dios,* it is true! Oh, that vile wretch! Oh, that miserable thief! How I would love to have his throat in my hands!"

"WHAT IN THE name of hell is all this that you're whispering about?" Brill demanded.

"What! That *ladrón* Bridges, that dog of a robber, who leaped upon me in the hall as I crept out of your office when Jim was gone and laughed in my face, holding the muzzle of his gun against my breast, and swore he, Les Bridges, should be paid for our having taken his gun and thrown him in jail, and snatched from me both money and bonds!"

"You mean you haven't *them?*" Pete hissed.

"No. Alas, no, Pete. It is as I say: I got them, but this scoundrel of a puncher sprang upon me and with a pistol to my heart took them."

"You're lying! You're trying to double-cross me and keep all the stuff for yourself!"

"Pete, never," Valdez spoke, vehemently. "I swear to you I speak the truth. Bridges has the money and bonds."

"You treacherous hound, I'll shoot you full of holes if you don't come across with that plunder when we reach town!"

"Would I be such a fool as to try to deceive you, Pete?"

"You're trying it now, by God!"

"No, no, no!"

"Yes!"

"I? No. Only the truth I speak, only the truth. Stop and consider what happened, how this Bridges attacked us before, swore to get us, hung about and listened to our plans, and—"

"You— Shut up, someone is passing. Can't stand here longer. But after supper we'll talk and, by the Eternal, I'll get satisfaction or know the reason why."

Their fierce whisperings in the darkness ended and they moved toward the mess house where the other men were gathering. But they did not eat there. Should not the owners of the Box U eat their meal in the ranch house? As to the Underwoods' feelings in the matter, Brill was in a mood now to trample them under foot regardless; and where Brill led, Valdez followed. Thus it was that Betty and her father had no opportunity to inform the Sheriff then, as they had none later that evening, of the desperate plight in which the cowman was involved.

"Ridin' with me to town?" Condon questioned of the two unwelcome guests, as all rose at the end of supper.

"Yes, yes," Valdez, assented, quickly.

"Might as well," Brill replied, giving the Mexican a level look.

"We'll start as soon as our meal's settled."

Betty plucked the Sheriff's sleeve as the three moved toward the door. He made an excuse to delay.

"Dad and I will be in tomorrow to see you," she informed him, when sure the others were gone. "It's important, terribly important. About the killing of Bill. But don't mention it to a soul. We can't tell you now because none here must suspect, especially those two who've just left. Now go before they miss you."

With a sharp regard of her flushed face, then a glance at Underwood's harassed countenance, he nodded and turned. Outside he halted to think. Here was more mystery. He thought, "A hell of a lot has been happenin' since I went after that horsethief the other side of the county—a bad killin', a big robbery, and a hatful of false clues and simmerin' secrets."

Off by the bunkhouse and the smaller corral he could hear the punchers and their visitors talking and see the burning ends of cigarettes glow. Pete Brill and Valdez had gone down there too. That pair, now! That Masked Rider yarn!

A hard metal end was jabbed into his ribs.

"Don't yelp or try nothin', Sheriff," came the tense command. "Move back slow, step by step, toward the creek."

"All right, boy," Condon answered, calmly. "I never argufy with a gun that has the drop on me."

A MINUTE AFTERWARD he was halted near a clump of underbrush.

"This is Les Bridges talkin' to you, Sheriff."

"I know. Rec'nized your voice. Kinda been wantin' a private palaver with you myself; I ain't of a mind to gather you in—yet. You can let down that bolt, or whatever it is you're pretendin' is a gun, Les, for it ain't deceivin' me none. I know the feel of the real thing."

"Shucks! And I thought all the time I was smart!"

"Never mind, Les," the Sheriff said. "Too many men around for us to waste time, so we'll get to the point. You're a murderer, a robber, The Masked Rider, a rustler, a fence-cutter, and a chicken-thief, by the tell—all since I left Chavo four days ago. You've straddled sin and are ridin' it high, wide, and handsome. Been disappointed in love?"

"For the love of Mike, Sheriff, be serious!" the youth exclaimed, appealingly. "I'm in a hell of a fix. They've made me a outlaw, they've got me on the run, they've—"

"Keep your voice low," the other admonished. "And pass up the sorrows of your case. Give me your side of the story, startin' with your comin' to town; and make it brief."

Thereupon Les burst into hurried narrative, relating step by step the succession of mystifying events, inexplicable misadventures, hazards, captures, and escapes, that had dogged him until the present moment.

"So," said Condon, meditatively, "so."

"Yeah, just so."

"And you don't have the least idea who killed Bill Lawson?"

"No."

"And you don't know who released you from jail and locked up Joe Mallett in your place?"

"Hey, did the fella do that? That's rich. No; don't know."

"And you were gone before the robbery?"

"Must've been. Left town fifteen minutes after mixin' it with Brill and Valdez in Brill's office."

"And you figger that disguise was planted in your cabin?"

"You bet your life! Had to be."

"If that's the case, how do you explain their waitin' for you to come back to the house?" Condon inquired. "They would know you weren't the robber and didn't have the loot."

"The three boneheads makin' up the rest of the posse wouldn't," Les said, acutely.

"That's true." Condon paused, then continued, "Now about this painted medicine wagon, sick doctor, Grantly, and a strange doctor lookin' after the others. You say the stranger told you Grantly had been shot at and creased?"

"Yeah."

"Curious. Like to talk with this Wayne Morgan; mebbe he could remember, with promptin', something about the ambusher from the glimpse he had. Curious, and more'n curious, Grantly bein' shot at when he knew something suspicious about Pete, as you say he hinted. Well, we must get on. You was chased, and doubled back to your cabin, and put the disguise in your sack, and was pursued again, and caught here, and confronted with the evidence, and was tied up in the blacksmith shop, and was cut loose by Betty. Sure it was Betty?"

"She was all wrapped up in a black cloak, but it couldn't be anybody else," Les declared. "She just showed up like a shadow at my side, cut my bonds, and faded away. Too dark for me to see plain, but it was her all right, all right."

"Well, boy, I reckon you can continue as a free outlaw till I want you," the Sheriff announced. "When I do, I'll send you word through Gus Burney. Stay hid here till we're gone, then you can slip down for your horse. After that keep back safe in the peaks, outa trouble. When you move 'round, you simply can't remain outa grief."

Les uttered a grunt, then a hiss of excitement.

"Something crossed before that window, something like a billowing black shadow!" he whispered. "And look, there it is by another; you can just see it at the edge of the lamplight kinda dim. Betty in the cloak again, I'm guessin'. But what in tarnation is she wrapped up for that-away now and peerin' in a window of her own house?"

"She ain't the only one," Condon murmured. "There's a man by the other window watchin' her. The light's showin' him plainer as he bends forward."

SILENTLY THEY OBSERVED the partially silhouetted figures, curious, intent, wondering what was the significance of the shadowed pantomime.

"The man is Joe Mallett," Les said low, presently.

"So I make him out."

"Mebbe he thinks it's me he's seein', me in another black outfit. You can always figger that skunk's sneakin' 'round somewhere meddlin' with what ain't his business. Look! Oh, my God, he's goin' to shoot her!"

By the lamplight they beheld Mallett's right arm raised with hand holding gun, the long barrel of which had been elevated but at the instant was being slowly lowered for an aim at the other scarcely visible form, the indistinct cloaked person gazing into the room through the window. The night quiet, the shadowy shapes, the deadly menace in that wordless pantomime, all were horrifying.

The Sheriff swiftly swept his own six-shooter from holster; Les gasped a choked cry. But no death flamed from the steel barrel pointed at the intended victim. Something gleamed and passed instantaneously in the lamplight of the window by which the Deputy stood and struck in the man's throat. At the same time a low animal snarl sounded in the darkness near the house; and the cloaked figure vanished.

The gun fell from Mallett's raised hand. His fingers clutched and fumbled at the object protruding from his throat, then he swayed, pawed blindly at the air and fell forward.

"Knifed, by God!" Condon exclaimed. "By a blade flung from the dark!"

"Come on," said Les.

"Stay, you idiot! Haven't you any sense? Head away from the ranch as fast as you can leg it; they'll fasten this on you sure, and they'll believe I'm lyin' merely to save you if I say I was here with you. That'll have to wait. Get goin' and don't show hide or hair till I let you know it's safe."

"Who could have done it?"

"Can't even guess. But I'm goin' to find out. Skip now. I've got to get to Joe and call the men. The way he went down, he's done for."

He left at a run, shouting for help. He was kneeling by the Deputy's body when the crowd drawn by his call came pounding up to the house. A chorus of excited questions assailed him as punchers and possemen grouped themselves about the spot.

"Joe. Killed by a knife. Bring a lamp from the house," said the Sheriff. "I was yonder and happened to look this way and saw him against the light go down when struck. The knife is still sticking in his throat up to the hilt. You there, Underwood? Didn't chance to see or hear anything, you—or Betty?"

"Not a thing. We were busy talkin' over some business, until you shouted."

"You weren't outside a-tall, girl?"

"I? No, Sheriff. Dad and I've been in the living room discussing things ever since you left."

There was no questioning the sincerity of Betty's words or expression. If she had been inside all the while, as appeared, then whose was the cloaked figure? Condon's mouth became grim, for now a new mystery was added to the rest and one with a diabolical quality.

"You men were at the bunkhouse and the corral, eh?" he queried. "Anyone know of a man who wasn't?"

A barrage of assertions and statements and verifications and confirmations soon established the presence of everyone of the punchers and visitors, and even the cook, at one place or the other.

"Best go into the house, Betty," the Sheriff advised, as a lamp was brought. "No need for you to see such an ugly sight."

THE DISTORTED FACE and bloody throat and projecting knife handle indeed made a horrible picture. After holding the lamp and examining the wound, Condon gave the light to Underwood and rose.

"We'll borrow a team and wagon from you, Clem, to take the body to town," said he. "Saddle up men; we'll start with it at once. Mort, you will stay here and in the mornin' lead the Box U boys in a search for the killer, whoever he is. It's useless seekin' him tonight, and it's goin' to be hard enough by day, not havin' any notion of who he is. Come mornin', perhaps you can pick up some sign, though."

A derisive snort sounded from Pete Brill.

"Sign!" he barked. "They don't need sign, Sheriff. We all can make one guess as to the killer and not miss the mark, and I reckon we've all done it already. Who killed Bill Lawson? Who robbed my office? Who was caught here with a disguise? Who had been tied up by Joe? Who swore to get even with him? Who was it thirsting for Joe's blood—and spilled it? We don't even have to guess, we *know*. Les Bridges."

A hoarse growl from the throats of a score of men affirmed this denunciation.

" 'Pears that way, barrin' proof," the Sheriff returned. "Anyway, you can bear Les in mind, Mart."

"If Bridges escapes, you'll never serve another term as Sheriff, I'll see to that," Brill roared.

Condon moved finger towards the form on the ground.

"Bring the body, some of you," said he. "A year till election, Pete. Before then I may be as dead as Joe here, I—*or you!*" With which he walked off.

CHAPTER X

GONE ASTRAY

WAYNE MORGAN AND Blue Hawk were riding for the box canyon. The first rays of the sun were tipping the pine tops with gold, but in ravines and under the trees there was still only pale dawn light. Immediately after Blue Hawk's knife had saved his friend they had slipped away from the Box U Ranch, got their horses and headed for the ford of Agate Creek, where they slept on the wooded ridge above, since it would be arduous to find their camp in the darkness.

Morgan experienced no regrets over the Deputy's death. Joe Mallett's intention to kill the unsuspecting watcher by the house was, though the Deputy doubtless believed him to be Les Bridges, an illegal, cold-blooded, venomous purpose. Law officer though he was, it was naught but a wolfish determination on murder. A rattlesnake coiled in the mantle of the law would be less evil: it would at least give a warning before it struck. He were better dead.

Nevertheless from this justified killing real danger would arise, to say nothing of the thicket of difficulties in which Morgan would find himself in his effort to help the Underwoods and Les Bridges. He felt that, putting it plainly, it had spilled the beans. For one thing, the ranch now was too hot a spot for him to venture near again at present; so he had given over his design of meeting Betty. For another, it would put a strong weapon in Brill's hand. Worst of all, the Sheriff when he heard the cowman's and his daughter's story would deduce that The Masked Rider was responsible for his Deputy's death and refuse to hold his hand.

But when obstacles and perils would have deterred a less bold man than Morgan, they but challenged his spirit and hardened him in his resolve to see justice done. And it was in such mood that he entered, with his companion, the box canyon.

At the last bend Blue Hawk drew rein in the shelter of a copse of aspens. This was in accordance with the cautious policy the two men ever followed to obviate risk of their secret relation becoming known. No telling if one patient or other had regained consciousness. When Morgan signalled all well, the Mexican Indian would join him.

The first proceeded alone. At the jackpines screening the camp Morgan dismounted, left his horse and made his way between the dense growth of conifers and cliff to the hidden space within. Passing the wagon, he stopped in surprise. Then he made a swift and silent search of the place and next of the canyon about.

One blanket bed was empty—Grantly was gone! On his improvised pallet the stricken doctor lay, but of the newspaper editor there was not a sign.

A beckoning hand brought Blue Hawk to him.

"Grantly isn't here," he announced, anxiously.

"And the médico?"

"Still here."

"Then it is that the camp has not been found by someone and the man carried away, *señor*," the Yaqui stated, "but the man awoke and went off on his own legs. Perhaps he is yet near; I must not be seen by him."

"His blankets are cold."

"His boots, clothes?"

"Gone too."

"Let us look there again." And when they had made a fresh inspection of the camp, the Indian presently grunted and called attention to their sack of provisions. "It is not as it was left. He woke up hungry, he has eaten of the cold meat and *frijoles*."

"How long ago, can you tell?"

BLUE HAWK DREW forth and unwrapped the chunk of roasted beef and pan of beans, scrutinized them, and spoke:

"Neither the meat where it is cut nor the beans where taken are dried over. An hour, perhaps two hours ago he ate; certainly this morning. At daybreak let us say, *señor*."

"A long start."

"But he would be weak. Besides, not knowing where he was he would not go straight but wander seeking."

"That's the devil of it, Blue Hawk; he may lose himself altogether," Morgan exclaimed, anxiously. "If by luck he finds his way down to the road, he'll likely make for town, which is the worst thing he can do. He won't know what happened to him. He'll be puzzled over what amounts to a loss of memory, over finding himself here, and all the other circumstances; but he has no knowledge how he got his wound or that his murder was attempted. Yes, if he gets out of the hills he'll head straight for home to solve the riddle."

"*Si,*" the other agreed.

"He must not get there; he'll be killed for sure. Besides, I need him. He has proof of Brill's embezzlement. And I must have that for use. We'll eat, then you get to work and see if you can't pick up his trail. I'm going to drive the doctor to the neighborhood of the Box U and leave him to the care of the Underwoods. May be hazardous, but I must risk it. He's rallying, his fever's down, he's sleeping naturally; nursing will bring him around soon and the girl can give him that. With things as critical as they are I can't be encumbered with a sick man. When I've delivered him there, I'll strike for town to try to meet Grantly and take him in charge again. He must be intercepted and warned."

"This going of yours to the ranch so soon I like not, *señor*," said Blue Hawk. "It is putting not only one foot but both into a wolf-trap."

"Have to do it, that's all, *amigo*," Morgan replied, frowning. "So let's eat."

The meal was quickly disposed of. Afterwards they packed their slender supply of provisions and utensils, hitched the team to the painted wagon, placed the doctor in its bed on pine boughs and blankets, fastened Morgan's saddled stallion behind, and leaving the garishly lettered cases of patent medicine by the jackpines, departed. Morgan drove out of the canyon, followed by Blue Hawk on his sorrel.

"Here's soft earth before the canyon's mouth," the driver said. "And aren't those boot imprints just there? Our eyes are growing dull, Indian; we should have noticed them when we rode in."

"I was thinking of a dead man."

"Never mind. We don't often slip like that. Which recalls to me another's tracks; keep an eye open for those of the ambusher. My first guess is that he will turn out to have been Joe Mallett, if we learn at all."

"He was a killer, yes."

"Well, I owe you a good knife, Blue Hawk, for last night."

"I have another," was the laconic response. "See, the tracks lead off. I will follow till I come up with him; a child could do that with such a plain trail." Whereupon the speaker veered aside.

The sun stood at noon when Wayne Morgan came down to the ford, for the going had been rough and he drove with care not to shake up the sick man. Luck was with him for the time being; he encountered no one on the road to the Box U Ranch. From a distance he observed the buildings, which might have been untenanted for any indication of persons he saw. The Underwoods would be in town, and the punchers must be absent. If anyone were there, he would be the cook. No sign even of him was apparent when Morgan, playing a hunch, stopped the wagon by the corral.

AN INVESTIGATION CONFIRMED his belief that everybody was away. He unharnessed the team and turned the pair of horses into the corral, pitched them some hay. After that he picked the lock of the kitchen door and bore the ailing doctor within the house, where after bestowing him in a bed he perceived the sick man's condition no worse for the journey. He placed Chessington's valise by the chair on which rested his clothes, left his wallet, watch, papers, and other personal possessions on a stand, and going out relocked the kitchen door.

A slight smile rested on his lips as he rode off on his black stallion. Surprises were due for the Box U "family." He could imagine the cowpunchers' amazement at seeing the gaudy wagon by the corral. He pictured the even greater astonishment of the cowman and his daughter when they discovered the plump invalid in one of their beds.

But he too was to be surprised. Far down the road he saw a cloud of dust raised by horsemen, whereupon he wheeled his mount toward the hill and sent it racing across the creek and up a brushy draw. He was looking down from timber when the party of riders galloped up to the ranch. They were Box U punchers led by a man he did not know but evidently in charge, and in their midst was a prisoner. Morgan did not have to look twice to identify the bound, disheveled youth.

"That damned Les again!" the watcher exclaimed, in disgust. "No matter how often he's hit, he just keeps poking up his head for more!"

CHAPTER XI

A RISING STORM

IN THE BLAZING sunlight, the mountains seemed to crouch and retreat on the desert—distant sage clumps and taller cacti quivered and stretched upward until they showed strangely elongated shapes floating on mirage lakes.

Chavo baked in the fierce heat. Against the sides of Mexicans' 'dobe houses chickens nested in the dust for relief, burros stood drooping, and goats lay sleeping in the shade in brush pens. It was the period of late afternoon when usually the town, sluggish and inert, awaited the coolness of evening to revive.

On this day, however, Chavo was, despite the heat, in a state of ebullition and ferment. It was thronged with ranchers, cowboys, homesteaders, miners, Mexicans from distant creeks and villages, and general nondescripts, who, informed by the swift "grapevine telegraph" of such communities, had been drawn in to town by a common curiosity and interest. The Big 9 Saloon was packed by patrons' thirst for liquor and news. The two *cantinas* were filled with excited, gesticulating natives. So too, in the street and at the Court House men continually came and went, met, formed groups, parted, circulated anew, and eddied to and fro; all with questions, all worried, restless and ireful.

Over and over, events and rumors and surmises were told, repeated, discussed, debated, revised, enlarged, more highly colored. Each hour the crimes appeared blacker and the bankruptcy of the County more complete. One cowman irefully and drily tallied the scores of the happenings. His reckoning was:

One big cattleman—rumored in financial trouble.

One newspaper editor—missing.

One County Treasurer—safe empty.

One robbery—hundred forty thousand dollars.

One ranch foreman—murdered.

One Deputy Sheriff—murdered.

One murderer—uncaught.

Another murderer—ditto.

One Masked Rider—probably imaginary.

One assembly of inhabitants—bloodthirsty.

This salty summary had point, but it omitted the effect in general feeling, except in the last word. "Bloodthirsty" expressed that exactly and fully. The crowd burned to lay hands on the murderer and thief, who was no other by overwhelming evidence than the young puncher and rancher, Les Bridges. Pete Brill had made that clear time and again, and whiskey and inflamed talk had augmented the public wrath against the youth. Nor was he the only one to suffer from this; hints grew that Clem Underwood was somehow involved with the favored suitor of his daughter in the ugly business, while rumors ran that the Sheriff, on his part, was staying in town when he should be leading the hunt, was "holding back," was for some reason postponing the inquests and not doing his duty.

Condon had noted the growing mob spirit and personal criticism. All day he had been hard at work striving to dig out information about Bill Lawson's doings in town the night he was slain, and all sorts of facts pertaining to persons and happenings on the night of the robbery, investigating the two lines simultaneously; questioning men, seeking possible unknown witnesses, listening to all sorts of accounts, and endeavoring to winnow real grain from the heap of chaff.

Who had killed Joe Mallett, he had not even a suspicion—but he knew absolutely that it was not Les Bridges. Who had shot Bill Lawson, he could not even guess—but he was convinced in his own mind that it was no more the boy in this case than in the other. And who had robbed the County Treasurer's safe, he had no actual indication as yet—but he had a hunch that Pete Brill and Carlos Valdez held the secret of that.

At noon the Sheriff had met Clem Underwood and Betty in the street and being pressed by a hundred matters had arranged to meet with them later, he suggested that they had best stay in the hotel where he would join them about five o'clock. At that hour the three sat down in a private room to talk.

"Now let's have it," he said. "What you know 'bout Bill Lawson's killin'."

HE HAD EXPECTED to be told something that might give him a pointer in the affair, but he was not prepared for the gruff confession made by the cattleman nor the strange story related by the girl. These recitals lasted for more than an hour. During the whole time the law officer never uttered a word, sitting quiet, listening with grim intentness, his own actions an occasional lift of eyebrows or a slow stroking of his gray moustache.

He remarked at the conclusion, "This all sounds like a nightmare."

"It isn't," Betty assured him. "Here's the deed."

He nodded. "I'll ask some questions, first. You don't rec'lect pullin' your gun on Bill, Clem? No? Had you ever experienced before that swimmin' dizziness you speak of? No? Well, did you notice any peculiar taste to the liquor you had that you say made you feel sick?"

"Come to think of it, I remember it had a kinda different taste what even the likker didn't hide," Underwood answered, thoughtfully. "Like aloes, or something."

"Anything else you noticed?"

"No. Unless I had a dim feeling of being helped to my feet before finding the gun in my hand."

The Sheriff leaned back in his chair. "Ah, just so!" he said, and smiled a hard smile.

"You think it means something?" Betty asked.

"It kinda lets light in. Now, the deed. In Brill's handwritin', I perceive, except your signature and the witnesses'. The witnesses are Joe Mallett and that drunken Mexican Jose Ortez. Thought you told me, Clem, there was nobody there but Brill and Valdez and of course Bill Lawson."

"There wasn't; by the Great Horned Bull, there wasn't! The paper wasn't witnessed in my presence at all, I recall."

"Afterwards, then. Joe would've done anything Brill bade and Ortez couldn't read, only scrawl his name. Brill's own seal used, too. Goin' back, I reckon you sat there while the deed was drawn, which must've been some time as it fills this entire sheet of legal cap."

"Wait. Let me think," the cowman said, putting hand to brow. "All kinda far off. But no. I didn't have to sit and— Why, the deed was already drawn! They told me

I'd murdered Bill, but the matter wouldn't come out if I squared 'em; and they pulled the deed on me immediate and eventually I signed it. By God, they knew beforehand!"

"You can put outa your mind that you killed Bill," the Sheriff rejoined. "We'll let the matter rest there for the time, and get along. Now, girl, 'bout this mysterious gent who converses with you. I'm opinin' that our neck of the woods is being visited by that famous outlaw we've all heard bout. The Masked Rider. And it explains a number of things heretofore obscure. Still I don't know how he learned your father didn't kill Bill but was tricked instead. As for the deed, he got it of course when he robbed the safe."

"He said he didn't rob the safe," Betty protested. "And I've a feeling that he was speaking the truth."

"Some reports of him asserts he doesn't lie, but we don't know for sure," the Sheriff mused. "Repeat them words he spoke."

"Those queer ones? They were, 'What was in a false hand fell into a true. What was stolen was saved.'"

"I'll have to ponder 'em to extract the meanin'. Now we won't talk no more. Clem, you and Betty head for home; hell is goin' to pop in the town tonight, I'm afraid. There's feelin' against you, against me, and against Les. Brill's ridin' the top of the wave and workin' up sentiment against me all the time. And I can't do a thing to check him until I get proof that he engineered Bill's death, said proof havin' to be positive, final, and absolute. Comin' down to it, he may have me whipped out by the mob if he suspects I'm after him. But I'll get him. First, I'll take a posse of the more reliable men and go after that Masked Rider."

"Oh, no. He has helped us," Betty exclaimed. "Wait, anyway. He said he would find the proof."

"Can't wait. He stole the County funds."

"But—"

"And he knows who killed Joe Mallett."

"He?"

"Yes. He was by your house when the knife was thrown. Haven't mentioned it, but I was talking with Les at the moment a little way off and we both saw him." The Sheriff rose to his feet.

"I promised to get you to wait for a day or two more," Betty pleaded.

"GIRL, DO YOU want Les hanged?" Condon asked, gravely. "I've got to act to save him, and the first thing is, if possible, to catch The Masked Rider. When it's known I have the Court House robber, the fury of the crowd will be turned away from Les, for the time bein' at least."

"To the other man, yes. Probably they would take him out of your hands and lynch him."

"Will have to risk that. I'm goin' out now to tell men The Masked Rider actually is the robber, in the hope of checkin' the feelin' against the boy."

"They can't do anything to him; he's hiding in the mountains."

The look the Sheriff directed at her was commiserating.

"Les has been caught again," said he, gently. "The news was brought to me by one of your punchers just before I came here and the men in the street already had it. They're cryin' for his head. Mort Jones is keepin' him at the Box U until he gets orders from me, for fear of a lynchin' if he brings him in. I'm sendin' word for him to hold him there.

So you see, girl, why I have to go huntin' The Masked Rider, though a blind hunt it will be in the dark. It's to save Les Bridges."

"Yes; you must save Les," she whispered, in fear.

"You'll be goin' home at once?"

"We'll start right away," the cowman replied. "Best thing to do."

CHAPTER XII

PETE BRILL

A BOUT SIX O'CLOCK Pete Brill forced his way through the pack of men at the Big 9 bar and there tossed down a drink of whiskey. At intervals throughout the day he had whipped up his energies with the fiery liquor as the strain under which he worked to achieve his malevolent ends sapped his strength. His narrow hawkish face had deeper lines, his thin mouth a more cruel expression, and his eyes a hard glitter. What with excitement and whiskey and a feeling of power to sway the passions of the men thronging the town, his blood sang in his veins. He foresaw his cunning aims consummated and all danger dissipated—the Box U Ranch and herd his, the stolen money and bonds in his pocket, Betty Underwood willingly or unwillingly his wife, Les Bridges hanged, the Sheriff forced to resign office, his double-crossing secret partner wrung dry and if necessary "removed," nesters and other cowmen eventually his prey, and his undisputed mastery of property and lives in the region complete.

Men spoke to him, he answered, but his mind was absorbed with its humming schemes. He scarcely noted the saloonman, his two regular bartenders and two others hired to help handle the rush of business. He did not perceive Mike Grogan's cynical smile turned on him when he slid a bottle forward at Brill's second order, or a man with a yellow protruding fang watching him, or a tall dark stranger who stood inconspicuously a little way off. Had he, for that matter, seen Grogan's expression or Fang Nully's fixed stare or Wayne Morgan's surreptitious regard, he would have made nothing of them in that vehement, jostling crowd.

"Ain't we goin' to meet that murderin' wolf with a rope as he comes in?" a man demanded of him. Other voices took up the cry.

"The Sheriff may have something to say about that," Pete snapped out.

"To hell with the Sheriff! We'll be the law!"

"We're needing a new Sheriff who don't shield his friends," Brill answered. "But we'll give him a last chance to act. If later nothing is done by Condon, or if he's holding Bridges at the Box U Ranch as I suspect, we'll go get him, the cursed killer and thief! And I'll lead you! When a Sheriff fails in his duty, then citizens have to enforce the law."

A roar of approval greeted this assertion.

"You got any idea, Pete, where the stolen money is hid?" Grogan asked.

"I'll get it back into my hands if I have to tear the heart out of the man," was the answer, uttered with pretended ferocity.

"I believe you. Boys, give Pete a cheer; he's the one county officer who can be trusted."

The cheer was given. Fang Nully, who alone of all the rest realized the irony in the words, parted his lips in a mirthless grin. Then he caught a furtive signalling motion of Grogan's head as Brill pushed a way out of the saloon, and drifted after the County Treasurer. Behind Fang, Wayne Morgan drifted in a casual manner that left him unnoticed.

Pete's progress was slow. He talked with individuals, he joined vociferous groups, and at one place harangued a small crowd of avid listeners about the enormity of Les Bridges' crimes, the County's terrific loss, and the Sheriff's dereliction. The sun was setting when at length he neared the hotel, which was at the lower end of the street.

THE SHERIFF WAS just coming out of the building and a moment later they met. Their looks crashed.

"You sure are puttin' your knife into me today, ain't you, Pete!" Condon stated, curtly.

"One would almost think that some of the stolen money was to come into your hands, by the way you're holding back on the thief," Brill retorted.

"You know better than that," was the enigmatical reply.

"Why isn't Bridges here by now?"

"To make a lynchin'?"

"There wouldn't be a lynching."

"You're a liar clear down to your toes," the Sheriff said, from compressed lips. "But there isn't goin' to be no impromptu stranglin' in Chavo or anywhere, not while I'm ridin' the law—and I'm ridin' it still. Any hangin' that occurs will be legal. And there's goin' to be legal punishment for the guilty for both the robbery and the murder, you can stake your bets on that!" With which the speaker strode up the street.

Brill scowled after him. A disagreeable apprehension flashed through his mind; the old Sheriff had, after all, a habit of digging up the truth, an uncanny ability to make the most of the clues, a long record of running down crooks and outlaws. Did his final declaration indicate knowledge of Brill's perfidy? Pete cast out the idea. Impossible for

Condon to know anything. He was only talking boldly to hide his resentment.

He saw Clem Underwood and Betty come out of the hotel and start across the street toward the livery stable. Instantly he advanced, halted them.

"Come back into the hotel," he bade.

"No; we're heading for home," the cowman stated, curtly.

"The Sheriff was seeing you, eh? What about?"

Underwood's face grew thunderous with wrath at the insolent questions, but Betty's hand laid warningly on his arm prevented an outburst.

"Told us about Les Bridges being caught again at the ranch," he said. "We came to town because with the Box U deeded to you we had to send letters to relations in the East where we might live in case we had to go, as appears likely. Have to throw ourselves on 'em. I'm too old to start new again in the cow business."

"You can stay at the Box U. I have plans for that."

"Based on marrying my daughter, so I understand," Underwood growled. "She told me you asked her and threatened her yesterday. Well, you'll never marry her."

"Never!" Betty exclaimed.

"You think not?" Pete Brill grated forth. "Think again. I'll marry her, or you'll suffer. But this is no place to talk; come back into the hotel. I want that bill of sale now, and as the deed you gave me was taken from the safe along with the cash and bonds I want another. You're taking orders now, Underwood, and you know what's waiting for you if you don't." He beckoned forward some men standing a short distance apart. "Will you go in, or shall I tell them?"

Underwood was in a quandary. Innocent as he now

knew himself to be, he realized that Brill's lies would be more quickly believed than his own denials.

"We'll go in, but you come after a while," he said. "Betty and I will talk things over."

This suited the other, as he imagined the cowman would accede to his demands as he had before; there would be plenty of time to make Underwood bend his neck. On the other hand, he wanted at the moment to get to Valdez. The wily Mexican might decide to skip out; the stolen money and bonds must be forced from him without loss of an hour. So he ordered two of the men to stand guard in front and the other two in the rear and not allow the Underwoods to depart from the hotel; they were being held, he explained, as important witnesses against the young scoundrel Bridges.

The cowman and his daughter returned inside, the guards took their posts, and Brill set off for Valdez' store. By now the sun had set and dusk was falling. On the way he was met by the Mexican's clerk, who gave him word that the merchant was anxious to see him. On his return journey he did not allow men to stop him. No one was in the place but a Mexican Indian who was indolently bargaining for a shirt.

"Send your clerk away and get rid of this customer," Pete addressed his mine partner.

VALDEZ LEANED OVER the counter and caught Brill by the arm, repressed excitement causing his huge moustache to bristle.

"He is not dead, he has come back," the merchant ejaculated. "I saw him. Not more than ten minutes ago I saw him pass the door."

"Who?"

"He, the newspaper man. The *diarisa!*"

"You're crazy, Carlos."

"No, no, no. He passed. About his head was bound a white cloth and he wore no hat. If it were not he, then it was his ghost."

Pete's lips clamped together and his eyes flashed evilly.

"Well, I'll see him at once," he rasped forth. "No, not at once. That can wait until we've transacted our business."

"But, Pete—"

"I'll attend to him, I say. Nothing is so important as our affair. Your clerk's gone. This fellow, send him away. Who is he? Never saw him before. But drive him out."

"You, I am busy now," Valdez told the strange Mexican. "Already you have wasted much of my time. You can come back later. In an hour."

With an impassive face, Blue Hawk, who had pretended to have no interest in the other pair's sharp colloquy, laid down the garment and slouched forth.

"Bolt the door, Valdez," Brill ordered. "We want no interruptions. Now let's get down to it; I've had enough of your evasion and false stories."

"Pete, I swear to you—"

And thereupon began a hot dispute, with accusations and savage threats on one side and with tremulous denials and passionate pleadings on the other. This continued for three-quarters of an hour, when Brill suddenly drew from his waistband a six shooter and pointed it at the Mexican's heart.

"Come across with that money and packet, or I'll let daylight through you," he barked.

"Hey, what's the row 'bout?" a hoarse voice broke in upon the quarrel.

The two men in the store wheeled swiftly toward a window, where they beheld the faces of two half-drunken punchers. The lower sash was raised.

"There's no row," Pete announced, in an altered tone. "I was showing Carlos how I'm going to make Les Bridges deliver his plunder."

"We pounded on the door, but I reckon you didn't hear us," was the statement. "Seeing you inside we came 'round here and raised the window to make you notice. Want ammunition and rope."

"All the ammunition is sold out," Pete replied. "Use your las' rope."

The puncher's companion spoke, "Been tellin' you that, Ike. Come on away."

They went off arguing. Pete put away his gun and gave Valdez an inimical stare. "I'm leaving you for the time, but I'll be back later; I have to find that damned Grantly before he starts talking. Listen; you have the stuff handy when I come. And don't get the notion you can run out on me with it; I'll track you to the end of the earth if necessary. You can't double-cross me, you fat greaser!"

After he had departed Valdez leaned weakly against a showcase and closed his eyes. He was terrified. Finally he dragged himself to his bedroom in the rear of the building, where with shaking hand he poured himself a drink of *tequila* and gulped the liquor down.

"*Dios,* I am lost!" he moaned.

He did not hear the door of the store softly opened and as carefully bolted, nor hear the windows closed and fastened. He was too absorbed by fear and despair even to detect the cautious tread in his bed chamber.

All at once a strange feeling made him lift his gaze. Two

men with bandanna masks concealing their faces stood before him, six-guns aimed at his breast.

"Hoist your paws, Mister Masked Rider," one commanded. "Don't yelp or make any false moves; the buildin's shut tight and we've got you. We're goin' to relieve you of that stuff you lifted from the Court House safe. You needn't lie none 'bout not havin' it, for we follered you here when you brought it night before last. We'll just rope you to start with."

Valdez stood frozen with fresh terror.

CHAPTER XIII

QUICK ACTION

O N LEAVING THE store the Mexican Indian had walked but a few steps when a tossed pebble lightly struck his shoulder. At once he veered aside into a vacant lot, where he halted and turned. A shadowy form joined him in the darkness.

"Blue Hawk," came Wayne Morgan's whisper.

"*Si, señor.* I was about to seek you."

"Speak low. Another is close by, who watches the store. Why I know not."

"I saw him, standing close against the front. As you are aware, my eyes are the eyes of a cat for the dark."

"Since you are here, Blue Hawk, it means that Grantly must have come."

"Yes. His trail led me to the Basin, the trail of a man uncertain of his way. I saw him talking with the rancher who lives in the uppermost house. Creeping near in cover, I heard their talk, which ended in the rancher agreeing to drive the injured *diarista* to Chavo. Why wait when one knows another's destination! I crawled back to my horse and came before them. You, I looked for but did not find. I came to the store to wait and watch. Only now one came who by his name Pete and his manner to the merchant I perceived to be your enemy Brill."

"I followed him here."

"He is also the ambusher of Grantly," Blue Hawk stated.

"What, Brill?"

"The rider who shot the man of the newspaper from the edge of the forest above the ford had bootheels worn in a way that you would not find on boots among ten thousand *caballeros*. The right bootheel was worn on the inside, the left on the outside. Since coming to Chavo, I have looked at many boots. I regarded the boots of this Pete as he stood in the store. His heels are worn so, and his knees are both bent a little to the left, which is the cause."

"That's sufficient proof."

"Also there is the fear of Grantly. That dead one, that mule of a Deputy, would not be in these cunning *hombres'* secrets. That leaves but the two of them. This Valdez is only a pig; this Pete is a *tigre*. It was the tiger that was at the ford."

"And it was not the pig but the tiger that killed Bill Dawson, naturally."

"*Si, señor.*"

"They spoke of Grantly?"

"Valdez had seen him pass and he was *mucho* scared he told Pete. Presently, Pete goes to kill the man."

"We must prevent that," Wayne Morgan said, "we must warn Grantly. There are the Underwoods to be got out of Brill's hands too; the girl and her father are being held at the hotel. Where's your sorrel?"

"Standing among other horses before a *cantina*."

"Get it and wait for me well back in the greasewood behind the printing office. Mine is in the livery stable; I'll come to you with him. We'll have to work fast; hell is ready to boil over any minute, now night has come. Brill and whisky and robbery and murder have made an infernal brew. Listen to it seething."

A murmur interspersed with drunken shouts rose and fell, the confused sound of hundreds of exasperated and impassioned voices. Through the bars of lamplight falling outward from lighted doorways and windows men surged back and forth the length of the street; in and out of drinking places figures thrust themselves; and now at one spot and now at another, forms swarmed.

"All that's needed is the spark to set them off," Morgan said, grimly, "and Brill will strike that when he's ready. I'm wondering if Brill will go for Grantly alone, or with new lies set the mob on him. The latter would be the shrewder move, and Brill's a crafty devil. Well, go, Blue Hawk. If I can, I'll somehow start a back fire."

ON HIS WAY Morgan ventured once more into the Big 9 saloon; Grantly might be there. For that matter, anywhere. He was not in the riotous crowd that was drinking heavily. As he was glancing about the interior, Mike Grogan and a man with a yellow tusk brushed past him going out; the saloonman shaking himself free from a clutching hand explained that he couldn't stop to talk because he was going to supper.

Morgan, always alert and tensed when with others because of the possibility that someone from his past might recognize him, gave them a sharp look from under down-drawn hatbrim, as he did with everyone who came close. For men seeking only food, he thought their hard-gleaming eyes and set mouths and air of furtive purpose strange. But they passed out, and he made nothing of it, and a moment afterwards he himself withdrew.

He was caught in an eddy of the tumultuous crowd and

swept across the street before he could extricate himself. Anything could happen on such a mad night, he thought, anyone sacrificed against whom the lust and fury of this mob should be swung.

The editor's building was dark. He made a circuit of it, entered by the unlocked rear door and called Grantly by name. No reply. No result, either, to a quick search with lighted matches through rooms and printing office.

Perhaps the man was safe, perhaps he was in a secure refuge. But did he know his peril? Not fully, in any case; not at all, most likely.

So Morgan went hastily through the crowd, peering into open doorways and among the noisy throng, until at last giving it up as a bad job he stopped before the livery stable. Turning eyes upon the hotel, he saw it peacefully quiet in comparison with the main business section. The mob did not reach here. He entered the long stable. No one was there; doubtless the owner and his attendant had been sucked away by the excitement, but as he had paid for the stabling and feed of his horse in advance it was not necessary to hunt for them or await their return to make payment.

Swiftly he saddled his black stallion and led it out the big rear door, where he anchored it by dropping the lines. Reentering, he caught up a lighted lantern resting on a box at the front, with which he passed between the double line of stalls inspecting the horses they contained. In one he came on a harnessed team of trim shiny bays bearing the Box U brand.

Leading the team out behind, he left it to seek the vehicle that the Underwoods had used. This he found to be a buckboard standing with two others near a front corner of the stable, identified by a Box U stamp burned in the dash board. He hauled it back and hitched up the team. Then he returned the lantern to its place, tied the stallion at the end gate of the buckboard, and drove southward until he could cross the road and turn up east of the town without being seen.

Two hundred yards back of the hotel he drew rein, fastened the team by shortened reins to a thick sagebrush root. From under his saddle he drew forth his black cloak, head hood, and gloves, which he donned. Loosening his gun in its holster, he stole toward the rear of the hotel.

When within a score of paces of the building, he halted to listen to loud talk.

"What the hell! I ain't goin' to stay no longer, I'm tellin' you," spoke one voice. "We're missin' all the fun."

"Brill will be sore if we quit," the other replied.

"What do I care?"

"Better care, Mac. He made Joe Mallett let you go, remember, after you beat up that greaser on Sanchez Creek."

"Joe Mallett's dead."

"Brill ain't, and he can have you jailed yet for half-killin' that Mex a month ago; he prob'ly will if we let him down so these Underwoods get away. Pete don't forget either his friends or his foes. He'll be rulin' with a stronger hand than ever after tonight, for Condon's goin' to be kicked out as Sheriff. You stick by Pete's orders."

"Well, mebbe that's best."

Neither speaker heard or saw the shadow creeping on them from one side, not until a low threatening command stiffened them into silence and rigidity.

"Don't move. My gun's on you."

THE PAIR SAT on a wash bench by the rear door. They continued in perfect stillness and immobility to sit there, with eyes goggling at the indistinct cloaked, hatted form whose face was invisible. Indeed, to their startled gaze they appeared confronted by a dark and evil monster, dimly disclosed in the starlight.

"Who—who are you?" one stuttered, at last.

From the masked lips came a low laugh, then the words: "Satan, maybe!"

As if that were too much for one of the hearers, he dove headlong to pass the diabolical visitant, but The Masked Rider was too close. The man's shoulder lunged into him and, taking him by surprise, drove him back a step. As if contact with a solid form dispelled the guard's fright and restored his courage, he instantly clasped the unknown in a fierce hug pinning his arms to his sides.

"He's a liar, he's a man!" he yelped. "I've got him! Come on, Jack!"

The other guard came to life. He sprang up, cursing and clawing for his gun. A moment later its muzzle was jabbed against the prisoner's breast.

"Who are you, fella?"

But before the savage question could be answered the man's companion cried, "He's wearin' a cloak and mask and black hat."

"Like them young Bridges wore?"

"Yeah."

"Mebbe he's Bridges hisself. Hold him fast, Lon, till I look close. No; he's taller than that young puncher. Speak, fella, who are you!" And the gun pressed harder.

"I'm called The Masked Rider," was the slow rejoinder.

"You're lyin'!"

"I never lie."

"Jumpin' Mavericks, Lon, we caught a prize!" Jack exclaimed, exultantly. "This fella's head is worth an ore sack full of gold. We'll tie him up and keep him till we get the rewards. He's the biggest outlaw in the Southwest."

"Well, yes, I'm caught finally," The Masked Rider confessed, with pretended chagrin. "But I never met up with two men so fast moving or smart or strong as you, I admit. Looks like it's all over with me. However, you'll find I can swallow the bad medicine as good as the sweet."

"You ain't got a chance to get loose, Mister Masked Rider."

"Don't I know it?" he answered, plaintively.

He had let the other boast and had encouraged him in his confidence, meanwhile appearing to abandon hope of escape in order to make the man relax his first vigilance. Vanity is a weapon with edge turned toward its possessor. Jack began to preen himself on his prowess, and his feeling of triumph resulted in lessened caution and a withdrawal of his gun a few inches.

For something like this The Masked Rider was waiting. He was never so cool, never so dangerous, as when the odds against him were greatest or when the situation was most desperate. As the pressure of the gun ceased, he dropped like a plummet to his knees, smashed Lon across the left ankle bone with the barrel of his six-shooter, and rolled sidewise. A yell of pain rang out from Lon and his hold slipped, while at the same time a bullet from Jack's gun jerked a waving fold of The Masked Rider's cloak.

Without stopping in his roll The Masked Rider bounded to his feet and with two lightning-like chopping movements of his gun smashed Lon over the head and shot the guard Jack through his right shoulder. Jack's revolver exploded harmlessly as it fell from the man's fingers, his arm numbed by bullet shock; the fellow himself with a howl of terror fled around a corner of the building. As for the second guard, he lay unconscious where he had dropped.

THE MASKED RIDER darted through the hotel door. He found himself in a dimly-lit narrow hallway, with four doors on either side, which one after another he flung open alternately only to find the bedrooms dark, until he penetrated the third at his right.

This room was lighted. A cheap bed, a battered washstand with chipped pitcher and a bowl, a rag carpet and two pine chairs furnished the place, as The Masked Rider saw in his quick sweeping glance. In the middle of the chamber Clem Underwood and Betty stood, wonderment in their faces.

The second the girl beheld the tall masked and cloaked visitor she gasped:

"You?"

"Yes, I, The Masked Rider."

"There was a pistol shot!"

"The two guards interfered with me," said he, abruptly. "One's wounded, not bad; he's fled. The other's napping from a rap on the skull. No one dead."

"Was it necessary?" she quavered.

"Good God, girl, you ask that?" he exclaimed, harshly. "Do you think I like to strike men just for sport? There's no time for thinking. Come, grab your hats; we must get out of here. Your team and buckboard are back in the sagebrush, ready. That man who's shot is at the street by now and will bring the other guards. Quick. Fly, both of you."

He led them at a run along the hall and out the back door. They had not yet reached the spot where the buckboard stood when a bunch of men ran around from in front and with calls and cries of "Find him," and "Get The Masked Rider," flitted to and fro across the lighted doorway in their frantic search.

The hooded bandit untied the reins and handed them to the cowman, who with Betty mounted to the seat of the buckboard.

"Stay here till they have left," said he. "They will not come this far back. If they hear you they might shoot."

"Oh, sir, we owe you a debt we can never pay for all you've done for Father and me!" the girl said, in a tremulous voice.

"It's little enough, forget it," was the curt response. "There's a light yonder at Grantly's building. Listen, the man is in danger of being killed. Brill wants him dead. Will you take him with you!"

"Yes," said the cowman. "Bring him."

"If you can do so without noise, move your rig up behind his place but remain as far back as you are now. Time presses. Brill may attack him any minute. I'm going there now."

He rode off, slanting toward the place where Blue Hawk should be. Shortly he uttered a low animal cry and received answer. The Yaqui and his horse met him.

"Grantly is there?" The Masked Rider asked.

"Yes. For half an hour he has been in the house. When the light appeared, I left my sorrel and moved to a window to see. It was he."

"We'll push our horses closer and to the right, for the cowman and his girl will soon be waiting near. We must not be seen together; you must not be seen at all."

"No."

"This is close enough. Now I'll go get him and take him to the Underwoods."

"But he's not alone, *amigo.*"

"Not alone?"

"With him is another, the gray Sheriff."

"The Devil!" came in tones of consternation.

Blue Hawk emitted a chuckle.

"Do you speak of yourself, *caballero?*" he queried. "At least you are the dark one. And when did The Masked Rider ever give a snap of fingers for a Sheriff?"

The other dismounted.

"Never in a crisis," said he. Then he added in a tone of irony. "Perhaps this Sheriff would like a good look at the *real* Masked Rider, perhaps he will be so charmed by my regalia he'll want to clasp my hands—with handcuffs."

CHAPTER XIV

THE EDITOR'S STORY

CRIMES MAY BE committed and mob rule threatened, but Sheriffs must eat. Condon had gone home at supper time, where he partook of the hot supper his wife had prepared and strove to allay her fears.

"Women have told me folks have all turned against you, Amos," she stated, in trepidation.

"Not all. I've still friends left among the steadier cowmen and punchers and townsmen," he remarked, as he finished. "They ain't all bein' swayed by Pete Brill. Some of 'em have assured me they'd back me in a pinch, and they know of more who will; but I admit that Pete's got most of the crowd believin' his lies. A number always go with the majority. Of course the riffraff and toughs and ignorant are strong for him, and they swing a good many 'long with 'em. For the moment, anyway. But don't you worry, Em. Things are goin' to come out all right in the end, as they always do."

An insistent knock sounded at the kitchen door and his wife went to see who was there. It proved to be an urchin, the small son of a widow who set a table for a few boarders.

"Ma sent me over," he announced, large eyed and breathless from running. "Mr. Grantly come back, with his head all tied up. He won't say how he hurt it, but he was awful hungry and Ma has been feeding him. He wants you to meet him at our house and go with him to his printing office. Has something terrible important to tell you, he says. It won't wait, he says. Come right now, he says."

"Comin', Sonny," Condon rejoined. "You skip 'long and tell him I'll be with him in two minutes."

The boy ran out. Buckling on his gun belt and taking his hat, the Sheriff told his wife not to wait up for him and followed. Grantly and the urchin were expectantly watching for his coming.

"Don't you get hurt no more," the boy warned, as the two men started for the newspaper office.

"I won't, Billy," Grantly promised. Then to Condon, "I won't begin what I have to tell until we get to the office, except this much: somebody tried to murder me two days ago as I was on my way to the Bar U Ranch. You can be studying that over while we walk. What's all this about Brill's safe being robbed, and young Les Bridges being guilty? Never was so surprised in my life as when I came back this afternoon and saw the hullabaloo in Chavo. I started down the street, but shied off after getting a look. Mrs. Dexter back there told me the little I've learned."

"That better wait too until we're in your office."

"Very well."

When they entered the building and, the editor having lighted a lamp, they saw the overturned chairs, disordered type cases, spilled type and printer's ink and scattered papers, the men were dumbfounded.

"Somebody has torn the place to pieces looking for something," Grantly said, wrathfully. "And I know what they were after, and I know who was after it. Well, let the mess lie. I'll lock the door and pull down the shades." He did so. "Take a chair, Sheriff; you're going to get an earful.

Wait till I get a pipe going. Hell's Delight, that mob in the street is ripe, by the sound, to turn the whole town over!"

"Never mind it for now; get to your story."

Grantly drew at his pipe, nodded.

"Here goes," said he. "I should have gone to you first thing with what I'd learned about Brill, but I waited in the hope of getting more on him. It was Ralph Simmons, Brill's clerk, who gave me the stuff.

"Heard he'd been hintin' things wasn't right in the accounts, but he left Chavo before anything reached me."

"GOT THE JITTERS and ducked," said the newspaper man. "Wise thing too. I overheard him in the Big 9 one night when he was half-seas over bragging what he could tell about Brill if he wanted to, but nobody paid much attention to him except me. I decided to go to work on him. Brought him here, plied him with whiskey till he told me he had discovered that Pete Brill was short forty thousand in his accounts and was covering up with false entries. Well, I put the screws on him then. Made him believe he'd be sent to prison along with Brill unless he made a sworn statement as to the facts, wrote it out, and got it signed and sealed and witnessed. The notary and witnesses weren't allowed to see the contents of the statement, but Simmons must've let out to someone what he had done. It got to Brill's ears, evidently. Simmons was gone by then, but the paper wasn't. That explains the ransacking of this place. Brill, of course. Let me see if he found the evidence."

He rose and went to the printing press. He reached a hand under the solid frame and extracted a tightly rolled sheet of white paper.

"Hidden in a bolt hole, the last place anyone would look.

Glance it over," he continued. "Then put it in your pocket to keep. Brill might yet get me killed."

"I'll be closin' in on Pete before that happens," the Sheriff stated. "I'll look this over when I have more time. Proceed."

"The next step in my private campaign against our thrifty County Treasurer was to start watching him," Grantly said. "Spent evenings shadowing him and his partner Valdez. The embezzled money had gone into their mine, I concluded, after getting from their superintendent an idea of the extent of the developing. A lot of money had been poured into that hole. Two nights ago I was at the Court House circulating around because there was a light in Brill's office burning late. Pete and Valdez and Clem Underwood were playing poker. I moved back by the jail and had a smoke. After while I went forward again and saw the game had stopped; the cattleman was asleep, his arms on the table and his head on his arms. Drunk. Never had seen him drunk before. He raised his head and gazed wearily around and let it down again. Then Bill Lawson came in for him,"

"Yes?" the Sheriff questioned, eagerly.

"Well, at that time I moved off, for I decided that nothing I was interested in would be said until the Box U foreman had taken his boss away. Men dead drunk don't appeal to me."

"Clem wasn't drunk?"

"He certainly appeared that way."

"Go ahead. You're reachin' a vital point, the one where Bill Lawson was killed."

"Ah, so you know he was killed there instead of in the street, as the report was spread next morning?" the journalist exclaimed.

"Certainly do, Ed. And I hope to heaven you saw the shooting. I need a witness to that bad—and that's all I do need to break down the charges of murder against Les Bridges and put a stop to this lawlessness in Chavo."

"Hard luck, Sheriff; I didn't see the shot fired. I was standing off and in fact staring away. When I got back to the window and hauled myself up for a squint inside, Bill Lawson lay dead on the floor, Underwood was on his feet looking at the gun he held, bewildered, and Brill and Valdez were supporting him one on each side and saying he had killed his foreman. Sheriff, the rancher couldn't have killed the man; he was too drunk. He couldn't hold the gun and it fell. His head kept sagging to his breast. His knees bent and gave, and if the other two hadn't held him up he would've collapsed on the floor. It was impossible. There was something phoney about the whole matter."

"Sure, sure. What more did you see inside?"

"NOTHING. VALDEZ BEGGED Brill to make sure no one was around the building who might have seen, and Brill made straight for the window to look outside. I dropped, legged it away. Thought I hadn't been seen. But Brill must have seen and recognized me and sent some killer to lay for me, for I was shot at Agate Creek ford. Anyway, that's the last I remember. When I came to, I imagined I'd fallen from my horse and struck my head on a rock and been knocked silly; and only learned differently today."

"How's that?" the Sheriff inquired.

"Was told by Gus Burney when I found my way to his Agate Basin ranch, who was told by Les Bridges, who was told by the man who saw me shot and afterwards picked me up and cared for me, a partner of that little Doc Chessington, who was here, you remember. Doc was there sick too with me."

"I don't recall Doc having a partner," the Sheriff mused. "Didn't see him, at any rate."

"Neither did I," Grantly said. "Probably he showed up only when Doc got sick. When I came to this morning, I found myself in a camp in a box canyon up in the mountains, with my head bandaged and lying on a blanket all wrapped up. Doc was stretched in another bed on the ground. His wagon and medicine cases were there, but not his partner. You can guess how mystified I was to wake up like that. Felt dizzy when I sat up, but after eating some food my head cleared and I decided I had to get along to the Bar U or back to town; that Court House shooting and the lie spread was disturbing my mind. I knew Brill's foxy hand was in it."

Condon nodded.

"The lie that Lawson was killed in the street wasn't the only one; Brill and Valdez laid the murder on Les Bridges."

"I learned he was considered guilty," Grantly replied. "Mrs. Dexter informed me of that; and she said too that he was accused of robbing Brill's safe of all its cash and bonds. You can never make me believe Les did that. It was Brill, if anybody."

"You're wrong there; it was the notorious Masked Rider."

"What! Was he here?"

"Yes."

"Then why is Bridges accused?"

"Because only Betty Underwood, her father, and I know about The Masked Rider. He told Betty he had the loot. He appeared before her on a hill back of the ranch, unexpectedly as he always does to people, and gave her a deed

THE MASKED RIDER ARCHIVES VOL. 4

that Brill and Valdez had blackmailed Underwood out of, on threat of making it known he murdered Bill Lawson. The deed was for the Box U Ranch."

"The scoundrels! So that was their game! For heaven's sake, Sheriff, throw them in jail and stop their plundering!"

Condon's face was rueful.

"If you had seen what happened in Brill's office that night I'd do it this minute," he declared. "But I haven't proof of their guilt. I can't strike until I have it. And I was hoping you had seen! But without a witness—"

Grantly sprang up.

"There was a witness," he cried.

"Are you sure, man?" the Sheriff demanded, rising too. "Who was it?"

"That little Doc Chessington. Good Lord, and he in the mountains sick!"

"I'll get to him. Quick, tell me the rest."

"He was at the window that night. When he got there, I don't know; but there he was when at the shot I looked round toward the office. I ran toward him, saw him for a minute peeping in, his head and shoulders outlined against the light. Apparently he had been stealing glimpses there without my noticing him, but in the excitement of what he saw had lifted himself right up in view, at least in my view."

"You would swear it was this doctor?"

"Swear to it a dozen times," Grantly affirmed. "I'm dead certain, even if he was there but half a minute or less. Next he slid down and went hurrying away."

SATISFACTION GLOWED ON the Sheriff's bronzed features.

"He's the key," he asserted, "and with him on the witness

stand we'll send Brill and Valdez to the gallows. *They* killed Lawson to trick Clem Underwood. Man, what you've told has put the whole game into my hands. Except the part pertaining to the safe robbery. For that I must catch The Masked Rider."

"No Sheriff or other law officer has caught him yet, Condon."

"I'll have to. The County will be broke if I don't. Let me get only a smell of his trail, let me get but a single clue to where he is, let me get only within reach of the thief, and I"—the officer raised right hand and slowly shut the fingers of it in a tight, talon-like grip—"and I, on my oath, will hold him like that. Yes; I'll bring him in and—"

He broke off. Framed in the inner doorway was a silent figure garbed in black from crown to bootsole—hat, hood, flowing mantle, gloves, clothes, boots, even the gun in his hand. Black, all.

"Save yourself the bother of hunting me, Sheriff, "the visitor spoke. "Here I am."

"The outlaw!" Grantly gasped.

"The Masked Rider himself!" Condon exclaimed, amazed.

Yes, he was here, within sight, almost within the Sheriff's reach. But Condon didn't make his savage clutch. He said:

"After all, the money's as safe with you as with Brill."

"Sheriff, you're flattering me," The Masked Rider said, satirically, "when you rank me with your high-minded, true-hearted, noble-souled County Treasurer. No, no; I don't deserve that honor. However, I agree with you that the County funds, what Brill has left of them, are as safe in my hands as in his. Yet there was a dry tone in your voice. Could I have been mistaken in what you meant? Could it be possible that you were taking a crack at me and really meant the money and bonds are no safer with me than with Pete?"

Condon's mouth hardened and his eyes smoldered.

"I ain't in the habit of payin' outlaws compliments," he replied. "Neither outlaws nor killers."

"Are you implying that I'm a killer?"

"My Deputy was killed close by you."

"How do you know?"

"I was lookin' at him and at you at the time."

"But I didn't kill him."

"You were by a window of the Box U Ranch house next to where he stood when it was done. I saw the knife thrown."

Under the black hood the outlaw's lips tightened. This was so like many other charges against him: a crime was committed and he was present; no further proof. He said:

"Did you see me throw it?"

Condon hesitated. "Well, no. I admit it came from another direction."

"Then I'm cleared of that charge," The Masked Rider declared. "The fact is, Sheriff, I never knew your Deputy was there until I saw him knifed. That's the absolute truth. Somebody in the dark flung the knife. Have you discovered who it was?"

"Not yet."

"At any rate, you can cross me off as the killer."

CHAPTER XV

THE STORM BURSTS

To THAT THE law officer did not immediately respond. He had in dealing with this notorious character a sense of confronting an enigma, baffling to solve and impossible to judge. The Masked Rider's unseen goings and comings, his mysterious knowledge of secret affairs, his strange motives, his disregard for law and his own notion of justice, his solitary existence, his uncanny ability to evade proof of guilt, his mingled guile and boldness, his successes, his escapes, his ringing deeds,—all made him a man out of the range of understanding. And his face, so far as known, no man had seen.

Condon considered. Be what he might, the unknown was after all an outlaw, a wanted man. The rewards on The Masked Rider's head did not weigh with the old Sheriff, but the feat of his lawlessness did. Had he not manifested it here in Chavo? Had he not been guilty in one act, if never in another? And on that act Condon clamped his mind.

"I will cross you off the list as a killer," said he, "but never as a safe-robber."

"What safe did I rob?" the other demanded.

"The County Treasurer's safe."

"I deny it."

"You admitted it to Betty Underwood."

"No."

"Yes."

"No. Again, no."

"You played with words in tellin' her of it, but you don't deceive me none in that."

"Sheriffs are all alike," was the retort. "Strong for law, weak for justice; quick to believe appearances, slow to learn the truth. Or most of them are so. I thought from what the girl said that you might be different."

"I grant that you've helped Clem Underwood and his daughter and given me a line on Brill's scheme, too," Condon answered. "But just the same I'm not to be swerved by that from doing my duty in arrestin' you when I'm able. What little good you done for the cowman don't weigh in the balance a-tall against the harm you've done to the mass of people in this County, for the most part poor, hardworkin' folks."

A mocking laugh came from The Masked Rider.

"When I came in here, Sheriff, I heard you and this man talking," he stated. "I learned he is the newspaper man here. I learned he had been shot because of a confession he had got from Brill's clerk. I learned that Underwood had been drugged—"

"Drugged!" Grantly exclaimed.

"Sure. Two drinks of whiskey don't put a man in the condition he was in. Yes, drugged so that Brill and Valdez could get from him his ranch and herd. What then do we have? Brill short in his accounts, Brill and Valdez squeezing Underwood, Brill—" He paused, regarding them intently through the holes of his hood. "Brill doing what next, with cash and bonds still in his safe?"

"Pete was in the Big 9 at the time of the robbery," Condon snapped.

"And where was Valdez?"

"At the saloon, too."

"Wrong again, Sheriff."

"I checked up on him as well as Brill."

"He was at the Court House in a disguise of black hat, black handkerchief mask, black mantilla, and black gloves, impersonating The Masked Rider."

"How would you know?" the Sheriff questioned, quickly.

"I saw him."

"Two Masked Riders is one too many," was the sceptical response.

"I agree with you. One too many when the other is Valdez. Well, answer this: How did that garb happen to be found by the Mexican at Bridges' cabin?"

CONDON STARTED. HE had forgotten that circumstance. Now as he recalled it and his discovery of Valdez' price tag on the mantilla, all his earlier suspicions of Brill and his mining partner flashed full-winged into his mind. The fact that the articles had disappeared from the ranch mess house the night Mallett was killed also told against the two men. No one else had a motive for getting rid of the evidence.

"You're not lyin'?" he asked, feebly. "Haven't you heard that The Masked Rider never lies?"

"Yes; I've heard that."

It was true. Whatever question there might be as to the man's guilt or innocence in crimes alleged against him, report had it that he was one of his word.

"Brill planned the robbery, and Valdez carried it out."

"Took the cash and bonds?"

"Not farther than the hall."

"How's that?"

"The real Masked Robber halted him there."

"Hark!" Grantly cried.

A sudden roar in the street before the building caused all three to listen. In it was a deep fierce note that revealed the long-seething wrath of the crowd come at last, to a head. A stone crashed through a front window, shattering glass and jerking the shade; human bodies thudded against the door.

"They're after you, Grantly," The Masked Rider said, sharply. "Brill was warned you were in town. He's set his pack after you. I knew it would happen, I came to get you away. The Underwoods are waiting for you in the sage a couple of hundred yards straight back to take you to the Box U out of danger. Come. You too, Sheriff. Our lives won't last a minute if they catch us here. Out we go before they get to the back."

The door of the office crashed even as they darted out at the rear. The mob had burst in. And as they ran, shouts and howls and crashing sounds came from the building, while about its front the uproar increased.

When well eastward in the sagebrush Condon began to call Underwood's name and heard the cowman's answering call.

"Hell's poppin', Clem," the Sheriff said. "Here's your passenger. Climb in, Ed, and keep at the ranch until you hear from me."

"Hadn't you best come, also?" Betty asked, anxiously. "There's strong feeling against you."

"I'm stayin', girl. There's still a few men who aren't drunk and crazy, and I'm goin' to gather 'em up to try to stop this spree. Hello, your place has been set on fire, Ed!"

Smoke and flames had begun to edge the windows of the building, while a dull crimson glow began to illumine the night and show past the open spaces on either side of the structure the heads of the tumultuous mob packed in the street.

"There goes the *Chavo Vigilante*," Grantly said, bitterly.

"How mad, how cruel!" Betty answered.

Condon looked about him.

"Where's The Masked Rider?" he asked. "I thought he came with us. Well, he's gone. But I'm hopin' to see him again and see if I can't talk him into returnin' that money. Meanwhile I've plenty to do. You better be drivin' on."

The Sheriff took a direction that would lead him into the street above the Big 9 saloon. He was lucky enough to find a group of cowmen before the door, good friends, who were gazing at the howling pack down the street. He joined them.

"Time to act," said he. "How many more can we get to back me up?"

"Twenty or so, cowmen and punchers."

"Go get them. It'll take some time. We'll meet in front of the Court House; and bring your horses. We'll ride through that mob and rip it to pieces, and I'm goin' to throw Brill and Valdez into jail and hold 'em. They're responsible for this."

"Pete's been fomentin' it all day," one spoke.

"That isn't all he's been doing," the Sheriff grated forth. "I'm tellin' you men facts now. They been blackmailin' Underwood, they killed his foreman Bill Lawson, they cooked up these false charges against young Bridges, and they robbed the County."

"No!"

"As soon as we're organized, we're goin' to grab those two wolves."

"Anything you say, Amos," another spoke. "We'll stand by you through thick and thin."

THE TALK WAS interrupted by the appearance of two punchers running into the light before the doorway, who stopped at sight of the men. One peered at Condon, and said:

"That you, Sheriff? We was huntin' you. For the love of Gabriel, come back with us to Valdez' store!"

The speaker was the same cowboy who with his companion had bibulously demanded of the merchant ammunition and rope through the window. He was cold sober now, but nevertheless full of repressed excitement.

"What am I to come for?" Condon queried.

"Valdez is dead. Been shot through the heart, murdered. He's lyin' there across the bed in a mess of blood."

"What in hell will happen next?" the Sheriff ejaculated, his mind racing in possible surmises. "All right. Come 'long, men; this killin' ties in somewhere with what I've just told you."

The big Mexican was stretched on the bed in his sleeping room as the puncher had described. He lay on his back with eyes staring, his great black moustache extending over his cheeks, and his mouth open in a terrified grimace. The terror he experienced when he died was still stamped in his lineaments.

"How did you happen to find him, Jerry?" the Sheriff

asked of his informant, after a swift examination of the slain man.

"Earlier we'd come to the store to get some ammunition and—well, some rope," was the cowboy's sheepish response. "We'd been drinkin' and got a kinda irresponsible notion into our damned heads. The front door was locked, but we saw Valdez was inside. So we went 'round to a window what was unfastened and told him from there what we was after. We was told to use our las' ropes. Well, we went off and had some more drinks, but the idea of usin' my own rope to do strangler work went against the grain with me; some ways I'm fastidious. Well, as time passes I gets more mulish 'bout it. Well, 'bout the time the party begun down the street, me and Sam heads once more for the store."

"I went 'long to see Jerry didn't get in no fight," the second cowboy explained. "His eyes was growin' red."

"The hell you say!" Jerry scowled at his friend. "Well, when we got here the lights was still burnin', and the door was still locked and so was the windows. Well, we didn't see nothin' of nobody. Well, I was after rope and goes prowlin' 'round and finds the back door standin' ajar and so we goes in. This door was open, too. Well, we seen him this-away and yells at him and then perceeds in to rouse him. Well, one look was plenty. We departs on the high lope huntin' you, all the likker evaporated out of us complete and our rope errand forgot."

"No sign of anybody 'round?"

"No," said Jerry.

"No," added Sam, emphatically.

"But there's something else—" Jerry began, hesitatingly.

"Shut up 'bout that!" Sam barked.

"Mebbe I'd best keep still."

Their eyes crossed, held together for a little; and then both looked away with an elaborate air of casualness. The Sheriff struck one palm against the other in a savage slap.

"You're talkin'!" he roared. "No holdin' back. This is a murder. I want 'something' immediate."

"We don't want Brill turnin' on us," Sam stated, shaking his head. "What's the word of a couple of dumb cowpokes 'gainst his?"

"It goes with us," Condon asseverated. "So Pete Brill is mixed in it; I suspected as much. Come on, out with what you know!"

After a few minutes of further stalling on the part of the cowboys, Jerry related how they had seen Brill menacing the storekeeper with his gun when they looked in at the window and the explanation the County Treasurer had made on learning that his actions were witnessed.

"At the time we swallered that," the cowboy concluded, "but when we found Valdez lyin' here we draws a diff'rent picture of it."

TURNING, THE SHERIFF regarded the listening cowmen with a grim visage.

"Knowin' the real facts, there ain't no doubt about Pete havin' murdered his minin' partner," he said. "Recall what I told you. I comprehend now how they worked it. They framed the Court House robbery to cover Brill's embezzlement, Valdez riggin' himself up as The Masked Rider and cleanin' out the safe after openin' it with the combination Pete gave him. Brill is showin' himself in the Big 9 at the arranged time of the plunderin'. He sends old Jim the swamper up to get his specs that he has conveniently forgot and left in the office, timin' it so old Jim meets up with Valdez who is disguised in a black hat and mask and mantilla and who tells him he's The Masked Rider, where-upon old Jim runs back to the Big 9 with his news. And Brill leads the hunt for the outlaw, knowin' all the while he won't be caught."

"Lordy, is that the way of it?" Jerry exclaimed.

"The actual story, boy."

"But why should Pete kill Valdez if they were in it together?" a cowman questioned.

"Because Valdez wouldn't turn over the loot to him."

"We heard him say," Sam interrupted, now as hot at Brill as he had before been cold. "For the Mexican to hand over to him the money and packet of bonds. You're right. Valdez must have tried to hold out on him."

"No," said Condon. "He wasn't double crossin' Pete; Valdez didn't have the money and bonds, but Pete didn't know that, or wouldn't believe it when told. So he killed his partner."

"How come Valdez didn't have the stuff?" the cowman asked. "Sounds queer."

A sour grin appeared on the Sheriff's face.

"It's queerer than it sounds," he announced. "When the Mexican came out of Brill's office with the loot, he wasn't the only masked robber on hand. The real Masked Rider was waitin' for him in the hall."

"Him?" Jerry yelped. "Has the fella turned up here?"

"He lifted the cash and bonds from Valdez."

"Gollamighty!"

"Valdez must've been scared that Pete wouldn't believe it," Condon explained. "Which is why he took his black outfit to Bridges' cabin and pretended to discover it there. No doubt he figgered he could fool Brill into thinkin' Les had dressed up in black and robbed him, when he couldn't get him to accept a story 'bout the real Masked Rider. Les had been in the office only a half hour before threatenin' them, which would add an air of plausibility to that yarn."

"If The Masked Rider has our money and bonds," a cowman said, dejectedly. "We may as well kiss 'em goodby."

"I ain't givin' up hope," the Sheriff answered.

"Nobody ever laid hands on him."

"Mebbe he ain't as black as the rig he wears; I've some new ideas 'bout that. Well, we can catch and hang Brill for this murder, anyway. No use in stayin' here longer. And the riotin' has to be ended and Pete seized, which won't be easy. We may hear lead flyin' before the night's over. I'll throw a sheet over Valdez, then we'll go."

Presently they were standing before the store and measuring their task. The flames of the burning building that had housed Grantly's printing office were leaping high and the street was lighted up. The mob's yells had died down and for the moment the packed crowd was still, listening to a haranguing voice.

Suddenly this ceased. A wild exultant roar broke out and the mob surged and milled about and then disintegrated as its members ran apart.

"What now?" asked one of the cowmen of Condon's little company, in wonderment.

"They're runnin' to get their horses," Sam said.

"What's that they're yellin'?"

ALL HARKENED. CALLS and shouts were flung back and forth as men mounted the lines of horses that filled the borders of the street, and presently voices of the nearer horsemen made the mob's purpose clear.

"By heaven, we're too late!" the Sheriff exclaimed. "They're ridin' to the Box U Ranch to string up Les Bridges."

"The hellions! More of Brill's work!" a rancher cried. "Mebbe if we start throwin' lead it will stop 'em."

"They'd only ride us down and wipe us out. No; we need more men than us to brave 'em. But we ain't through, only checked. Get down there and collect what others will be left; all won't share in that lawlessness. We'll follow 'em and strike when they don't expect it. The law ain't dead in this County yet. Hell's Bells, they're comin'! Get back!"

In the street the horsemen had massed and then at some word of command had started. Like a horde of howling bloodlustful Tartars, they rushed forward up the crimson lighted street in a long irregular column of wild riders and swept thundering by into the dark night.

"Brill! In the lead!" Sam ejaculated.

The Sheriff did not reply—only gazed after him, his look narrowed and his jaw outthrust and his gun-hand half-raised. He too had seen the mob's leader gallop past with eyes bright and head high.

CHAPTER XVI

"*STRANGLERS*"

U NDERWOOD'S BAYS MADE fast time travelling to the
ranch, for the cowman drove them hard. He was still
shaken by the sight of the mob that held sway in Chavo
and felt that only on his own property, in his own home,
would he have security. There were his men, there was his
fortress, there was he rooted, there armed in his rights. So
in a little over an hour his fast stepping team brought him
to the Box U.

Punchers were smoking in the starlight before the bunk
house. Two of them came to unhitch the team, one of them
Lafe.

"Holding Les here, I understand," Clem Underwood
said, after the three in the buckboard had alighted.

"Yeah. Sheriff's orders; Lanky brought 'em out after
reportin' the boy's capture again," Lafe rejoined.

"Where is Les?" Betty asked, quickly.

"With the boys by the bunk house. Never knew such
a fella for hard luck. We was ridin' 'round kinda makin'
believe we was huntin' him and tellin' Mort Jones what a
smart Deputy he was, and as we was headin' up a draw I'm
danged if that kid didn't blunder outa some brush right
into the middle of us. Well, of course that tied it. All the
afternoon we tried to lure Mort away on one excuse or

another so Les would have a chance to make a break up the canyon. But that damned Deputy wouldn't lure; he clings to that boy like he was a long-lost brother. Awful sorry, Betty, the cards fell that away."

"Don't you worry, Lafe," said she. "As long as he stays with us, nothing will happen to him; and the Sheriff will keep him here until he's cleared, I know. He knows Les isn't guilty of anything. This is Mr. Grantly with us; he's in trouble too. We're late, for that wretched Pete Brill tried to hold us in the hotel in town. Fortunately a friend appeared and disposed of two of the guards and got us away; I say friend, and that's what he's proved himself to be to us—The Masked Rider."

"Who'd you say?"

"The Masked Rider."

"Another one besides Les?"

"You know Les never was one. I'm speaking of the real Masked Rider, the famous outlaw. He was at the ranch yesterday and in town tonight, and he it was who took us out of Pete Brill's hands and aided Mr. Grantly in his escape. A friend, yes."

Lafe gave a low whistle of surprise.

"What's that standing there by the corral?" Betty inquired, peering. "A little wagon?"

"A little painted wagon. Mort says it belongs to a quack doctor who has been in town sellin' bottled doses. When we came back this afternoon with Les, there she sat. How she came there we don't know. The team was in the corral. Where the Doc is we don't know, either. Mebbe out collectin' herbs. Why she is there, we've argued a lot. My notion is that the team strayed in with the wagon, unhitched themselves likin' the looks of the place, and is sayin' nothin'."

"Of all things. Well, tell Les I'll come and talk with him after I run into the house for a minute. Coming, Dad?"

They entered by the living room door and Betty lighted a lamp, opened windows for fresh air.

"Sit down, Mr. Grantly," she addressed their guest. "You must be tired, poor man."

"My head is aching a little."

Clem Underwood, who was moving toward his customary seat, the homemade cowhide chair that suited his bulk, stopped and turned toward the part of the house in which were located the bed rooms. He listened for a moment.

"I thought I heard a call," said he.

"Your ears must have tricked you."

THE COWMAN LIFTED silencing hand, again harkened.

"There. Kinda muffled."

"Yes," she agreed. "But it would not be a call. I expect it's Baldy's tabby that must of have got in and been locked up without our knowing it when we left. I'll take another lamp and go look."

She had been gone in her search for but a moment when the two men were startled by a little shriek and the sound of her running feet. Bursting in on them with eyes and mouth of amazement, she gasped:

"A man—a strange man! In bed in one of the spare rooms! At first I didn't see him, was looking around on the floor when I went in, and had just set the lamp on the stand when he spoke. Then I saw him! In the bed, in *our* bed! A total stranger! I froze. He said, 'Damned poor service in this hotel, girl. Bring me some cold water to drink; I'm burning up.' I squealed and ran out. In our house and bed! Of all things!"

The cowman stared.

"Well, I'll find out what this means," he said, at last. "Come with me, Grantly; I may need help."

"Perhaps that wagon by the corral may give you a clue to his presence," the journalist suggested.

"You mean he may be the quack doctor?" Betty asked.

"That's my guess."

"But to be in one of our beds!"

"He doesn't know that, apparently," was the reply. "Evidently he imagines himself somewhere in a hotel, to judge by his words to you. Did he strike you as being drunk?"

"More as if he were ill. His face was flushed and his voice weak."

"Let's be getting in to him," her father said. "Then we'll learn."

Curious and on the part of the Underwoods, resentful, the three of them traversed the vestibule until Betty led them into the particular bed room where the surprising guest lay. Going close to the bed, they gazed down at him, receiving in return a blinking regard.

"You two doctors?" the stranger questioned, restlessly. "This a consultation? I feel as if I had typhoid, or endemic, or spotted fever, or something similar. Been out of my head, I reckon. Last I remember was starting from Chavo and being on the road and then I went under."

"You don't know when or how you got here?" the cowman asked.

"No. Came to and here I was. Isn't this a hotel somewhere?"

"You're at the Box U Ranch. My name's Underwood."

The sick man brushed hand across his eyes as if to clear them of cobwebs and weakly regarded the speaker.

"I remember you now," he said. "I saw you at the Court House the night—the night—"

"The night he was drugged and made to believe he had killed a man," Grantly took him up quickly.

"Then you know they used that stuff Brill got from me!" the little doctor groaned. "You must believe I never dreamed he was going to use it in your drink, Mr. Underwood. He had come to my wagon several times while I was in town and we got to talking of dope and I showed him a medicine made from a plant by an Indian in Mexico, what plant he wouldn't tell me, that stupefied without rendering whoever took it entirely unconscious. It had been used by the Aztecs to drug victims intended for sacrifice, the Indian told me. Brill asked for some of it to use on an old dog that must be put out of misery, he said, and I gave him a little. He lied to me, as I realized when I looked through the window and saw what was happening. I recognized its effects in your condition, for I had tried it on myself and so knew them."

"Don't hold it against me, Underwood," he begged, after a pause to restore his strength. "He tricked me, the same as he tricked you, only worse. I wasn't myself that night, or I'd have told you about it afterward. For two days I'd been coming down with this fever; I was so hot and distressed that evening that I couldn't sleep and I was moving around aimlessly for relief when I glimpsed your heads in the office and, growing curious, pulled myself up at the window to see what was going on. You were groggy. Your man came in for you. He thought they had made you drunk to flimflam you at cards and started for Brill mad as hell and Brill shot him. Next instant I knew from what Brill said to the Mexican that the whole business, the drugging and shooting, was a trap to get you in their power, Underwood."

HIS FEVER-BRIGHT EYES were fixed on the cowman.

"I dropped to the ground and ran, for I realized I'd been witnessing a planned murder and if I was seen I should be killed too by Brill, like a rat. All the rest of the night I cowered in the darkness away from my wagon. By morning the fever had me in its grip; I was so weak and dizzy I could hardly hitch up my team and strike camp. I was having fever fancies by then, also. I thought Brill and the Mexican were hunting me, I imagined I saw them lurking at corners of the Court House, I was possessed by only one purpose. To flee, to get away, to escape from the murderers. I gave my team the whip and raced off from the Court House and over the bridge above town and north along the road, almost out of my head with fever and fear; and then somewhere on the trail I must have gone out of my head for sure. I remember nothing from that time until I woke up here an hour ago."

His listeners exchanged significant looks. Here was the man who had seen, the key witness. The plotters' dastardly crime was exposed in all its hideous nakedness. Brill and Valdez stood irrefutably damned by the sick man's evidence.

"You can rest easy in mind about my feelings," Clem Underwood said, heartily. "You were unwittingly tangled in the web and so no responsibility attaches to you. And your chancing to be on hand to see the actual shooting, that I hold as a great piece of luck for me. The way this has turned out, I'm glad your partner brought you here."

"Partner! I haven't any partner."

Grantly spoke. "A man found you delirious at the ford and took you for care into the woods above. We had the impression he was another doctor and associated with you. Les Bridges, who ran across him tending you and me—I was in his care too—guessed he was. It apparently was only a guess. Anyway, the man, likely a stranger passing through, was a Good Samaritan. No other way of accounting for your coming here except by his aid. But the matter's not important, not important enough to keep you talking."

He turned to the cowman, after feeling Doc Chessington's skin and taking his pulse.

"Fever still up," said he. "But if I'm any judge, not so high as it must have been to keep him unconscious. With nursing you'll come along nicely, doctor."

"He shall have the best," Betty asserted.

"You can begin by bringing me some water," the patient stated, "and I'm begging your pardon, Miss, for ordering you about as I did at first."

"You're excused," she smiled. "And you shall have a cold drink at once."

"Best he should talk no more," Grantly advised. "Water and sleep and quiet, that's what he needs. Doc, you're a lucky dog to have Miss Betty for your nurse."

"No need of telling me that, Mister," was the response, weak but assertive.

The cowman and the newspaper editor returned to the living room. Betty gave Chessington water to drink, bathed his hot face and wrists, and then went to prepare supper, which neither she nor her father had had.

While she was engaged at this, Lafe put head into the kitchen.

"Call the Old Man," he exclaimed.

"What's up, Lafe?"

"Red Glasser, of the Walkin' A outfit, just come with a

warnin' that the mob what's been raisin' hell in Chavo is comin' here. Rode his horse to a fare-ye-well gettin' himself to the Box U ahead of 'em. Yeah, they're comin'. A mob of stranglers!"

"To hang Les?" she cried.

"Yes."

"Hurry in and tell Dad. I'm going to Les. He must be taken back somewhere safe in the hills."

"My notion, but he won't go."

"Why?"

"Says he's done all the runnin' he's goin' to. Set as a mule 'bout it."

"He must!"

"Mebbe you can persuade him."

"I shall."

SHE FLEW OUT of the door to go to the prisoner. The puncher made for the living room, and there told Underwood the bad news. The cowman's eyes flashed and he smote his chair arm with fist.

"Stranglers headed for the Box U, you say!" he roared. "By God, I'm not going to take any more from Brill! They don't string up Les and they don't work any mischief here! Round up the boys, bring 'em into the house with their rifles and shot guns! If Brill and his gang want trouble, we sure will give 'em a bellyful!" The quick change of events had fully revived him. He was once more strong and masterful.

CHAPTER XVII

HELL BROKE LOOSE

N O LIGHT SHOWED. The ranch buildings crouched silent and dark under the stars, and their very stillness and vagueness had on more than one of the lawless company of halted horsemen, peering and muttering, an effect at once sinister and foreboding.

"Why we waitin'?" ran the nervous question low-toned from rider to rider.

"For a haystack to be fired," was the word passed back from the front.

Two of the party had been sent creeping forward to scout the grounds and touch match to a stack of hay by the smaller corral. Minutes dragged by. Then appeared a flickering crimson tongue of fire ahead in the gloom, that edged higher and spread and finally burst into mounting flames and smoke. In the ruddy light cast by the burning haystack the buildings and corrals were revealed.

"Not a horse in either corral," a man spoke.

"Nor anyone in sight," said another.

"What if Bridges or nobody else is here?"

"We'll rip the place to pieces."

"Hand me your bottle again."

"Leave some. I want another drink, too."

Men drank and pushed their horses slowly forward

impatiently and growled fierce, senseless curses. Their momentary uneasiness at the ranch's quiet had passed. Whiskey and the wild leap of flames and the prospect of a lawless hanging again roused the beast in them.

The two scouts came running back and swung up into their saddles.

"Not a soul anywhere 'round," one declared. "What'll we do?"

"Search. Someone's here. We'll dig him out and learn where Bridges and the rest are."

It was Pete Brill who uttered the terse statements and the command. As with his followers, liquor was in his brain and the smell of incendiary smoke in his nostrils. He was half-drunk with whiskey and wholly drunk with power.

With a rush the more than a hundred riders swept up the creek trail and jerked their mounts to a sliding stop between corral and house. There they massed, a savage company of horses and armed outlaws—for outlaws they had become—glaring this way and that. The flames' lurid light struck the horde aglow.

"Come out, come out, damn you!" a rider howled, shaking fist at the ranch house. "Bring that hound Bridges and turn him over to us, or we'll swing you all!"

"None of that," Brill ordered sharply.

"You say!"

"Yes. I say!" the leader shouted. "You'll leave the Underwoods and their boys alone."

"Ain't they shelterin' that murderin' skunk?"

"No. Mort Jones is keepin' him here."

"Let him bring him out, then."

"They ain't here," a second man exclaimed, wrathfully.

"Well make sure," Brill said. "Start hunting through the buildings, but leave the ranch house to me."

A dozen riders wheeled horses and galloped to the bunk house. Others to the mess house, the blacksmith shop, the granary, and smaller outbuildings. Others to search the trees and underbrush bordering the creek. When the dozen or so remaining with Brill moved to advance upon the house, he checked them.

"Wait," said he.

They sat watching their fellows, who ransacked the structures they entered and in their fury of disappointment at not finding whom they sought, threw out bedding, broke windows, hurled out pots and pans, pitched over the cook stove, smashed tables and chairs, scattered tools, and wasted grain. Some of the more ruthless spirits, aflame with lust of destruction, tore rails from the corral and flung them upon the burning haystack, while another group, drunk and howling Mexicans these, ran the itinerant doctor's painted wagon to the fire.

THEY ONLY PAUSED in their frenzy of demolishment and havoc to tilt bottles and gulp down whiskey. Alcohol and fire, the twin devils of lawlessness whipped them on. Two stacks of hay beside the larger corral were fired and then the granary. The air became hazy and pungent with burning straw, the crimson flare brighter, the running, yelling, working figures more demoniac.

Brill and his squad sat motionless.

"Looks like you lost control, Pete," one said.

"No."

"Well, I didn't figger we was comin' here to burn out Underwood. You stated yourself he wasn't shelterin' Bridges. Things are goin' too far."

"I feel the same," remarked another rider.

"Here, too," a third added.

"You do, eh?" Brill answered, with a snarl. "Well, I've changed my mind. This is what Underwood needs to make him toe the mark in the future. And if you think you can buck me tonight, just start in."

The protesters held their peace. Brill had indeed altered his view of the proceedings as he sat there watching. The latent cruelty of the man came alive and stretched its claws and licked its chops. A malicious satisfaction filled him as he saw the hay and painted wagon and corral poles and grain go up in smoke, for at bottom he hated the simplicity and bluff honesty inherent in the nature of the cowman; as, too, he hated while admiring, resented while lustfully desiring, the pure, proud young mistress of the ranch. What he was allowing to go on would at any rate make them fear him. And yield to him. Yes, they should yield!

And what of the little party in the ranch house?

Gathered in the living room the members of the group, with the exception of the sick man who had fallen into a troubled sleep, watched through the windows. Underwood glowered without speaking. Betty was furious. Grantly made bitter remarks. Lafe and the other punchers discussed among themselves what positions they should take when an attack was made. Baldy, the cook, cursed fluently. Lee Bridges was by turns vocal and sulky. The Deputy Sheriff, Mort Jones, ordinarily indolent and passive, had developed an unexpected force and authority.

"Give me a rifle and let me put a bullet through Pete Brill," Les exclaimed, hotly. "If you had any gumption, you'd do it yourself, Mort. He's leadin' this mob, he's the ringleader. He's nothin' now but an outlaw bustin' all the laws wide open. And you talk of arrestin' him!"

"You're little better than they are," the Deputy replied. "Brill come to murder you, and now you wanta murder him. The law is, every man is entitled to a fair trial whatever he's done. Mebbe the law's broke down in Chavo and it's bein' bent hard here, but it ain't gone entire. Not while I'm standin' on my legs. It's prevailin' here inside the house if nowhere else. No, Les, you can't throw a gun down on Brill or any of them other fellas till they throw lead at us. Then, says the law, all gents can go for their guns, the game bein' wide-open with the Joker runnin' wild." In the darkness he clapped Bridges on the shoulder, and concluded. "Boy, hold your horses. You'll get your shootin' before long."

Several minutes passed, then Brill was seen by those on watch within to signal an advance upon the house.

"Time to move back from them windows," the Deputy said. "I ain't much at speakin' and I never attempted to handle a mob before, but I'm goin' to have a try at both."

"They won't listen to you, and they may shoot you down first thing," Les answered. "If you wanta talk to 'em, talk from inside the door with me behind you holdin' down on 'em with a gun."

"I reckon the Sheriff would go out and speak to 'em."

"You ain't the Sheriff."

"Not by a long ways, but just the same I aim to do what he would do, which is to speak 'em peaceful, point out they're breakin' the law and order 'em to quit under penalty of bein' jailed."

"You goin' to jail 'em all by yourself, Mort?" Baldy jeered.

"I reckon we won't get that far. I reckon I'll be divin' back inside 'bout then, evadin' lead."

"You never spoke truer word."

ON THAT, A profound hush rested in the room, for the danger was imminent and their fate in the balance. No, their fate was not even in the balance. For when the approaching horsemen demanded Les Bridges, they would of course be refused; and when they were refused, their demand would be followed by an attack. That would result in a fight. Once bullets were flying and blood spilled, the fury of the mob until now satisfied by pillage and fire would be fully unleashed.

None in the room spoke of the almost inevitable outcome. A hundred against ten! A fight, a siege if necessary, repeated assaults at doors and windows, a last storming through rooms of the house by the drunken, maddened "stranglers," and then the floor piled with the Box U dead and the bodies of slain invaders! But the picture haunted the minds of all.

"Well, they've come," Lafe remarked. "Goin' out, Mort?"

"Yeah."

"And if they shoot?"

"Don't pay no attention to me if I drop; pour it into the coyotes."

"All right, Mort. But we'll leave the door ajar and you stand close to it and jump back pronto if you see a gun drawn. Get to the windows, men, and kneel down ready. Never mind the glass; shoot right through it. Huh, they're callin' to learn if we're in here. Now's as good a time as any, Mort, to speak your little piece."

The Deputy quickly swung back the door and stepped out, pulling the door after him. His sudden appearance resulted in quick silence on the part of the shouting riders facing the house.

"What do you want?" Jones asked, quietly.

"The robber of my safe and the murderer of Bill Lawson and Joe Mallett, young Bridges," Pete Brill stated, with arrogance. "Hand him over, then go in and you and the rest of you stay there."

"He's in the hands of the law."

"You fool, we're the law now!"

"Is smashin' and burnin' Clem Underwood's property your way of sustainin' the law?" the Deputy questioned.

"Don't get smart, fella. Bring that young wolf out."

"I'm repeatin', he's in the hands of a legal officer. You and your men are breakin' the law. I'm warnin' you to quit and go away. You may be County Treasurer, but you can't break laws no more than anybody else without sufferin' for it. Mebbe you think you can get away with this, but you won't. The people—"

"The people are here, you swelled-up bag of wind!" the other barked. "The Sheriff's out, you're out, and we're runnin' things. We're takin' Bridges and puttin' him on trial and then stringin' him up for his crimes."

"Stranglers' court."

"The people's court. Enough of this talk. Are you goin' to give him, or no?"

"No."

"Then we'll tear him out of that house. Tell Underwood that."

"Underwood is backin' me up. Wait; I'm doin' the talkin' right how. You say you're the law. You ain't the law, Brill; you're a damned outlaw and before you're done with this you'll be swingin' from the gallows yourself. Now move back. My hand is on my gun, as you see, and I can shoot from the hip."

"Pull back, men," Pete Brill ordered, instantly. "He's got me straight in line. We'll take care of him when we've called up the rest of the men."

The horsemen at his imperious gesture backed their mounts farther off from the house. For a few seconds Mort Jones stood watching them, then stepped quickly back inside and closed the door.

"Some day you'll be pinnin' on a Sheriff's star, fella," said Baldy. "With them guts of yours."

"I was scared stiff."

"Like a fightin' wildcat's scared."

"Well, we'll all have to be wildcats from now on," the Deputy remarked. "They're ridin' round and callin' in the rest of the mob. When they start, we'll think hell's broke loose."

AS HE SAID, the horsemen who had been with Brill were galloping about and collecting the rest of the crowd from their work of destruction. Presently they all were assembled where their leader sat his horse and they listened to his orders. Next, they mounted and while a score or more of them rode to encircle the ranch house at a distance, the rest moved off into darkness; when the latter reappeared they were on foot and scattering to approach the dwelling from all sides.

Underwood, Mort Jones, and Lafe conferred hastily regarding the dangers of this new situation. Finally the sick man was brought into the living room and placed in a corner safe from direct gunfire, after which all doors to the room were locked and together with windows barricaded thick and high with mattresses and furniture. Their force was too small to defend the whole length of house with the many windows, but behind this room's defenses they would be able to make a deadly and prolonged fight.

The attack was not delayed. First came a fusillade of shots that did no damage, only striking the adobe walls and thudding through doors and windows into the raised barriers. This was followed by a rush at the front. Through the narrow openings left for use above the upper edges of the mattresses the punchers, two at each window, delivered a rapid return fire with their six-guns. Yells and groans answered. Three men had fallen; one of them lay dead, one sat clasping his stomach, and the third was crawling off. Others were fleeing.

"The fools hadn't sense enough to keep out of the light and come at the building where it's dark," Lafe remarked. "First blood for us. They won't make that mistake again, though, likely. You gents at the inner doors prick your ears and listen for 'em."

That presently some of the mob had ventured into the dwelling became evident when muffled sounds of bodies stumbling over furniture in a bedroom were heard. The shooting outside increased. The end of the building where the kitchen and the dining room were located was being subjected to a heavy rifle fire.

"That's to draw our attention," Underwood said. "So they'll be coming from the other end."

Two of the cowboys, experienced fighters and dead shots, replaced Grantly and Baldy, who had been guarding the door between the living room and the hall leading to the bed chambers. That this was wise was proved when several volleys thundered in the pent space of the vestibule and bullets splintered door panels and shook the mattresses propped up there.

The punchers' guns roared in answer. Came a muffled thud of a falling body, a curse, and the sound of retreating feet. The two cowboys laughed. Through the darkness of the room seeped the acrid fumes of powder smoke.

After some time there came another attack upon the inner doors, both the one from the dining room and that from the hallway, this time with pieces of timber used as battering rams and then bullets. The doors were half broken in, wrenched partially from their hinges, and the barricades disturbed. A withering fire from the defenders at each place blasted the assailants and ended the double assault. Handicapped as were the occupants of the room by lack of light, the men who attempted to force their way in were worse off, since they had not only to crawl forward and grope and make their effort in darkness but were hampered by unfamiliarity with the house.

Perhaps an hour later, a third and worse assault was made: two parties fighting to break through the inner doorways as before, while men on foot and on horses swept the front of the building with continual gunfire. Lead began to enter. A bullet wounded Les Bridges in the left shoulder and another gashed a puncher's cheek.

"If we could only have a light!" Betty exclaimed, as kneeling beside the injured youth she fumbled at binding up his hurt with a strip torn from a sheet. "Poor boy, you won't be able to fight any more."

"The deuce I won't!" he grunted. "Nothing the matter with my right arm or hand. I keep shootin' at 'em even if I have to hold my gun in my teeth. No time to quit now; every fella's needed."

"Seems like we've been here for ages cooped up in the dark and stifling reek."

"Not more'n an hour and a half since the first shot was fired."

"Oh, they're attacking more fiercely all the time, Les! Oh, my dear, hold me for a minute! I shudder to think they may get in, that we may fall into their hands."

"We won't fall into their hands, not alive," said he, between his teeth. "And we'll take a lot of 'em 'long with us. But we ain't goin' to die. All we've got to do is hold 'em off till help comes, and we'll do that if we have to stick here a week. Mort says the Sheriff will surely be showin' up in time with some men. If I could only get a shot at Pete Brill!"

WOOD POPPED, MATTRESSES danced, plaster dust trickled down under the rain of lead, the steady roar persisted and the smoke thickened. A puncher slid down to the floor and lay in the darkness, until Lafe moving about found him, bent ear to his breast to listen for a heartbeat and then rose to take his place. Baldy snapped out an oath as a bullet smacked his hip.

"Them mattresses are gettin' ripped all to pieces," he growled. "Hey, Betty, when you get done with that fella, tie up my leg. Wait a minute. See one of the bunch out there sneakin' along in range." His rifle pommed. "Got him. That's better'n salve for my hurt. Well, gents and ladies, we beat 'em off again. Gettin' peaceful and calm-like."

The furious assault had ended and the gunfire died slowly down.

"A breathin' spell only," said Lafe. "Won't last long. But we can fix up our bulwarks, as they say, and get set for the next barbecue. Keep watch on the hall, Jess, while I move Lanky. He's gone. And no better boy ever lived."

Minute after minute passed without the attack being

resumed. Those in the dark little stronghold grew anxious. What diabolical trick were their assailants preparing?

On a sudden Mort Jones, who was observing the foreground through a window slit above its buttressing mattress, said:

"None I can see are near. They're gatherin' yonder beyond the burnin' haystack by the small corral. Something must've happened, for they're talkin' and showin' excitement."

CHAPTER XVIII

AN OUTLAW UNMASKED

WHAT THE DEPUTY Sheriff saw was an impromptu conference that grew from the refusal of several Mexicans to risk their lives in another assault. The word spread about that men were quitting and resulted in others withdrawing to the spot, until at last most of the mob were assembled there. The dispute waxed hot as the mutinous group gained adherents with fresh arrivals.

A mob's spirit if fierce is fickle. Some men believed the defenders could not be routed out, some were shaken by their losses, some counted the heavy price yet to be paid for success, some had sobered and were fearful of the penalty for this lawlessness, some were natural cowards and thought of their own skin, some were sated with excitement, and nearly all were tired. After all, they owed nothing to Pete Brill.

Throughout the argument the County Treasurer's voice had not been heard. What did he have to say about it? Calls rose for Pete to speak. Why was he silent? Where was he? Who had seen him last? What had become of him, anyway? No one recalled seeing him any time during the last attack, in fact, during the last half hour.

"If he ain't here, it means he's quit," a man exclaimed.

But Pete Brill had not removed himself from the scene

of conflict; he had been removed, and if not actually from the scene yet from its active midst.

The manner of it was this. Always careful of his own safety, as he was careless of that of others, he had made a pretense of heading the party on foot and on horse that attacked in front; but before entering the lighted zone of fire, slowed down and when behind the rest had wheeled his horse and galloped back to the bunk house. Pulling up behind this, he sat his mount and watched the progress of the fight from a corner of the building out of line of bullets.

Nor did the light from the burning haystacks fall there. No one could see him, or so he thought. Darkness hid him. His men supposed him taking part in the action. Like a wise general, he commanded and maneuvered his forces from behind the lines. Nevertheless Brill felt no complacency. In truth, the stiff resistance of the ranch house defenders and the deadly toll they were taking among his followers aroused mingled fears, rage, and a thirst. The last he satisfied from a flask. The second he fed with curses. The first he could not allay, for the prospect that Underwood and Betty would be slain and he thus prevented from obtaining the ranch and the girl appeared certain. He had counted on frightening them with a little gunfire and forcing them to yield, and here the cowman and his friends were fighting desperately.

So intent in his watch and so much a prey to his feelings was he, he was unaware of a horse with rider that came slowly and stealthily alongside him. The first the leader knew that he was not alone was when a hand seized his reins.

"I've come for you, Brill."

The hearer started around in his saddle. He beheld leaning close to him the dim shape of a rider swathed in black; that was his first dismayed impression. Then he was able to see that the other wore a black hat, a hood through the eyeholes of which he caught the gleam of eyes; and a voluminous cloak; and despite the callous hardiness of his nature his skin crawled with fear. In the black garb, in the gleaming black eyes, in the other's very forward leaning, there was a cold ominousness of purpose that held something deadly.

"A masked rider!" he gasped, in a whistling whisper.

"*The* Masked Rider," was the chill response.

"What—what do you want?"

"You."

BRILL DID NOT believe in apparitions, and he now knew this unwelcome companion for a man, even if one of wide notoriety.

"So you've turned up here, eh?" he stated, after getting a grip on himself. "The famous outlaw himself!"

"And just in time. You're coming with me."

"Sorry I can't oblige you, Mister Masked Rider," he sneered. "Important business is occupying my attention at present."

"Hellish business, you mean."

"That comes fine from the lips of the outlaw who has done all you've done."

"Keep that hand still!" the order was hissed. "Try to reach your holster again and you'll never swing from the rope that's waiting for you! My gun's pointing at your dirty liver and my finger's twitching on the trigger. I've the eyes of a cat, and I can smell your every intention. If I didn't choose to let you live long enough to get your last rites on a gallows, I'd end you and your devilment this minute. You persuaded your scoundrel of a partner to impersonate me and rob your safe after you'd killed Underwood's man, you accuse a young rancher of being the masked thief and of having been the murderer and set this mob after him— well, your crimes have forced me to take a hand in your damnable game. You're dealing now with no masquerading Mexican or lie-dressed boy; you're under the gun of the real McCoy in the way of Masked Riders."

The harsh, low-spoken words, full of menace, dissipated Pete Brill's self-confidence as an icy blast does mist.

"Where you taking me?" he asked, dry-mouthed.

"Farther back."

"You intend to kill me, by God!"

"If that was my mind, you'd be a corpse now."

"Listen. Let me have my say—"

"No." The word was iron-hard in its finality. "No pleading with me."

"Let me go and I'll take my crowd away."

"With you gone, it will go. Come."

"You're holding me for the law?"

"For the gallows. No more talk."

They rode away knee to knee until at The Masked Rider's command they stopped out of reach of the crimson light. Three times Brill had steeled himself to make a break for freedom, but each time the hooded outlaw seemed to divine his purpose and to grasp tighter the reins of Pete's horse and to lean threateningly nearer, so that each resolve faltered and failed in the crook's soul. Like a cat, the cloaked and hooded rider watched him. Like a black devil with death directed straight and sharp, the masked man gripped him fast.

"We sit here, we wait," spoke The Masked Rider.

"For what?"

"For the hangman!"

Brill felt a gun muzzle settle firmly against his back. He shivered. Thus they sat motionless and silent with the stars making their slow wheel overhead.

Up the creek trail were galloping the Sheriff and a posse of forty men whom after delay he had raked together in Chavo. Good men, loyal men, men armed with guns and a righteous wrath. They swept around a hill where the burning haystacks and illuminated ranch buildings came in view, which set them spurring their mounts and racing at top speed for the place.

THEY CAME WITH a thunderous roll of hoofs into the light and at sight of them pouring forward in a solid column, the mob half-raised their guns, milled in confusion, then broke and fled for the horses and the darkness. When the Sheriff and his riders came to a sliding stop by bunkhouse and corral, the scattered fugitives were flying each for himself into the hills or the desert.

From the ranch house the defenders ran forth.

"Thank God, you've come!" the cowman exclaimed, fervently. "We were about at the last breath."

"Came as soon as we could," was the answer. "But I see some bodies on the ground; you used your stinger."

"They was after Les Bridges," Mort Jones said.

"And you didn't give him up, naturally."

"No. They demanded him, and I warned them they was vi'latin' the law and ordered 'em to quit. That brought on the fight." He wiped mouth with back of hand. "They didn't get Les, but they got plenty of lead. The dead ain't all out here; there's more in the house."

"Any of your party killed, Clem?"

"Lanky. Les and Baldy wounded, and some others scratched."

"You should have taken to the canyon."

"No," the cowman said, stoutly. "I won't be driven off the Box U. Grantly's safe, too, you see, and so is Doc Chessington who was brought here sick."

"What? He here? The most important witness against Brill? Good. Betty, I'm sure sorry you had to go through what you have."

"Well, we beat them back and now we've won," said she. "I hope you can round up and punish these snakes. They did a lot of damage, you can see. The house inside is wrecked. And Lanky's dead."

"I'll round up the worst of 'em, anyway."

"Especially Pete Brill, the sidewinder!" Les Bridges ejaculated.

"Never you worry, I won't," the Sheriff answered, grimly. "He's billed for hangin'. Killed not only Bill Lawson night before last, but Carlos Valdez this evenin'."

A murmur of surprise greeted this news.

"What for?" Underwood inquired.

"For the stolen bonds and money. It was Valdez took it from the safe in Pete's office, with Pete's connivance, and Pete thought he was bein' double-crossed when Valdez said he didn't have the loot, or so I figger it went, and Pete killed him. He was kinda killed by mistake." He concluded by giving Underwood and Betty a warning look.

"You're startin' to hunt Brill?" Les asked, eagerly. "Well, I'm goin' with you."

"You're not, Les," Betty cried. "Wounded as you are, no."

"No, boy," Condon added. "You're remainin' here if you have to be hogtied. You're too damned unlucky, and I don't want whatever little luck we may have ruined by you. So you will stay."

To this order, which the youth considered an insult, Les made a hot rejoiner as to his "luck" and several reflections upon the Sheriff's recent misjudgments. But the Sheriff refused to be baited or bothered.

"We'll look around and see who's dead and if any wounded are lyin' about, as is likely," he stated, "then we'll high-tail it back to Chavo. Pete will certainly go there to get what money he can grab if he plans to skip out. But mebbe he won't skip out; he may yet figger he's got influence enough to outride the storm. I'm hopin' so, I sure am hopin' so. Fact is, I'm kinda hopin' he'll take the notion to chance a draw 'gainst me when I arrest him, though of course I'd enjoy more seein' him stretch hemp."

"Hadn't we oughta look 'round here for him first before startin' back!" the puncher Jerry questioned. "He may still be lurkin' in the background somewhere."

"We'll go through the motions, yes," Condon rejoined. "But I expect nothin' from it. Knowin' Pete, I know he'd be the first to depart when he saw the game was up at this end."

UNQUESTIONABLY HE HAD the crafty County Treasurer sized up correctly. Had Pete been able to exercise his free will, that is. He was not in a position to do so, of course. The Masked Rider's gun and own compelling will had held him mercilessly in the saddle at the spot where the two waited.

But when the posse had put in an appearance and the lawless gang had fled, The Masked Rider had uttered a derisive laugh that filled his prisoner with fresh apprehension. Jamming the gun savagely against Pete's ribs, the man issued some instructions and proceeded to array Brill's person in ignominy. Then The Masked Rider forced Brill ahead of him toward the bunk house.

The Sheriff was on the point of bidding his men assist the cowman's punchers to collect the dead and wounded when the thing happened. At the corner of the bunk house a quirt slashed across a horse's flank, and into the crimson light the animal with its rider leaped forward toward the group. It plunged to a stop almost in the midst of the startled company.

"The Masked Rider!" Betty cried.

"So it is," the Sheriff echoed, and drew and presented his six-gun with lightning rapidity at the breast of the horseman garbed in black hat, black hood with eyeholes, black gloves, and black mantilla at the hem of which hung one of Valdez', red grilled price tags.

"The Masked Rider!" a score of voices muttered, amazed.

The Sheriff's mouth hardened in a tight line, his jaw jutted forward, and his grip tightened about the butt of his revolver.

"This time you don't fade away," he said, "and what's more I'm takin' a look at you."

Reaching forward, he seized and jerked up the other's hood. Then he stared at the face he saw in bewilderment, exclaiming:

"Pete Brill!"

CHAPTER XIX

THE LAST JEST

I T WAS THE next afternoon. Betty Underwood had gone up to her favorite resort when wanting to be alone and think—the slab of rock on the ridge overlooking the canyon. So much had happened, so much that was exciting, that was sorrowful, that was terrible, that was reassuring, that gave her happiness, she felt she must be by herself for awhile.

Except for the lost bonds and money, all the issues of the crimes had been settled or were in the way of being rightly terminated. The Sheriff, who had come from town to the ranch at noon and who was still there, had brought news of Brill. The man on the way to Chavo had escaped. He had reached town, where a strange thing occurred. Only Mike Grogan, the saloonkeeper, was a witness of the event, and he apparently was mystified by its peculiar circumstance. By his story, he was alone in his place and on the point of closing when two men slipped in, one a man with a yellow fang whom he had never seen before and the other Pete Brill, and they broke into a furious quarrel over the stolen County money and bonds and both drew and shot each other, falling dead. That was all he could tell. He had run out into the street immediately, calling men. The whole business was queer. He suggested that, perhaps, the man with the fang was a secret friend of Brill's and that on Pete's escaping and getting to town ahead of the posse he had gone to Valdez' store, met the stranger there, searched for the money, and the pair not finding it had come quarreling to the saloon and there killed each other. This opinion had been generally adopted.

"Thinking it all over, Miss Betty?" a familiar voice said.

She faced quickly about. There stood The Masked Rider.

"Yes," said she.

"The masquerade of outlaws in Chavo is over."

"That may be," said she, "but it isn't over as far as you're concerned. The Sheriff will hunt you down if he can. He's at the ranch house now, so it isn't safe for you. He eyed me curiously when I started off up the canyon."

"You don't want the robber of the safe caught, it seems."

"No, I don't want you caught, that's true. Perhaps I'm wrong in warning you of danger; my duty in the matter is mixed up with my sense of gratitude for what you did for Dad and me and our friends. I would feel badly if you were captured, even if you have the stolen bonds and money. You see, I'm pulled two opposite ways over that."

"An outlaw's expenses are heavy, girl."

"No doubt."

"And sometimes his tastes are expensive, too."

She regarded his hooded face in an effort to penetrate through its web, but all she perceived through the holes were his enigmatical eyes.

"I find it difficult to understand you," said she. "You do noble things, and at the same time ignoble ones."

"What, for instance?"

"You're keeping money that doesn't belong to you but to the people of this County, many of them who have paid in their share only with sacrifice."

"I haven't the money."

"You're jesting."

"I seldom jest."

"You played a grim joke last night on Pete Brill, certainly," she asserted. "Pitching him to the Sheriff as The Masked Rider."

"Well, perhaps," he admitted, laughing a little. "But coming back to the money—"

HE BROKE OFF and stood unspeaking, his head turned a trifle to the right and his eyes gazing at a dense thicket of junipers a few yards off. Thither the girl's look went too.

"You can come out, Sheriff," said The Masked Rider.

Condon came forth from his screen, on his face a mixture of chagrin and determination. In his hand was his gun.

"So you followed me!" Betty addressed him, indignantly.

"Doin' my duty."

"The Masked Rider will imagine me guilty of plotting with you for his capture."

"Did he know you were comin' here?" the Sheriff asked.

"Well, no. I don't see how."

"Then your conscience needn't be uneasy 'bout your share in the matter. I read your eyes. You come sorta hopin' to see him once more so you could thank him. Right?"

"Yes."

"Same with me."

He holstered his gun. Drawing from vest pocket tobacco and papers, he made a smoke and struck match.

"There's outlaws and outlaws," he remarked. "Pete Brill was one kind, and mebbe—"

"Was?" The Masked Rider queried.

"Pete is dead. Killed late last night."

"Just as well."

"Yeah; saves expense of a trial," Condon said, slowly. "The County bein' broke has to get along without a lot of things it used to could afford."

"That means you'll have to dig up, eh?"

"And tough diggin' it's goin' to be for everyone, too," the Sheriff affirmed.

Again The Masked Rider laughed; and Condon's face flushed as he felt its mockery.

"Depends where you dig, Sheriff," said the laugher.

"We have to dig down in empty pockets."

"Why not first try digging under that flat stone Miss Betty's feet are resting on?"

Betty jumped up from her seat and regarded the piece of rock mentioned as if it were a puzzle. Condon took a step forward, glanced at it, and then fixed on the hooded outlaw a level, measuring look.

"Turn that stone over, girl!" he exclaimed excitedly, at last.

Dropping to her knees, Betty did so. Under it in a hole rested the steel box and the packet Valdez had removed from the County Treasurer's safe. Condon too went down on knees to lift out the stolen funds.

When he had them and when he and the girl raised their eyes, The Masked Rider was no longer there. They saw him instead down in the hollow, swinging up to a seat on his mount, which was screened by brush and obviously prancing about, fretting to go. The Black Caballero looked up at them. His hand was flung up in a wave, a triumphant laugh travelled to their ears. Betty smiled and waved in return. The Sheriff grinned. Even an outlaw should be allowed his little jest.

Then the stallion leaped forward in a great bound and whipped behind a great clump of mountain maple, heading up the hollow. The watchers remained unmoving, unbreathing. Came the distant cry of a mountain lion. The cloaked and hooded horseman, The Masked Rider, had gone from Chavo.

WIDE OPEN TOWN

BY JACK DRUMMOND

CHAPTER I

DEATH STRIKES

THE LONG FINGERS of dusk reached out, masked the last glowing shades of a flaming sunset and condensed to usher in the night which promised to be black and mysterious, relieved only by star-strewn heavens. Later the heat-blistered, sandy wastes would cool; living creatures of the desert would stir, slither through the darkness on their forage for food and water and possible combat with hereditary enemies. But at this hour all was quiet; a strange, eerie pall hung in the air prolonging the lethargy of a long, hot day.

Paused close beside a water hole in the fringe of the dry sun-baked hills that marked the lower reaches of the Peso Mountains, two men hovered close to a small mesquite fire. While one prepared their evening meal the other squatted on his heels close by, thoughtfully smoking a cigarette.

Both were tall, dark, and virile, young in the prime years of life, but that is where the resemblance ceased. It was plain by the glow of the fire which played on their grave features that the man smoking the meditative cigarette had acquired his deep bronze from long exposure to the desert suns and the hot, shriveling winds, while the other had inherited his sharp, swarthy features from a parentage found south of the Rio Grande.

His coloring was Mexican; but the lithe, straight body,

the extremely high cheek bones, and the dashing black eyes which gave hint of the wild and untamed, were truly Yaqui. Pride of his Aztec ancestors was Blue Hawk's; yet for Wayne Morgan, the white man squatting there beside him, he bore a reverent respect that bordered close on idolatry.

While the Yaqui tended the food, Wayne Morgan stared moodily into the fire, apparently mulling over some troublesome problem. His bronzed forehead, shaded beneath the brim of a dusty black hat, was furrowed with wrinkles. Below this was a face etched with deep lines that bordered on hardness except for the network of crowsfeet around his wide-spread eyes which bespoke of a droll sense of humor and an amused, if slightly sardonic, outlook on life. A cynical glint marred the depths of his brown eyes as he pulled them from the fire and raised them to the Indian's face.

"Once again the gold on my head has tempted the greed of men, Hawk," he drawled in a voice that came deep and soft, yet one that harbored a tang of bitterness. "Posse's dog our trail and so to avoid them we take to the desert. Our horses are none too fresh, but we'll have to start pushing

them across the sandy wastes tonight. With luck we'll make Skeleton Springs by daylight where we'll rest up until the following night when we will push on into Nevada."

"*Si señor,*" Blue Hawk nodded without looking up from the sizzling bacon that he was frying. "It is only fools who travel the desert in the summer sun and we are not fools."

"I wonder?" mused Morgan, taking a contemplative pull at his cigarette. "Maybe in Nevada the sheriff will be waiting for us. Then what?"

"*Quien sabe?*" shrugged the Yaqui. "Perhaps we ride some more. But here, *señor,* we know there is danger. There, maybe not."

Morgan laughed dryly, "No such luck, Hawk. There isn't a sheriff in all the west who hasn't got his office papered with reward posters for The Masked Rider dead or alive." A philosophic mood took hold of him. "Life is a funny thing when you come to think of it, Hawk."

"It is not life, *señor,* it is the people who live it"

"Maybe you're right at that. Anyway it's funny how a little notoriety will add to a man's value to this old world. As Wayne Morgan I'm not worth a thin dime to anybody, but as The Masked Rider I'm worth *mucha dinero* to anyone who is lucky enough to sink a slug in me."

"Perhaps if it was known that Wayne Morgan and The Masked Rider are one and the same, *señor*—"

"But it isn't and thereby hangs my silver thread of life. Once it is learned that it is my face behind the black hood my string will be played out. It's the mystery of the man inside the hooded, black cape that makes men fear him, Hawk. Remove that mystery and you likewise take away the fear."

The Yaqui looked up, the hint of a smile broke across his thin lips.

"Your mood, it is what you call whimsical, *señor,*" he reproved gently. "You smoke and look into the fire too long. You dream. Better that we eat and be gone. Danger lurks—"

HIS WORDS TRAILED off, his head jerked around and his black eyes peered up along the black depths of the north slope of the wash.

"Somebody comes," he said in a low, guttural voice.

Morgan, too, was listening, but as yet heard nothing. However, it was characteristic of him that he accepted the Yaqui's words without question. He snapped his cigarette butt into the fire, came to his full height and quickly faded away from the fire back into the black maw of the wash where their horses had been staked to forage on the rank growth of salt grass.

Stooping low, Blue Hawk gathered up the two rifles which had been stacked against their saddles and followed. A dozen paces back from the fire, swallowed up by the gloom, Morgan paused, loosened the two heavy .45s that were snuggled low against his lean thighs and opening the front of his shirt, brought forth a folded, black hood. When this had been pulled over his head and the eye slits adjusted, he slipped into a mantilla that flowed down around his shoulders in a long cape. In the space of a moment Wayne Morgan had been transformed into the notorious and universally feared outlaw, The Masked Rider.

The Yaqui again struck a listening pose beside the hooded man and suddenly gripped his arm.

"You hear?" he whispered close to one cloth-covered ear.

This time the other did hear. Sounds which at first came

faintly, grew louder and could be distinguished as the hoof-beats of a horse picking its way along the backbone of the sloping ridge. Closer they came and when directly above the two in the draw they halted abruptly. For a moment silence, broken only by the jingle of bridle irons, settled down on the wash. Then suddenly the horse was put to the slope and came sliding down toward them amidst an avalanche of loose dirt and rock.

With nerves tense and eyes straining to pierce the darkness the masked man and the Indian waited. As the plunging horse leveled off on the bottom of the wash and moved into the circle of light cast out by the small fire a hail crackled against the night air.

"Anybody here!"

The words were tremulous, high-pitched, lacking the heavy timber of maturity.

"A *nino*," whispered the Indian.

"Yeah—just a boy," replied the masked man, his eyes taking in every detail of the horse and rider.

When no answer came to his hail the youth in the saddle flashed a desperate, panicky glance in all directions and tried again, this time with a distinct note of anguish in his voice.

"Please come out. I'm—I'm in trouble!"

The last was almost an hysterical sob. That frightened note of appeal sent an odd thrill coursing through the masked man's veins. Impulsively he took a step toward the fire.

"Have a care, *señor*," cautioned the Yaqui laying a restraining hand on his arm. "It may be a trick."

"I'll chance that," murmured the other. "You wait here and keep your rifle handy."

He faded away, but paused again just outside the circle of light.

"Hello, son," he drawled. "You kind of gave me a scare riding up like that. Light and let me look at you."

The drawling voice coming at him out of the dark startled the boy. He jerked in the saddle, stared hard in the direction it had come from.

"Where—are you?" he stammered.

"Right here," replied The Rider. "Don't get excited. I'm not going to hurt you."

"Why don't you come out here?" questioned the youth, logically enough.

"I will, maybe, after I get a good look at you," drawled the hidden man. "Light and step up close to the fire where I can see you plain."

The youngster hesitated. For a second it looked as if he was going to bolt in panic. Then he got hold of himself and did as he was bid. As the light played full on his face, The Masked Rider saw that he was younger than he had first suspected. He was little more than a child, his years numbering less than a dozen. Standing there nervously, unable to see the man who he knew was looking him over, his face was chalkwhite with fear, his eyes round with apprehension.

"Looks like something has scared the living hell out of you," the masked man summed up his observations. "I'm not going to show myself yet but figure me a friend and tell me all about it, son."

THERE WAS SOMETHING about that soft, friendly voice that impressed the boy, quelled his fears. He found reassurance in it even though the owner of it was loathe to expose himself. To the boy's tortured mind this was enough to make him suddenly give way to a flood of emotions which panic and fear had held in check for so long. Tears welled up in his eyes, a choking sob burst from his lips and he cried openly and unashamed.

"My mom an' paw," he choked between sobs. "He k— killed them both!"

As the anguished words hammered against The Masked Rider's ears a cold chill surged the length of his body, pulled at the roots of his hair until his head tingled. Impulsively he moved to join the grief-stricken youth, then the caution of a hunted man checked him in time. After all this might be a trap set by those who sought him. Also it would help the boy none to join him now; might frighten him further if The Masked Rider was to expose himself garbed as he was, in the flowing black mantilla. So he remained concealed and spoke his sympathy from a distance.

"Better tell me all about it, son," he drawled. "If something has happened to your mother and father I don't blame you for crying. But you'll have to buck up and tell me about it before I can help you."

The low words had a quieting effect on the youngster. After a moment his sobs ceased and he wiped away the tears with the knuckles of two tiny fists. Trying vainly to pierce the darkness and catch sight of his new-found friend he started talking and blurted a story of wanton, cold-blooded murder that jolted even The Masked Rider's hardened senses.

In broken, sobbing speech he told of a man who had come to the small ranch house of his father suffering from a bullet wound in his side. He was weak from loss of blood and in the grip of the first stages of fever when Tom Aiken, the boy's father, helped him from the saddle and put him to bed. Then followed a week when Aiken and his wife sat with him night and day fighting to save his life.

Aiken thought of riding the thirty miles to the closest town where there was a doctor, but decided against this after listening to the man's delirious ravings. From them Aiken learned that he was an outlaw—a bandit, for he spoke of train holdups and bank robberies in Arizona and California. He repeated again conversations he had had with different men, apparently other members of an outlaw gang. He blurted names, none of which meant anything to Aiken, except one. It was when the name of Gage Dampier rolled from the raving man's lips that Aiken decided against bringing a doctor to his place.

Aiken knew of Dampier—knew that he was a big cattleman who owned and controlled the Burnt River Valley and most of the country surrounding it high up in the Cayuse Mountains. What Gage Dampier's connection with the gang might be Aiken could only guess but hearing the cowman's name spoken by the delirious man was enough to make him decide to doctor the man himself and send him on his way when he got better or bury him secretly if he died.

"Don't pay to get mixed up in a thing like this," he told his wife. "Gage Dampier is supposed to be a respectable cowman, but he runs things to suit himself up in Burnt River. I ain't hankering to bring him and his crew down here on my neck."

"But this man is an outlaw—a train robber," protested his wife.

"I don't own no banks or trains neither," replied Aiken.

"That's the law's lookout. Best way to handle this is to know nothin' an' say nuthin'."

Aiken's wife didn't agree with his policies but she said nothing more at the time. They finally succeeded in breaking the fever and from then on the outlaw recuperated fast. In another week he was on his feet and taking walks to regain his strength. He was surly and suspicious, offering no thanks for what they had done for him. His biggest worry seemed to be that he might have talked when he was delirious. He questioned Aiken about this several times and always received the answer that he had said nothing intelligible.

IT WAS ONE day while the outlaw was on one of his walks that Aiken's wife again spoke about notifying the authorities. An argument ensued, during which the outlaw appeared at the door. He held his gun balanced in his hand and it was plain from the snarling expression on his face that he had crept close and heard much of what had been said.

"He told them they knew too much an' then shot them—killed them both," cried the boy. "I was in the kitchen when he done it an' I ducked down cellar an' closed the door. Guess he heard the door shut an' figured I'd gone outside 'cause I heard him run across the floor over my head an' go outside. He come back after a while an' started lookin' through the house for me. I crawled up under the floors an' laid there without breathin' when he came down in the cellar. I was scared he'd find me, but he didn't.

"After he went away I stayed there a long time an' then crawled out. From the kitchen winder I seen him just ridin' away on his horse, goin' east. I waited till he got outa sight an' then went down an' saddled a horse an' started ridin' to tell the sheriff. Reckon he musta seen me or was figurin' I'd do that an' was layin' for me. But I seen him before I got too close. He shot at me but I reckon I was too far away. Knowed I couldn't git around him an' git to the sheriff so I headed east into the hills, figurin' I could lose him.

"When dark come I kinda got lost myself an' then I seen your fire. Was scared to come down at first, but figured that feller wouldn't be squattin' 'round no fire. I'm glad I didn't git scared an' ride by, mister. You'll help me, won'tcha?"

"I sure will, son," promised the masked man. "What's the outlaw's name?"

"Dunno. He never said. He talked about a lotta fellers, maybe he's one of them."

"Remember any of the names he mentioned?"

"Kinda. Besides Gage Dampier he was talkin' about a feller named Hutch somethin' an' another'n he called Jim an' another'n that was Blalock or Malott or somethin' like that."

"What did he look like?" The Masked Rider next questioned.

"He was short an' kinda chunky an' his skin was dark."

"Mexicano?"

"I don't think so. Looked like he mighta been mixed with negro. His face was kinda brown an' his eyes was—"

The rest of his speech was chopped off abruptly as the sharp report of a heavy sixshooter rolled down from the ridge above. The Masked Rider whirled. His guns leapt into his hands and rolled lead toward the crest of the ridge. The deep bellow of a rifle told that Blue Hawk had also gone into action.

But the damage had been done. That first bullet had been aimed with cold deadly accuracy. It's doubtful if the boy ever knew what struck him as he pitched face forward to the ground. Blue Hawk and The Masked Rider had no way of knowing at the moment whether their lead had taken effect, for after that first deadly shot no more explosions came from the ridge.

Reloading, The Masked Rider moved close to the Yaqui.

"Keep him stirred up," he hissed at the Indian and faded away in the dark, working back up the draw, his intentions being to circle the ambusher and come up on him from the rear.

Changing positions after every shot, Blue Hawk continued to sweep the ridge with lead. Cautiously the hooded man took to the slope and angled his way toward the crest. Banking on the thunder of Blue Hawk's rifle to conceal his move, he forsook the safety of a slower approach in his anxiety to reach the top of the ridge. He blundered at times and his boots found and loosened unsteady footing which otherwise would have been avoided.

It was this haste which was almost his undoing, for suddenly, not over twenty feet to the right of him, a burst of orange flame pierced the night and an angry, searching bullet ripped through the folds of the masked man's cape. Caught off balance and unaware, The Masked Rider held his fire until he had dropped flat and rolled. Then he sent four bullets, futile ones he suspected, at the spot where the orange flash had come from.

BLUE HAWK HAD also seen that flash, but had held his fire not knowing who it was that had fired. However, as The Masked Rider's two guns exploded Blue Hawk raked the ridge above him with rifle fire. With the rifle empty Blue Hawk reloaded, then settled down to await further developments. Too dangerous to send any more lead up on that ridge. The Masked Rider was close to the top and would be in range of it.

With the patience known only to his race Blue Hawk waited. Minutes dragged by, lengthened into an hour.

Then, suddenly the wailing, blood-chilling call of a mountain cat vibrated against the walls of the wash. Automatically the Indian got to his feet, cupped his hands to his mouth and sent an echoing call up the draw. Moments later The Masked Rider sidled up to him in the dark.

"Sloped, I reckon," were his words of explanation.

"I heard what I thought was a horse getting under way," said Blue Hawk.

"So did I, but I was too far away to do any damage," muttered the other. "Thought he might circle around, but I guess he kept on traveling. Have you looked at the boy?"

"I have not moved from here, *señor*, yet we shall surely find a dead *nino* by the coals of our dying fire."

"He went down like he was hit plumb center," said the masked man. "My fault, I reckon. I should have made him come away from the light of that fire. Had a hunch that killer was around here close," his voice grew husky. "Who is it that murders women and children, Hawk?"

"That we do not know, *señor*."

"Not right now but we'll be finding out," grated the hooded man. "We cross no desert tonight, Hawk. Our plans are changed."

An expression of quick apprehension came over the Yaqui's solemn features.

"That is not wise, *señor*," he cautioned earnestly. "We have many troubles without seeking others."

"Not seeking any," denied the hooded man. "This was

dumped right into our laps and we can't let it pass. A boy has been murdered, Hawk."

"Of a truth, *señor*. But we do the *muchacho* no good now. He is dead. Anything we can do will not give him new life."

"Maybe not, but I figure it's my fault he's dead," growled the hooded man. "We'll trail the killer till we find him."

"It is not wise," insisted Blue Hawk. "But if it is your wish then it shall be done."

"Do we ever do anything that is wise?" inquired the other. "You argue with me yet you would follow me to hell if I led the way."

"My life, it is yours," stated the Indian solemnly. "Many years ago you saved it and have since watched over it. But with your own you are careless, *amigo mio*. Too often you make the troubles of others your own. One day you shall stand up before a court of law and then will one of these men you have befriended come to your rescue?"

A slow, sardonic smile broke across the lips behind the mask.

"I doubt it, Hawk. But that makes no difference. I ask nothing in return for what I do for others. I demand nothing of life except the privilege of living it in my own way."

"Others do not wish that you live, compadre. Thousands of pesos hang over your head—rewards—blood money for crimes you never committed."

"What matter?" shrugged the other. "My conscience is clear. What others believe doesn't seem to worry me much. Well, we eat and ride, Hawk."

"And the *muchacho?*"

"You're going to take him down to the sheriff, Hawk, and tell him where the lad's mother and father can be found. Use your own judgment, but don't let them detain you."

"And you, my friend?"

"Will take the trail of the murderer."

"That is not as it should be, still I offer no protest."

"No. You'd do better with the trail than I," agreed The Rider. "But I cannot take the body into town, Hawk. We'll meet again up in the town of Twin Peaks."

"Where is that, *senor?*"

"Up in the Burnt River Valley. Must be close to sixty or seventy miles from here, north by west."

"You think that is where the trail will lead, *senor?*"

"I don't know. Anyway, it's where this Gage Dampier, the cowman that the boy mentioned, lives. I must see this man and talk with him. Train robbers and bandits do not speak of men like Dampier unless there is some connection between them, Hawk."

"Suppose the trail does not lead there, *senor?*"

"Then I'll leave the trail and seek identity of the killer through Dampier. Now, while you warm up the grub I'll saddle up. After I see you on your way I will move from this spot and wait for the coming of daylight when I'll pick up the trail of the killer. Vamoose!"

"At once, *senor,*" and Hawk moved off.

CHAPTER II

TWIN PEAKS

H IGH UP IN the Cayuse Mountains crowded hard against one of the sheltering hills which flanked the Burnt River Valley, lay the town of Twin Peaks. Deriving its name from two closely related peaks which loomed up at the head of the valley, the town first sprang into existence when the rush for precious metals was on. The boom, however, lasted only a short time until the decree handed down by the barren gravel bars and fruitless prospect holes which pockmarked the hills drove the restless, gold-greedy inhabitants and their following of riff raff to seek new fields.

With their departure the town, which had mushroomed into existence, might have degenerated into cobwebs and oblivion had it not been for the foresight of two brothers who saw in the wide, fertile valley, possibilities other than the disillusioned dream of rich ore.

When the horde of gold-seekers abandoned the town Gage Dampier and his brother Jesse stayed on. By an odd quirk of nature here was a valley, surrounded by supposedly mining country, which would graze many head of cattle, produce many tons of wild lush hay and it was theirs for the taking.

Though they had followed the rush on the opening of several new boom towns, greed for raw gold had never taken a firm grip on either one of the Dampiers. Rather, it was the excitement of a new town; the danger and uncertainty that appealed to their reckless natures. If the gaming tables and other sources not strictly square and aboveboard, furnished them with enough gold to live recklessly and well they gave little thought to resorting to pick and shovel or pan to produce the necessities of life.

The collapse of the Twin Peaks bubble marked a change in them, however. Having lived full lives well into their thirties, their ardor for excitement cooled somewhat when nature sounded the death-knell on the town. With the petering out of the boom they gave thought to the future and a comfortable living and it was then that the possibilities of turning the valley into one large cow ranch was opened to their eyes.

Two homesteads were easily acquired, but there they met with an obstacle. If they were to work the homesteads and acquire cattle they must have money and an inventory of their pooled possessions turned up a mere five hundred dollars. Two plodding men could have taken that five hundred and made a go of things, but the Dampier brothers were not plodders, they were born gamblers. With them it was either a case of make it big and quick or not at all and so for a time they disappeared from the valley and thirty days later showed up in Yucca, the county seat, with money belts bulging with wealth. How they had acquired this affluence none thought to question and the Dampier's offered no explanation.

Here they purchased a herd of breeders, saddle stock, work teams and various and sundry ranch implements. Hiring on two men they returned to the Burnt River Valley and started the job of putting up buildings and getting established. For a time it seemed they were to have things all their own way. Then, other eyes were opened and a mild invasion of homeseekers struck the valley. The Dampiers managed to stave off this threat with strong talk backed by menacing six-guns, forcing the newcomers to forsake the fertile bottom lands for the bordering hillsides which were broken and not so fertile. Later, through purchase and a long government lease, the Dampiers made legal their holdings in the valley and the sun-drenched south slopes.

The threat of open warfare passed and peace settled down on the community. But in many of the frustrated settlers envy and resentment was bedded deeply. Other settlers filtered into the district and with them came men who reopened the abandoned business houses in town. With this solid foundation to build from Twin Peaks took on new life and grew despite the fact that it was somewhat isolated from the outside world, its only connection being a weekly stage.

THE DAMPIERS MARRIED and prospered. The other settlers, primarily dirt farmers who soon learned that cattle were a much better bet in the rough hill country, fared as well as could be expected. Peace reigned for better than twenty years, due mostly to the fact that the Dampiers, after their initial belligerence in grabbing the valley, treated the others with much consideration and respect, lending a helping hand whenever it was needed.

A village government was set up in Twin Peaks with Gage Dampier at the head of it. A marshal was appointed who experienced little difficulty in maintaining peace and order in the town. In later years Gage Dampier erected a house in town and moved his family in from the ranch, the headquarters of which lay only two miles out. From then on he was looked upon as the father of the town. Many disputes, problems and differences were brought to him to thresh out which he did to the best of his ability, his ruling invariably being accepted as law.

The first dissenting factor in this setup came when Jesse Dampier, who had been left to oversee the ranch, suddenly died leaving behind an elderly widow and a step-son just entering his twenty-third year. Cole Dampier was a good looking youth, tall and straight and blessed with a code of strict morals and principles, yet he was inclined to be slightly reckless and headstrong at times. It was for this reason that Gage Dampier hesitated about installing him at the helm of the big Dampier spread. It was only after listening to the wishes of his wife and daughter in the matter that old Gage relented.

If Gage Dampier had a weakness in his makeup, it was his great devotion for his wife and daughter, upon whom he lavished an almost doting affection. Pride in his family was close to an obsession with him particularly where Rita, his only child, was concerned. Well along in her twentieth year, Rita was not a beautiful girl, yet the full bloom of healthy young womanhood was expounded in the glow of her smooth cheeks and the clear sparkle of her blue eyes which had been handed down to her by her father.

Between Cole and Rita there was a close understanding which held prospects of soon developing into marriage. Gage Dampier knew of this and secretly resented it, not because he held anything against his brother's step-son, but because of his blind, selfish love for his daughter. He wanted to share her affection with no man. It was this feeling which had kept the two men from really being close to each other.

But all these worries were catapulted far into the background one day by the arrival of two strangers in Twin

Peaks. Strangers were not unknown in the town. Many had drifted in through the years. Some had stayed, but most of them, typical range tramps and floaters, had found opportunities rather limited and drifted out again.

These two were different. There was nothing careless or easy-going about their appearance. Instead they exuded an efficient, prosperous air that had been sadly lacking in the others. Their horses were big and rangy with a depth of chest that denoted speed and endurance. The rigs they packed though slick and stained from hard usage were Porter saddles and the garb of the men was well-chosen and expensive from the toes of their Justin boots to the crowns of their gray Stetsons. Around the waist of each sagged a "shaped" belt supporting low slung holsters where walnut-handled .45s rode high.

The men themselves had the stamp of a rough, hardened existence about them as was evidenced by the grave lines in their weathered faces and the vigilant glint in their restless eyes. Both were short, slender and wiry, their movements cat-like. But where one was still young, the other was older by many years. On top his head was as bald as a billiard ball and lower down on the sides and back the growth of grayish hair was only meager. His face was lean and leathery—the bedding grounds for two deep-set gray eyes which peered out sharply from beneath the over-hanging ledge of a too prominent brow.

This one's name was Haze Blalock. The younger one went by the name of Monte Malott. That they were acquaintances of Gage Dampier became known their first day in town when they met the cowman in the Golden Eagle saloon.

Dampier had come in for his customary afternoon drink and found them standing close to the bar making idle talk with the bartender. Both turned at the cowman's approach and a slow grin of recognition came over Haze Blalock's face.

"Well, damned if it ain't Gage Dampier!" he exclaimed. "Or are you Jess? Never could keep you two jaspers separate."

DAMPIER HALTED IN his tracks and stared, blinked his eyes and stared again. Blalock's grin widened.

"What's the matter?" he queried, walking slowly toward the dazed cowman. "Don't you remember me? I'm Blalock—old Haze Blalock. Shucks, it must be twenty, twenty-five years since we last seen each other down Phoenix way. Remember the Gila Bend country, don't yuh?"

Dampier stared as one dumbfounded. He lifted a hand, brought it across his forehead, shielding his eyes as if to wipe out a bad dream. When he took it away his forehead pulled into a heavy scowl. A haunted expression burned deep in his eyes.

"Yes—I remember," he muttered, still in the grip of dulled senses, "It's been a long time. You've changed a lot, Cru—, Blalock."

Blalock jerked to attention, then as Dampier pronounced his name he smiled again.

"Gittin' old an' soft," he explained. "Lookin' for a place to squat an' live out the rest of my years kinda peaceful an' easy." He motioned toward the bar. "Drink?"

"That's what I came in here for," said Dampier and walked up to the bar where he was introduced to Monte Malott.

"My pardner," explained Blalock. "Right likely feller, Monte is. Handy with the cards—an' a lotta things."

As he talked Blalock's eyes were boring straight into the cowman's, holding him at attention.

"I hear you've done right well by yoreself, Gage," Blalock went on. "Looks like you mighta let yore friends know about the advantages of this valley. No man should hog a thing all by himself."

Dampier said nothing. He turned to the bar, poured himself a drink and gulped it down. The bartender looked at him oddly. He was accustomed to seeing Gage Dampier toy with his whiskey, drink it at his leisure.

"Let's take a bottle and go back to a table where we can kinda talk over old times," proposed Blalock.

Dampier's eyes raked his face. "No," he said. "We'll go up to my house where I usually talk over business." He flipped a coin on the bar to pay for the drinks.

Blalock caught it up and flipped it back at him. "My treat," he smiled thinly.

Dampier's eyes drove hard against his face for a moment and then without speaking further he turned and strode out of the saloon. Quickly the two men moved to flank him on either side and it was in this manner that they reached Dampier's big house sitting high up on the hillside.

Rita Dampier let them in and stepped to one side awaiting the expected introduction. None was forthcoming.

"I'll be busy and don't want to be interrupted, Rita," Dampier told her and led the way through the house to his den, somewhat segregated in the right wing of the house. The girl stared after him with a puzzled frown but said nothing and later joined her mother, where she expressed surprise at her father's apparent rudeness.

Inside the den, with the door closed tightly, Dampier

motioned the two men to chairs and dropped into one himself.

"Not a bad layout you've got here," remarked Monte Malott, his eyes darting about the room. "That yore daughter that let us in?"

Dampier ignored him completely to stare at the older man. "All right," he said. "Speak your piece, Crump or Blalock or whatever your right name is."

"I'm usin' Blalock right now," replied the other, grinning unabashed. He threw a glance around the room. "Like Monte, I figure this is a neat layout you've got, Gage. Must be a healthy climate up here. You don't show yore age much. Reckon that's what bein' a family man does for a feller. Well, I shore give yuh credit for havin' brains enough to come here an' grab up this valley. Quiet an' peaceful here an' from what I can learn yo're kinda the big push hereabouts, ain't you?"

DAMPIER LEANED FORWARD, rested both arms on the desk he was sitting in front of.

"Speak your piece, Blalock," he commanded sharply. "I know you didn't stumble in here by accident."

"I learned a long time ago that it ain't healthy to do things by accident," replied Blalock, sobering. "Nope, we come here on purpose, Gage, an' for a reason."

Dampier nodded, sat back in his chair and divided a glance between them.

"What I expected," he grunted. "You got wind somewhere that Gage Dampier was the Gage Harrison you knew down in Arizona and you came to hunt me out. All right," he bit his words off short. "How much do you want?"

Blalock feigned surprise. "I don't git you."

"Oh, yes you do," contradicted the cowman. "I can't hold you responsible for my mistakes so I'm willing to pay up. What's your price in cold, hard dollars to get out of here and stay out?"

"Hell, that ain't no way to talk to a friend," complained Blalock, getting jocular again. "If we aimed to leave this town we wouldn't have to be paid to go. Keep yore money, Gage. We ain't here to bleed yuh. All we want is to stay on here an' grow old peaceful an' quiet like you done."

Dampier eyed him suspiciously. "What's the rest of it?" he questioned.

"That's all there is," said Blalock. "We're tired of knockin' around first one place an' then another. We want a place we can kinda call home—a place where we can come to an' kinda take things easy till the storm blows over."

"I thought so," growled Dampier, his face flushing a deeper hue. "And what am I supposed to do?"

"Well, first we figured you might be kinda glad to give us a chunk of yore hill land where we can throw up a shack, run a few head of cow critters an' make it look like we're startin' out in the cow business. Might not look quite right if we was to loaf around here without no occupation. Some of yore friends might git suspicious an' start talkin'. But if we've got a little spread of our own they won't be so liable to start checkin' up on our movements."

"Which won't bear checking," growled Dampier. "Go ahead. Is that all of it? You'd just as well get it all out of your system at once."

"Well," drawled Blalock. "Seein' you kinda run things to suit yoreself in this country we figure to look to you to kinda keep things runnin' smooth for us. What I mean is, see that we don't git messed up with no local law an' head off any outside law from comin' in here. With yore standin' in the community you can do that easy."

"I could, probably, but I won't," stated Dampier firmly. "I owe you nothing, Blalock. If you think I'm going to get mixed up in a set-up like you mention, you've got another think coming."

Blalock laughed silently. "Maybe *you* better think again, Gage. The rest of the boys oughta be stragglin' in here in a few days. They'll expect me to have things all fixed up. Kind of a salty crew. Hutch Keever, Shine Tremaine, Buck Kemper, Jim Barr—you remember old Jim, don't cha? Tall an' skinny as ever, Jim is."

"An' cold-blooded as a fish," grinned Monte Malott.

"If you're tryin' to scare me, save your breath," snapped Dampier.

"Not tryin' to scare yuh," denied Blalock. "Just tryin' to talk reason to yuh is all. Fact is we're comin' in here whether you like it or not, Gage. Yuh might save yoreself some grief by playin' along with us."

"All bluff," snorted Dampier. "As you've said, my word carries a lot of weight in this town. One word from me and you'll be slapped behind bars, Blalock."

"Yeah, but you'll never say that word," Blalock stated confidently. "You know damn well you'd be shoving your own neck into a noose."

"More bluff," sneered the cowman. "You wouldn't take chances with your own neck just to tell what you know about me. It looks like a standoff, Blalock. I can't talk and neither can you, but if you try to crowd in here I'll turn my crew loose on you as sure as hell!"

"And they'd last about as long as a snowball in hell," sneered Blalock. "My boys ain't cowhands, Gage. They're picked men. Jim Barr is the only one you know but the others measure up pretty well to Jim. Figure it out an' you'll see that the cards kinda lay on my side."

"Then I'll use the law to stop you," growled Dampier.

"Oh, no yuh won't."

THERE WAS NO smile on the old outlaw's face now. It was cold sober and his gray eyes were like flint.

"We've got you where the hair's short, Gage. You stand pretty high around here an' I reckon yuh want to stay that way. Besides that you've got a wife an' daughter. Don't reckon they know that Gage Dampier was a—"

"That's enough!" thundered Dampier, coming to his feet, his eyes blazing with anger. "Name your price in gold and then get out!"

"It ain't gold we want," said Blalock. "We've got all the money we need for a while. What we want is a quiet place to squat between jobs an' yo're gonna give us that spot."

"It's no go," snapped the cowman. "Damned if I'll be mixed up in a deal like that."

"It's a go, all right," said Blalock, getting to his feet and preparing to leave. "We'll give you till tomorrow mornin' to think it over. I ain't bluffin', Gage. You buck me an' I'll tell what I know an' shoot my way out of this damned town."

A grayish pallor spread over Dampier's face as he stood there under the scorching gaze of the two men. He knew then that it was himself who had been doing the bluffing. There were only two courses open to him. One meant destruction, the tearing down of everything that it had taken years to build up. The other meant following Blalock's instructions.

"All right, Blalock," he finally muttered. "You win this

time but damn you, if I ever get the bulge on you I'll blast you into hell!"

"You'll never get that edge on me, Gage," sneered the outlaw. "You play this quiet an' square an' you ain't got no worries. If yuh don't—"

He left the rest to be guessed at as he turned and strode out of the room, Monte Malott following close on his heels. The following night it was known throughout the district that Gage Dampier had sold a good third of his mountain range to the two strangers. People wondered at this and wondering voiced their curiosity. Dampier had but one answer for them.

"Had more range than I needed. Was offered a good price so I sold."

This explanation, however, didn't set well with Cole Dampier.

"Instead of being flush with range we're short on it," he argued with Gage. "Our herds are growing and grazing isn't what it used to be. Besides that our lease ran out a year ago and can't be renewed. You know that. A lot of that valley land and some of the hill stuff we're using because the government hasn't got around to ordering us off it yet. But they'll decide what they're going to do one of these days and I've got a hunch they'll throw it open for home-steading. By the time a herd of new settlers get through coming in here our outfit will look kind of sick."

"We have plenty in the land we own," said Gage. "If we have to we'll cut down the herd. But if they took all of it we'd all still have enough money to live on comfortably the rest of our lives. While I think of it you'll find that five thousand dollars has been deposited to your account in the bank as your half of the price I received for the sale of the land and cattle."

"Do you mean you got ten thousand cash on the deal!" exclaimed Cole.

"I did," lied the older man. "And at the same rate I'd gladly sell the rest of the outfit."

"Sure, if we wanted to get rid of it, but we don't," muttered Cole. "I figure the outfit will be handed down to my kids."

A flash of quick anger came into Dampier's eyes, but his voice showed none of this when he spoke.

"Then maybe you better get back to the ranch and take care of what's left instead of worrying about what I just sold."

Soon other men of the same ilk as Blalock and Malott started filtering into Twin Peaks. They came singly and gave evidence of having put many hard, fast miles behind them. It was evident at a glance that they were not cowboys; yet Blalock and Malott, the two new ranchers in the district hired them on as fast as they got to town.

Others around Twin Peaks looked suspiciously upon these happenings. They didn't like the invasion of hard characters, but their fears were somewhat lulled for a time by the fact that all stayed pretty close to the Blalock ranch and when they did come to town they bothered nobody and had little to say.

BUT TIME RENDERED a change in this routine. Evidently the quiet, uneventful life in Twin Peaks palled on the newcomers and one day Monte Malott came to town, dickered with the owner of the Golden Eagle saloon and finally purchased the place. This marked the turning of another leaf in Twin Peaks history for from then on a great change came over the quiet little town.

Malott remodeled the Golden Eagle, installed new gambling paraphernalia, a dance floor and rooms overhead. Shortly, to the horror of the women of the town, girls were imported for entertainment purposes and the Golden Eagle became a noisy, blaring honky-tonk. Nights along main street became noisy, uproarious as whiskey-fired brains sought an outlet in coarse amusement or physical combat which, upon two occasions ended in gunplay that luckily didn't prove fatal to any of the parties concerned.

Dampier's riders and the younger element of the district welcomed this new state of affairs and entered into it wholeheartedly. Cowboys who previously had been mild-mannered and easy-going became belligerent and careless with a reckless abandon which thoroughly aroused the ire of the oldsters.

At first Abe Hazen, the marshal, made many arrests, but his prisoners never stayed in jail long or were never brought to trial, which fact was highly puzzling to the decent element of the town. It was evident to all that power and money were being used to obstruct justice and they could think of only one man in the community who could wield this power. As things grew steadily worse a committee approached Gage Dampier.

He listened to their complaints and promised to check things. And for a time conditions were better. But, apparently it was only the calm before the storm for suddenly they broke out with renewed vigor and this time even Gage Dampier seemed helpless to cope with the issue. Word trickled out and finally got to the sheriff down in Yucca who communicated with Dampier by mail and received a reply that things were a bit lively in Twin Peaks but there was nothing in the way of trouble that couldn't be handled by local authorities.

That was enough to satisfy the sheriff and he turned a deaf ear to further complaints that came drifting down out of the mountain town. When it seemed that Gage Dampier was helpless to control things the committee of business men, headed by Henry Holbrook, went directly to Monte Malott.

"What can I do?" defended Malott. "I keep an orderly place here. I'm not responsible for what comes off in the street an' that's where most of the fights come off."

"The town was all right till you came in here and opened up this den of hell," declared Holbrook. "We've got no objections to a saloon, but this place is nothing but a vice emporium. A cheap honky-tonk—a hang-out for criminals."

Malott's thin lips parted in a smirk. "The boys an' girls might not like it if they hear you calling them names like that. Anyway, what you squawkin' about? This place of mine has brought you all a good business. Even sinners have to eat, yuh know."

"We can get along without that kind of business," stated Holbrook. "We lived here before you came and we'll live after you leave."

"Didn't know I was leavin'."

"We're telling you to, unless you clean up this joint!" retorted Holbrook, who was the merchant of the town.

Malott's hard little eyes scorched Holbrook's face and shifted to take in the others.

"All right," he said. "Are you ready to buy me out?"

Those in the group exchanged glances.

"What's your price?" queried Holbrook.

"What's yore best offer?" countered Malott.

The storekeeper thought a moment and blurted: "Five thousand dollars."

"Slap a hundred thousand on top of that and the place is yours," grinned Malott.

"You must be crazy!"

"Just don't want to sell is all," smiled Malott. He came closer to the storekeeper. "You got any more squawks?"

"Yes," snapped Holbrook. "We're getting tired of having gunmen run the streets, to say nothing of the drunks and rowdies who insult our wives and daughters."

"Scared of them?" grinned Malott.

"That isn't the question."

"Reckon it is," corrected the saloon man. "If you're lookin' for protection why don't you go to Gage Dampier. He runs this town, don't he?"

"We will," asserted Holbrook.

MALOTT'S EYES NARROWED cannily. "Good idea," he drawled. "But don't be surprised if it costs yuh somethin' to git that protection."

"What do you mean by that?"

"You'll find out," smiled the other mysteriously. "It's a golden harvest that I reckon even Gage Dampier won't overlook. Come in again, gents, when you can drink more an' talk less."

Again Gage Dampier listened to the complaints, but not with his previous patience.

"It's no worse here than in a lot of other towns," he told them. "Trouble is we were buried up here for so many years we sort of went to sleep. A little activity won't hurt you."

It was peculiar talk coming from Gage Dampier.

"Activity is all right, but it's getting so it isn't safe to be out on the street at nights," complained Holbrook. "I look to be robbed or murdered most any time."

"Well, at least I can promise you that won't happen," returned Dampier. "As I see it the sensible thing to do is to not worry so much about those who drink and carouse a little. Tend strictly to your own business and I don't believe you will be bothered."

They left puzzled over this unusual stand taken by the old cowman. The following night several of them were visited by a man using a bandana to mask his face who informed them that the surest way to get protection was to buy it.

"Lay out twenty-five per cent of what you take in every week and I'll guarantee you won't be bothered by anybody."

"Who are you?" Holbrook demanded of the man.

"I represent the only man in these parts who can give you protection," said the masked man. "But it's going to take a little money. Yuh can't expect him to work for yore interests without gettin' paid for it."

"Got out!" bellowed Holbrook. "Before I knuckle down to a graft like that I'll strap on a gun myself and shoot the first one who makes a crooked move toward me."

"Better be shore yuh *sabe* how to use that gun 'fore yuh strap it on," cautioned the other. "Be kinda sad if you should wake up some mornin' to find yoreself dead."

"Get out!" roared Holbrook.

"I'll give you tonight an' tomorrow to think it over," said the other as he started to fade out the door. "Tomorrow night you take the money an' leave it in an empty can by the southwest corner of the corral in back of the stable. Get that straight—southwest corner an' be dang sure you've got the right amount. I might want to check over yore books if you've got any."

"I'll leave no money anywhere!" asserted Holbrook.

"Then there ain't no tellin' what might happen to yuh," returned the masked man and disappeared in the night.

True to his word, Holbrook left no money as did none of the others. The night following the deadline Holbrook was taken from his house by masked men, led back into the timber of the bordering slope and there beaten unmercifully with rope and quirt. Besides this assault on the man his store was robbed and looted.

This outrage created a furor of excitement in the town, but nothing was done about it for there was no conclusive evidence against anyone. Holbrook had recognized neither of the two men who had taken him from his house and administered the beating. Other men in the town received a second warning from the mystery man and the fact that the fate which had befallen Holbrook passed them by proved that they were meeting the demands and paying up.

From then on a reign of terror took hold of Twin Peaks as the decent element paid tidings and kept still, each keeping pretty much to himself, dubious about banding together to fight the scourge lest this hostile move would bring upon them the same fate which had befallen Holbrook or maybe worse.

In the short space of time since the coming of Blalock and his crew of hard, gimlet-eyed, thin-lipped gunslingers, the inhabitants of Twin Peaks sped from security and content to uncertainty, worry, and fear.

CHAPTER III

A STRANGER IN TWIN PEAKS

T HE BLACK STALLION pushed through the gap in the
hills, dropped with the pitch of a wooded ravine and
at length broke out on the wide floor of the Burnt River
Valley. Here the road curved to the south and the town
of Twin Peaks lay straight ahead at a distance of less than
a mile.

As he entered the outskirts Wayne Morgan rode
slouched in the saddle, a wheatstraw cigaret dangling from
his lips while half-closed eyes roved languidly over the
buildings. Straight to the stable he rode where the hostler,
hunkered down with his back against the big grain box,
cocked open one eye, took the measure of the newcomer
and pulled himself slowly to his feet.

Morgan ran an eye over his surroundings and stepped
to the ground.

"Want to put up my horse for the night," he told the
hostler.

"Yuh mean day an' night, don'tcha?" queried the hostler,
coming around to where Morgan was jerking loose the
latigo. "It's still mornin' or else I've plumb missed out on
my dinner."

"Have it your own way," shrugged Morgan. "But when

I say *up* I mean in a stall an' not turned loose in the corral with a lot of hammer-heads to fight."

"Sure," agreed the hostler, his eyes on the black. "But I don't reckon you'd have to worry about that hoss gettin' kicked around. More 'n likely you'd have a few of them hammer-heads yuh mentioned to pay for when this stallion got done with 'em. He'll have good care, feller."

"I know he will," replied Morgan. "I aim to take care of him myself. All you've got to do is keep a lookout that nobody steals him."

"If that's the way yuh feel about it, all right," grunted the other. "Yuh sleep with him or has he been weaned?"

Morgan whirled on him, stared a moment and then grinned slowly.

"I guess I had that coming," he said. "I'm kind of an old woman about this horse. He's been weaned and I might add that his habits aren't any too good around strangers. He kicks, bites and strikes."

"Outside o' that, I reckon he's plumb gentle," grinned the hostler. "Just lead him into that third stall back on yore left when you get around to it. It's where you'll find him when yuh get ready to take him out." His gaze traveled up over Morgan's person. "Cowpoke, eh?"

"Some."

"Comin', goin', or just lookin'?"

"Just lookin', I guess," grinned Morgan.

"Won't take long. Dampier outfit is the only one around here that amounts to a damn an' they're always full handed. Been a new one started up a while back, but it strikes me they've got more men than cows which likewise brings on the notion that Haze Blalock has got more money than cow sense."

"How's that?" asked Morgan carelessly.

"Well, first he lays out ten thousand iron men for five hundred acres of grazin' land and a hundred head of cows—mixed herd. Next he hires six men to haze them critters which don't need much hazin' at all, as is proved by the fact that them rannies of Blalock's spend a hell of a lotta time in the Golden Eagle. Strikes me funny—"

He broke off abruptly, looked surprised as though he had suddenly recalled something important and stood there with his mouth gaping open staring past Morgan out the big doorway of the barn. Wondering, Morgan turned, followed the direction of the man's gaze and seeing nothing except a large house nestled in the trees that lined the long, curving slope against which the town was nestled, turned back.

The hostler shook himself free from whatever mood had taken hold of him, closed his mouth and shifted nervously. His Adam's apple galloped up and down his scrawny throat as he gulped dryly and without further speech turned and made his way back through the stable where he picked up a pitchfork and went to work cleaning out a stall.

Wondering what had come over the man Morgan went on caring for his horse and when the black had been watered, rubbed down and fed he sauntered out of the barn and made his way back toward the main part of town. It was still too early for dinner so he wandered into the Golden Eagle, threw a lazy, disinterested glance around the room and went up to the bar where he ordered whiskey.

WHEN BOTTLE AND glass came sliding up to him he poured sparingly, paid for the drink and let it set while he engaged the bartender in idle conversation which had to do mostly with the prospects of finding a job. Other customers needing service soon interrupted this idle chatter and when the bartender next thought of him he found that Morgan had left the bar and crossed the room to a chair where he now sat tilted back against the wall smoking lazily while he looked over on a mild game of solo being indulged in by three old cronies.

As he went to take Morgan's bottle and glass from the bar he noticed that the glass was half full of whiskey. Few men sip their whiskey and Morgan had poured sparingly. The bar man arrived at the logical conclusion that the whiskey had not been touched. With this thought established in his mind, he looked across at Morgan with new interest, which, as he continued to stare, took on the aspects of suspicion.

Monte Malott appeared at the head of the stairs leading up to the floor above. A meaning glance passed between the saloon owner and the bartender and a few moments later they were closeted in Malott's room.

"Who's the stranger?" queried the saloon man.

The bartender shrugged. "Dunno. Claims he's a cowhand lookin' for a job."

"See the horse he rode in on?" asked Malott and continued without waiting for an answer. "Hell of a good looking animal for a tramp cowpoke to be riding."

"Yeah, an' busted-down cowpokes don't usually pay for drinks an' then leave 'em," added the bartender. "Somethin' funny about that jasper. Reckon he packs two guns so as to keep his balance in the saddle. You reckon some of these natives have been squawkin' so loud it's been heard on the outside?"

"Sheriff got wind of somethin' but Dampier fixed that," said Malott.

"Government man, maybe," suggested the bartender.

"What would bring one of them fellers in here?"

"Dunno unless he froze to the trail of one of the boys on the last job."

"That ain't likely with the job being pulled off clean down near Yuma. Buck an' Llano rolled in better than a week ago."

"Yeah, an' Shine come draggin' in yesterday with a bullet hole in him," pointed out the other.

"That's what held him up, Doc. Said it laid him low for a couple weeks."

"Where?" questioned Doc. "I had a look at that hole, Monte. It was a bad one an' showed signs of havin' a heap better care than Shine could have give it by himself."

"Yuh mean he had help?"

"Looks that way to me."

Malott shrugged carelessly. "Nothin' to worry about anyway. If this stranger is a government man or a railroad dick that's just his tough luck," he flashed a knowing grin. "I'll have Llano kinda watch his moves. Blalock will be in town tonight. He can smell a dick a mile off."

Unaware that he was the subject of puzzled speculation, Morgan presently left the saloon and sauntered down to the hotel where he engaged a room and washed off the trail dust before going down to the dining room for dinner. Later he sat out on the porch overlooking the town. While he smoked and listened to snatches of idle talk going on around him he stowed away in his memory the exact location and outstanding features of every building in town. His gaze rested for some time on Gage Dampier's spacious dwelling. A careless question to the man sitting next him apprised him of the ownership.

An hour later he was following the path leading up to the house. His knock brought Rita Dampier to the door. The unexpected sight of a girl opening the door to him confused Morgan for the moment. He swept off his hat and stared openly. As a red flush tinged his ears the girl's lips parted in a smile.

"How do you do," she said in a friendly, cultured voice.

MORGAN GAVE A short nod, muttered a low "hello" and fumbled with his hat. The movement distracted the girl's gaze from his face, lowered it to the two guns sagging low on his thighs. Her smile wavered, disappeared and when she looked up there was no longer a friendly crinkle at the corners of her eyes.

"I'll call father," she said coldly.

Morgan had regained his composure by this time. A slow grin cracked his features.

"I didn't know you were gun-shy or I'd have peeled them off before I came up here. Is Gage Dampier your father?"

She gave him an odd glance.

"You must be a stranger in town."

"I'm all of that," smiled the man. "Morgan is my name and it really isn't important that I see your father right now if he's busy."

"He isn't busy. Just step inside, Mr. Morgan, and I'll call him."

Without waiting to see whether he came in or stayed out she turned from the doorway, crossed the big room to an inner door and disappeared. Morgan stepped inside the large living room and treated himself to a look at the luxurious furnishings. Whatever Gage Dampier's shortcomings he was obviously a man of means who took great pride in his home, for the furnishings were well-chosen and costly, not those to be found in the average cowman's house.

Footsteps approaching jerked his eyes from the big, stone fireplace he had been inspecting and directed them toward the door where Rita Dampier had vanished. A stately, white-haired man had entered the room and was now coming toward him, a quizzical pucker on his brow. This was not at all the type of man Morgan had expected to see. None of the grizzled, rough-hewn cattleman here. Family influence, easy living and the pride of dominion had all served to put a polished veneer on Gage Dampier. Given a Vandyke and mustache and he would have looked the part of an old Southern Colonel.

"I couldn't remember the name and now I can't seem to recall your face," he mused, pausing close to Morgan.

Morgan smiled. "Maybe that's because you've never seen it before. I judge you're Gage Dampier?"

"I am."

The voice was questioning and the blue eyes seemed slightly puzzled as they ran over Morgan's person, missing nothing. Having come to the house merely to meet Dampier and see what type of man he was Morgan found it difficult to proceed. His smile took on a self-conscious quirk.

"It's kind of dawned on me all of a sudden that maybe I got off on the wrong foot by coming here, Mr. Dampier," he muttered. "Reckon your ranch would have been a better place to go and look for a job."

"Is that what you want—a job?" queried Dampier.

"Well, I like to eat pretty well," laughed Morgan.

The cowman looked at him a moment and smiled. "My nephew manages the ranch and usually takes care of all the hiring and firing. But it's all right. You probably saved yourself a ride by coming here. Conditions at the ranch right now seem to warrant firing instead of hiring."

Morgan nodded. "This is the slow time of year for a drifter. Besides I play a bum game of poker."

Dampier's eyes crinkled with amusement. He smiled knowingly and reached into his pocket.

"Broke?"

"Oh, no. Not that bad," protested Morgan as the cowman brought forth a handful of money. "I'm not putting up a hard luck story."

Dampier looked into his face, smiled again and shoved the money back into his pocket.

"Don't let pride make you miss any meals, son," he drawled. "Ride out to the ranch and rest up a few days anyway. Tell Cole that I sent you."

"Thanks. I might do that," said Morgan and determined not to be dismissed so soon, added: "Nice cow country you've got up here."

"I've found it so."

"I reckon you have," and Morgan threw a glance around the room. "There's a lot of outfits twice the size of yours that couldn't take money enough away from their herds to build a place like this."

DAMPIER SMILED HIS appreciation. "Perhaps that is because most stockmen believe that every dollar they make should be poured back to increase their herds far beyond grazing conditions. I throttled the increase when I reached the capacity of my range. I've found that it pays better to run a small herd on good feed than it does to run a big herd on poor feed."

From there on the talk naturally gravitated into the problems of stock raising and when, a half hour later, Morgan left he had safely stowed away a mental picture of the entire house and grounds. Besides that, he had enjoyed the opportunity of forming some shrewd opinions about Gage Dampier. To his puzzlement he found that these opinions didn't jibe at all with the conclusions he had previously formed without having seen the man.

If Gage Dampier had a criminal side to his nature he kept it well concealed for after their half hour acquaintance Morgan found that he liked the man and this didn't fit in at all with the picture he had previously formed from the words that had fallen from the Aiken boy's lips.

Something strange here, he told himself as he made his way back to the main part of town and into the Golden Eagle where he wore out the remainder of the afternoon playing a conservative hand in an uninteresting game of draw. Still, the day was not wasted for his sensitive ears picked up many snatches of conversation and his eyes looked covertly upon happenings which were puzzling yet none the less hinted a warning that he was a marked man in the town.

The supper hour found him back at the hotel partaking of the evening meal and later he walked through the gathering dusk to the stable to look after his horse. Voices raised in argument halted him beside the wide opening in the front of the barn and he hovered there for a time listening.

One he recognized as the voice of the stableman. The other strange to him.

"What do yuh mean—pay up my feed bill?" this unfamiliar voice was grumbling.

"Just what I said," came the stableman's voice. "You

knowed this ain't a free lodgin' place for hosses when yuh first started leavin' him here, didn't cha? I want my money."

"Aw, you'll get it," growled the other.

"Yeah, that's what you've been tellin' me for a couple weeks," retorted the other. "I want that money now. It's comin' to me an' I gotta have it."

"Just like that, huh?" There was a nasty slur to the man's words. "Now you listen to me, you long-geared barn dog. I ain't in the habit of havin' folks rag me about a couple lousy dollars I might owe them. You keep squawkin' an' I never will pay yuh. Hell! Way you rant a feller'd think I owed yuh a couple hundred in place of a measely ten."

"It means that much to me," declared the stableman. "I've got big expenses—I need that money bad, I tell yuh."

"Well, ain't that too bad? You'll maybe need it worse 'fore yuh git it. Now git outa my way. I got ridin' to do."

"Not till you pay up, Kemper!"

"Why you horse-faced—"

The words broke off and the sound of a heavy blow being struck came to Morgan's ears. Quickly he moved into the stable, saw two shapes milling back along the wide runway and continued on toward them. Another heavy blow thudded and the stableman dropped to the floor where the other man started putting the boots to him. Twice his toe drove against the helpless man's ribs before Morgan's low, sibilant voice stopped him, froze him in his tracks.

"Lay off there," hissed Morgan and as Kemper, mouthing a low, startled curse reached for his gun, Morgan moved in on him with the speed and agility of a mountain cat.

Kemper's gun never cleared leather before a hard fist drove straight into his jaw staggering him. Another in the same spot treated the man to a kaleidoscope of glittering lights and a third dropped him to the floor where he lay still. Morgan reached down, jerked loose his gun and punching out the loads shoved it back into the man's holster.

THEN HE LOOKED to the stableman and found that individual dragging himself slowly to his feet one hand gingerly caressing his ribs. Morgan helped him to an upright position.

"Hurt?" he queried.

"Kinda bruised up is all, I reckon," muttered the hostler. "Guess he'd of kicked my ribs clean in if you hadn't showed up, mister," his eyes darted along the runway and fell on Kemper's outstretched body. "Damn his dirty heart!" he cried. "I got a notion to stomp his guts out!"

"You've got a notion that beats that," said Morgan taking hold of his arm. "He's taken care of for a while. What was all the trouble about?"

"Money that he owes me," growled the hostler. "He keeps stallin' me off. He ain't the only one neither. Damn 'em. I know what's back of it. I ain't had money enough to pay up. They keep ridin' me, but I don't know how they figure I can pay when fellers like Kemper won't pay me."

"Who keeps riding you to pay up what?" questioned Morgan.

"I dunno. I—"

He broke off and the expression Morgan had seen appear on his face earlier that day was again resting there. Morgan watched him a moment and shrugged.

"You talk like something's got you scared plumb to death," he remarked. "Isn't there any law here in town to take care of fellows like Kemper?"

"Law— Sure, but it's all on the other side."

He threw a startled glance at Kemper, brought his eyes back to Morgan and bent toward him earnestly.

"You done me a good turn, stranger, now I'll do you one," he said. "Saddle up that black hoss of yourn an' see how damn fast he can pack yuh outa this country."

Morgan eyed him quizzically. "What's the rush?" he asked. "I just got here."

"An' you'll stay here permanent if yuh don't take my advice," stated the other. He pointed to Kemper. "After what yuh just done to him your life ain't worth a plugged nickel in these parts, mister. They'll git yuh sure as hell!"

"Who'll get me?"

"Kemper, Blalock—Monte Malott. Any of that gang. They're bad, I tell yuh. This town ain't fit for a white man to live in any more."

"Seems to be quite a few living here," pointed out Morgan.

"That's because they're payin' for that privilege."

"How do you mean—paying?"

The man's eyes scorched his face. "Payin' like I said. Every week he comes around to collect his percentage on what we take in."

"Who does?"

"I dunno. He keeps his face covered with a bandana."

"Sounds like you've been having a bad dream," scoffed Morgan, leading the man on.

"It ain't no dream, mister," the hostler assured him. "Ask any man in town that's got a business. But they wouldn't tell yuh. They know it ain't healthy to talk. So do I an' I'm a damn fool for doin' it, but I gotta git this outa my system.

Gittin' so a man can't even take a long breath hereabouts no more."

"If there's something like that going on, why don't you go to the law about it?"

The stableman laughed brittlely. "I done told yuh there ain't no law here for fellers like me."

"How about Gage Dampier?" prodded Morgan. "He's supposed to run the town, isn't he?"

"Reckon he does."

"You mean he's behind this graft?"

"You figure it out, feller, I give up tryin'. Them conditions are here an' that's all I know about it."

"Why don't you leave the country then?"

"Can't. Couldn't sell my stable and ain't got no other money. Besides that I've got a hunch they wouldn't let me git far. I'd take a gamble on sneakin' out anyway but I got a sick wife. That's what's been usin' up all my money so's I couldn't pay up. Nope, I'm stuck here, stranger, but you ain't an' you better be gittin' out before Kemper wakes up an' noises around what happened to him."

"I'm not a good runner," drawled Morgan.

"Stay here an' you'll be a corpse," prophesied the hostler. "Just like I'll be if anybody hears me talkin' to you. After what just come off in here I got a hunch I ain't goin' to live to see another sunrise."

"Don't talk foolish," rebuked Morgan.

"I ain't. Say, if you are dang fool enough to stay here an' don't git killed right off, kinda look after my wife in case my hunch is right. I live in that little shack in back here an' kinda off to the right."

"Sure," promised Morgan, "but don't loose your nerve, man."

A GROAN COMING from the man on the floor turned Morgan's attention toward him. Kemper shook the cobwebs from his head and sat up staring around groggily. Suddenly his eyes pierced the heavy gloom of the stable enough to recognize Morgan and with a curse falling from his lips he rolled and dragged out his gun.

"Look out!" cried the hostler diving low against Morgan's legs with force enough to upset him.

Kemper's gun was already out clicking spitefully as the hammer fell on empty cylinders.

"Don't wear out your thumb, Kemper," Morgan drawled, righting himself after the fall the hostler had given him. "I took the precaution to punch out the loads."

Muttering his wrath Kemper stood up. "You'll find it ain't healthy to horn into things around this town, stranger," he threatened.

"That all?" queried Morgan easily.

"I'm done talkin'," rasped the other.

"Good. Then I'll tell you something," retorted Morgan. "Twice you've pulled your gun on me and got away with it—the third time you won't."

For answer Kemper muttered an oath and strode up the darkened runway and out of the barn.

"You better drag it, stranger," the hostler muttered warning. "You don't know what you're tyin' into here. You might be handy with your guns but there's about six or seven gents in that gang that are likewise handy with guns."

"I'll play out the hand," grunted Morgan.

"Just the same I'm gonna sneak your hoss outa here an' tie him where you can get at him in a hurry in case yuh need him," declared the frightened stableman. "That jasper heard plenty, I'm thinkin'. I got a hunch he was fakin' that long snooze of his'n."

Morgan digested these words and reached one of his sudden decisions.

"Maybe I will drag it," he said. "No sense in kicking a hornet's nest just to see if there's hornets inside."

"Now you're talkin' sense, mister."

Morgan went up to his horse, cinched on his saddle and slipped the bridle in place. Leading the animal into the runway, he mounted, ducked low and touched the black with spurs. The stallion snorted, lunged and went thundering out of the barn into the darkened street. Expecting bullets to come swarming around him, Morgan swerved away from the town and headed up the valley.

To his surprise no bullets came nor did his move create any furore of excitement. After a short run he pulled the black down to a canter and at length bent him toward the hills, his intention being to circle the town, strike the out-going road below and ride out of the valley in the hopes of meeting Blue Hawk before the Indian could enter Twin Peaks.

He was high up on the wooded slopes when he rode past Twin Peaks letting the black pick his own course. It was after the road kinked into the deep ravine and lifted upward toward the gap that he struck it. Carved into the west side of the canyon the road was narrow and treacherous, the overthrown embankment pitching almost vertically down into the bottom.

Morgan was thinking of this—thinking how easy it would be for a green horse to make a misstep and go pitching down over the embankment when suddenly the black beneath him gave him his first warning of danger. It was no more than a quick up-toss of the head but it was enough to warn Morgan who instinctively dropped low over the horn and wheeled the stallion around directly away from the point of danger which he knew must lie ahead.

It was this mechanical coordination between man and beast that saved the rider from running his head directly into a noose that came hissing through the air toward him. But, bent as he was, the rope fell harmlessly across his back and at the same instant the black leapt away as he felt the touch of spurs.

A curse rent the air, followed by a quick shot and an ired command.

"Drop him!"

"What about—" a voice started to protest only to be silenced by the first speaker.

"To hell with orders. I'm running this show. Pour it into him!"

A BULLET SCREAMED over Morgan's head as he raced the stallion back in the direction of Twin Peaks. Another sliced the air to the right of him whining within an inch of the black stallion's ear. The horse instinctively swerved away from it, crowded over the edge of the embankment and tried to recover himself. But too late. Startled, Morgan threw his weight to help the beast but to no avail. In a second they were over the edge plunging down the dizzy, vertical descent into the yawning canyon.

Morgan jerked the black's head up, shot his stirrups forward and reared straight back, hard put to it to stay with the lurching, steep-pitched saddle. A cloud of dust swirled around them, billowing up to choke Morgan's nostrils. Giving little heed to the bullets that started falling around them, Morgan tied up all his hopes in the stallion's ability to keep his feet. Once they were swept from under him—the mad plunge would end in certain disaster for them both.

The plunging lurches finally slackened as the black horse got squared around with the acclivity, stiffened his forelegs and sat back on his hocks to slide with the avalanche of dirt they had loosened. The bottom of the canyon came suddenly and with a jolt that buckled the stallion's knees and all but tossed Morgan over his head. For a breathless second it seemed the horse would go down, then he righted himself, came to a dead stop and stood there quivering.

Morgan spoke a soothing word and lifted the reins. The horse would have lunged forward again but Morgan held him in check, working his way slowly across the bottom of the canyon. He paused finally in the shelter of a frowning ledge of rock on the opposite slope. A few bullets sprinkled the bottom of the canyon and then ceased as those back on the road possibly realized the futility of further shooting.

Morgan dismounted and started a careful exploration for cuts or bruises on the legs of his horse. He took his time about it feeling sure that none would follow him down that vertical pitch and to reach him otherwise they would have to ride all the way up to the gap where a crossing could be made or go back down to the valley where they could circle the mouth of the canyon and gain access to the slope he was now on. In either case he knew that he had at least a half hour's start on them.

When he mounted again and started up the slope at right angles to the fall of the canyon it was with the satisfying knowledge that his horse had come through the ordeal with nothing more serious than a couple small scratches. Reaching the top of the canyon wall he kept going in the same direction which presently brought him to a point where the lower end of Burnt Valley pinched in to start the river on a downward plunge through a long, rocky canyon. He crossed the river without mishap, took to the opposite hills and bent his horse with the widening contour of the valley on a course that would lead him back in the vicinity of Twin Peaks.

Wayne Morgan had left the Burnt River Valley for all time, but The Masked Rider was just arriving and before he was finished, the town of Twin Peaks was due to undergo a radical change.

CHAPTER IV

OUTLAW DISCORD

THE THREE MEN who rode back to Twin Peaks were in a grumbling, irritable mood; especially Buck Kemper who had seen the man he most wanted to kill slip through his fingers.

"If you fellers had unlimbered like I told yuh he'd never got away," he growled at Joe and Pete Colby, his two companions.

"We was followin' orders," replied Pete Colby. "Blalock said to take him alive an' that's what we aimed to do."

"Yeah, but you didn't take him an' now he's probably clean out of the country," complained Kemper. "Fool notion in the first place tryin' to toss a loop on him. "What did Blalock figure to win doin' that?"

"Aimed to pump him, I reckon. Figured he might be a government man, but, shucks, he wasn't no more a marshal or railroad dick than I am. He was plumb scared to death else he wouldn't never took to the canyon. I still can't *sabe* how he come outa that alive."

"How yuh know he wasn't a marshal?" growled Kemper. "Just because he run—"

"A marshal wouldn't quit the country an' that's what that feller Morgan done," said Pete.

"Yeah, he shore did quit the flat," put in Joe Colby, Pete's brother. "He never will stop goin'. Like Pete says, he wasn't no law hound. What Matt Gould, that stable feller, told him would have only made a marshal curious an' he'd stuck around to find out more instead of circlin' around to the road to get clear of the valley like Morgan done. Nope, I reckon Morgan was just what he claimed to be—a driftin' cow hazer who shore took a notion this valley was no place for him. But Gould now—"

"I'll take care of Gould," snarled Kemper.

"Better talk to Blalock about that first," hinted Pete Colby.

"I already know what he'll say," grumbled Kemper. "Don't know about you two but I figure Blalock has gone soft since he got here. Fool notion he had comin' up here in the first place. What do you fellers think about it?"

"Blalock's ramroddin' the spread," hinted Pete.

"Yeah, but me, for one, don't hanker for the way he's doin' it," blurted Kemper, who was a mouthy individual. "I figure there's a better man for the job."

Both Colby's turned to peer through the dark at the speaker's dark shape. Suddenly both laughed.

"Meanin' you?" sneered Pete.

"No." Kemper snapped. "Jim Barr."

A long, hushed silence followed this statement. Kemper waited for an opinion from the brothers and as none came said:

"Well?"

"Well, what?" grunted Pete.

"What do you think about it?"

"It ain't healthy to think out loud," said Pete. "Blalock is bossin' the gang an' as long as he's doin' it I'm takin' orders from him."

"Supposin' Jim was pushin' things?"

"He ain't," grunted Pete and that again brought on a long silence that was finally broken by Kemper just before they entered town.

"What in hell is it that Blalock's got on Gage Dampier?" he questioned, testifying to the fact that his mind had been busy mulling over things.

"Reckon only Blalock and Jim Barr know that an' neither one of them talk much, Buck," drawled Pete. "You'll probably live longer if you foller their example."

They reached town and went directly to the Golden Eagle where they looked around for Haze Blalock. Not seeing him anywhere Kemper made inquiry of the bartender.

"Upstairs with Monte," the bartender informed him.

"Reckon we better go up an' tell him we let Morgan make a sucker out of us," Kemper growled to his two companions.

"Go ahead," invited Pete. "It won't take all of us to do it an' you talk a sight better than me or Joe."

KEMPER FLASHED THEM an angry glance and climbed the stairs to Monte Malott's room where he found not only the saloon man and Blalock but also big Jim Barr and Shine Tremaine. A strained atmosphere clung about the room as though an argument of some sort had been in progress when Kemper burst into the room.

All had whirled on the door at his entrance, hands falling to guns.

"You're going to get your fool head blown off one of these days when you come bustin' in like that," growled Malott. "What's the news?"

"No dice," growled Kemper.

He went on to tell them what had happened.

"If he's a law hound," muttered Blalock when he had finished, "We can look for some grief."

"He ain't no law hound," declared Monte Malott. "Told yuh that when I first seen him. Nothin' but a thick-headed cowpoke who didn't like the smell of trouble an' sloped."

"Should have cracked down on him here in town an' been done with it," growled Kemper. "It's what I wanted to do."

"And have the whole town on our necks for a killing," snapped Blalock. "I tell you this rough stuff won't go. We had a good thing here if we'd played it right but it's fast petering out. If we ain't careful we'll have to shoot our way out of this town some day."

"Who's goin' to make that necessary?" inquired Shine Tremaine, a smirk on his heavy, rolled lips.

Shine Tremaine was short, stocky, his negro blood showing plain in his dark, coarse-featured face. Blalock turned to face him. He had never liked this man, having learned when it was too late that the muddy-eyed outlaw was as cold-blooded as a fish, inclined to be bull-headed and too quick on the trigger. Blalock had found him a hard man to handle.

"These natives," explained Blalock. "Gage Dampier and his crew."

Shine Tremaine's smirk widened into a sneer. "I've got a bullet marked for every one of them if they want to start anything," he said.

"Always ready to kill, ain't yuh?" snapped Blalock. "Had to unlimber your gun on the last job an' picked up a slug in your ribs for your trouble. I'm still wondering what happened to the feller who doctored that bullet hole for yuh an' pulled yuh through."

"You can quit wonderin' then," sneered Tremaine. "Dead men don't talk."

"They sometimes talk plenty if you leave them layin' around," growled Blalock, not pleased.

"Well, we don't have to worry about these billy goats in Twin Peaks," cut in Monte Malott. "We've got them scared stiff. Hell, they're even scared to breathe out loud."

"One of them wasn't," pointed out Blalock.

"He'll be taken care of," promised Shine Tremaine.

"Yeah—how?"

"Only one way to close a noisy mouth," declared Tremaine.

"Yeah, an' by closing that one we'd open up fifty others," argued Blalock.

"Suppose they do squawk?" said Malott. "Dampier has got a choke hold on the town an' we've got Dampier muzzled."

"For the time being, yes. But you can crowd a man only so far, Monte. You get a coyote into a corner an' he'll turn on you an' fight an' Gage Dampier ain't no coyote. He'll start fightin' before you get him walled in."

"Thought you had him cold," sneered Tremaine.

"An' so we have," spoke up Jim Barr, offering comment for the first time.

Jim Barr was tall, angular with a long thin face that seldom showed a vestige of emotion. His eyes were two fathomless pools of steel gray, cold, level and deadly. He spoke seldom but when he did speak his words usually carried weight. He and Haze Blalock had been together for many years. Between them they had organized several bands of outlaws, the present one included.

BLALOCK NOW LOOKED at this man to whom he seldom issued orders.

"You know Dampier as well as I do, Jim," he said in a softer tone of voice.

Jim Barr nodded. "I know Gage Dampier better than you do, Haze," he stated flatly. "He thinks pretty well of himself—Dampier does. He figures it was him built this country an' he's got kinda used to havin' folks hereabouts look up to him as the big push. He'll go a long way to keep 'em doin' that the same as he'll go a long ways to keep his family from knowin' he ain't the respectable cowman they think he is. Pride's a funny thing. Dampier ain't going to do anything that'll let his past life be noised around."

"If things keep gettin' worse for him he'll figure he ain't got a hell of a lot to lose," declared Blalock. "Folks around here don't look up to Dampier any more, they're beginning to hate him an' nobody knows it better than Gage himself. These natives don't blame you or me or any of the rest of us for what's happened to their town. They blame Dampier. They know damn well he's got the law sewed up an' they likewise know there's some good reason why Dampier won't shut down on things an' close up the Golden Eagle like they want. They figure he's gettin' paid to keep his paws off just like they figure it's him who's behind this graft of makin' them pay for protection. It ain't done his standing in this town any good, I'm tellin' yuh. He'll figure pretty soon he ain't got a whole lot to lose an' tell us to talk an' be damned."

"Well, if it's fight he wants we can give him that, I guess," spoke up Kemper.

Blalock whirled on him. "You keep your lip out of this. Buck, You've done enough damage for one night. You were crazy to get into an argument with Gould in the first place."

"Ridin' him a little is all," defended Kemper "He wasn't paid up an'—"

"Another crazy notion I shouldn't have listened to," growled Blalock. "We go ahead and spoil a good thing just to rake in the little two bit ante we get from these town folks. That money don't even make good pocket change for this crowd. It's like playin' poker for matches and a damn lousy business for a gang like this to be messed up with."

"It ain't the money that counts," explained Monte Malott. "It's just a good way of puttin' the fear of God in these whippoorwills an' keepin' them that way."

"No sense in scaring them in the first place,"snorted Blalock. "This thing ain't worked out at all."

"Yuh don't have to tell us that," growled Shine Tremaine. "I never did cotton to your idea about comin' up to this God-forsaken hole. You been in this game long enough to know better, Blalock. Maybe it was old age or somethin' creepin' in."

"An' maybe I got tired of jumpin' around," retorted the harried leader. "I figured if the gang had a permanent head-quarters it would beat layin' out on the desert or in the badlands between jobs. I got kinda tired of that after twen-ty-five years of it. My plan was a good one. We could have come here, played Dampier for a chunk of ground an' cows to make things look right an' lived here with some feelin' of security between jobs. It would have worked, too, if the rest of you hadn't gone off half-cocked."

"Still workin', ain't it?" asked Malott.

"Not the way I had it figured. We started out all right.

We come in here quiet an' for a while we stayed that way. Folks had got over bein' suspicious of us an' things were lookin' pretty till you jaspers got to honin' for excitement an' decided we should buy out the Golden Eagle an' liven the town up some."

"What do you expect us to do between jobs?" growled Malott, "Bury ourselves? What in hell good is our money if we can't spend it? What's the use of livin' at all if there ain't no excitement? Looks a heap to me like you got all messed up with some notion about bein' a respectable cattleman, Haze."

Blalock stared at the saloon man. "Just how do you mean that, Monte?"

BUT IT WAS Shine Tremaine who answered. "Maybe, like me, he figures that a man who ramrods an' outfit oughta ride with them, Haze," he said, making no attempt to hide his feelings in the matter. "Two rides have been made since we hit this country an' you ain't been on either one. It looks a heap to me like you aimed to just squat here shinin' up the seat of your pants while the rest of us do the work."

Blalock swept the ring of faces, probing each one. Finally his eyes centered on Jim Barr.

"Well, Jim," he drawled. "What do you think about it? Do you figure I'm lettin' you down?"

It was a long, thoughtful moment before Jim Barr replied. Then his words came flat, even.

"It strikes me you're hell-bent on reforming, Haze, an' I'm here to tell you it's too late to do that."

Blalock nodded. "It looks like a showdown, boys."

"Then I'm havin' a drink," said Jim Barr and pushed by

Blalock to a table slightly in back of him where bottle and glasses stood.

Blalock gave him a glance, then faced the others.

"I'm either bossin' this crowd or I ain't!" he asserted gruffly, his eyes flashing angrily. "Which is it going to be?"

"You ain't!"

The words came from Jim Barr and with them he whirled. A gun jumped into his hand and as Blalock turned in surprise the barrel of it crashed against his head with bone-splitting force. Blalock groaned, started to sag. Again that vicious gun was brought down on his head and as the outlaw leader dropped, Jim Barr menaced the rest of the room.

"I'm steppin' into Blalock's shoes," he stated evenly. "Any objections?"

He waited, but none came. Shine Tremaine was the first to break the spell. His heavy lips cracked into a grin.

"Why didn't yuh drill him an' be done with it?" he questioned.

"That whole gang downstairs would have been up here to see what the shootin' was about," explained Jim Barr. "This thing's going to be done quiet."

Monte Malott looked up from staring down at Blalock's bleeding head.

"Is he done for?" he questioned.

"Doubt it," grunted Jim Barr callously. "Blalock's head is hard," his cold level eyes fell on Shine Tremaine. "That's going to be your first job for me, Shine. You like killing, I don't. You an' Kemper get your hosses around back an' Monte an' me will lower the carcass down to yuh. Take him back in the hills away from town an' finish him any way yuh like only be damn shore yuh do a good job of it an' bury him so he won't be found."

"Bury him!" exclaimed Tremaine.

"That's what I said. Put him under the ground or a nest of rocks. It's going to be a mystery what happened to Haze Blalock outside of the four of us. Wait," he said as the two men started for the door. "Blalock was right when he said our string is playing out here, but before we go we'll make it pay big. When we leave there won't be nothin' left in this town except the buildings. You boys wanted action—you'll get it under me. First we're going to bleed Dampier out of every dime he owns and while we're doing it we'll work on the others hereabouts. It's one way of robbin' a bank without gettin' caught at it."

Tremaine grinned his appreciation. "Sounds good to me."

"And you?" queried Jim Barr laying his hard eyes on Kemper.

"You're the boss," grinned Kemper.

"I'm hopin' Llano an' Joe an' Pete Colby will figure the same without no grief," said Jim Barr. "While you're down at the stable gettin' your hoss, Shine, yuh might as well work on that Gould feller. We'll leave him as a good example for these natives that it don't pay to talk. You *sabe* what I mean, I reckon. Use the blade an' do it quiet. Now, get goin'."

CHAPTER V

GRISLY MURDER

TWIN PEAKS AWOKE the following morning to stark, violent tragedy in the form of Matt Gould's body, which was found thrown into a stall of the stable. Besides being stabbed in the heart the stableman's tongue had been cut out and placed on his chest, there to portray a horrible warning against talking. The shock of discovering the brutal murder silenced the town for a time, but as the horror of the mutilated body wore off murmurs of outraged humanity could be heard. Men formed in small groups. Their talk was low, secretive and many hostile glances were directed toward the Golden Eagle and Gage Dampier's house on the hill. True to Haze Blalock's prediction the closing of Matt Gould's mouth only served to open up many others.

"That's enough," decried Henry Holbrook to a small group in the back room of his store. "I've put up with a lot of things in the past few months for the sake of my family and my business, but I won't stand for murder!"

"What can we do?" bewailed one of the listeners. "We've appealed to the sheriff and it did no good. We appealed to Gage Dampier and he has done nothing."

Holbrook's eyes shot fire. "Why should Dampier do anything when he's behind this whole rotten mess?"

"But what's Dampier getting out of it?" protested one of the skeptical ones.

"Money!" cried Holbrook. "Some men will do anything for money."

"Then what about that gang that hangs around the Golden Eagle?" the other wanted to know. "Who are they—what are they doing here?"

"They're a crew of gunmen that Gage Dampier imported," snapped Holbrook.

"Imported for what?"

"To help him get control of this whole valley," asserted Holbrook. "He's always wanted it. Didn't he try to hog it all when he first came in here?"

"Yeah, but he didn't get it."

"He's getting it now. Already two of the small ranchers have left. More will follow them if things keep on as they have been. As fast as they leave Dampier will gobble up their land. His lease on a lot of the valley and some of the hill land has run out. One of these days the government will throw that land open for homesteading and Gage Dampier knows it. Land that Dampier has used for years he isn't liable to give up without a fight—he isn't giving it up. He's working right now to hold it against an invasion of new settlers."

"How can he hold it if the government throws it open for homestead?"

"By making this valley such a corner of hell that settlers will be afraid to come in here. It isn't the first time a cattleman has tried to keep settlers from coming in on open range land that they have been using. Gage Dampier is different only in that he has the foresight to start his dirty work before the invasion of settlers actually starts. It's deep planning. Only a man of Dampier's caliber would think of it."

"Makes sense," nodded one of the group.

"It makes our prospects of a decent existence damn slim unless we put a stop to it!" declared Holbrook.

"Have you got any ideas on how to go about that?" queried old man Harrison, the hotel owner. "None of us are gunmen. What chance would we have going up against men like Jim Barr, Shine Tremaine and that crowd? It's been proven to us that we can expect no help from the outside law and law here in Twin Peaks is a joke so far as we're concerned," he shook his head slowly. "It looks hopeless to me, Henry. Has from the first. I'm content to let things ride as they are."

HOLBROOK GLOWERED AT him. "That's a hell of a way for a man to talk who has just come from looking at Matt Gould's body. Who knows but what you might be the next to go the same way."

"Guess not as long as I keep my mouth shut," said the old man. "Poor Matt was a hand to talk. He talked too much."

"He was fighting against the injustice of being bled out of every cent of money he made!" barked Holbrook, now thoroughly fired up.

"Well, ain't you been payin' like the rest of us?" retorted Harrison. "You ain't forgot that beating they gave you, have you, Henry?"

"It was not myself I was thinking of when I decided to meet their demands," defended Holbrook. "I was thinking of my wife and family. I considered it the one way of making the town safe for them. I thought the sheriff or somebody would come in here to put a stop to Gage

Dampier's high-handed methods, but I see now if anything is to be done about it we will have to band together and do it ourselves. That's what I'm trying to do now—organize a vigilante committee to clean this town of the outlaw element that has crept in on us."

"It might turn out a noble experiment," warned Harrison. "I'm an old man and probably haven't got much left to live for, but even so I favor being a live coward instead of a dead hero. I'm making a living for myself and family. They haven't taken that away from me yet. Until they do I guess I'll rock along like I have been, paying my dues and keeping my mouth shut."

Holbrook's lip curled. "I never thought you were yellow, Harrison."

"I ain't yellow," denied the old man. "Just can't see sacrificing myself for a cause that is lost before we start. Suppose we did get together and decide to go after Dampier. What chance would we have against a half dozen fellows we *know* are gunmen and Dampier's crew along with them?"

"I'm not so sure Dampier's crew is with him," said Holbrook.

"Don't talk foolish," argued the hotel man. "Whoever heard of a cowman's crew being against him! Don't they come into the Golden Eagle and hoot and yell with the rest of them? Isn't Blalock and his gang out on a piece of land that Gage Dampier gave to him or sold him—whichever way you want to look at it? They're all in together. You said it yourself a while back."

"I said Dampier had hired Blalock and his gang of cutthroats to come in here," stated Holbrook. "The regular crew may be in with them, I don't know, but I'm almost positive that young Cole Dampier is *not!*"

"What makes you think that?"

"Because I know that Cole has had trouble with Gage. I've heard Cole drop remarks."

Harrison shrugged. "Maybe so, but if you figure to get Cole to go with you and fight Gage you've got another think coming. Cole is a Dampier."

"He's nothing of the kind," contradicted Holbrook. "Cole is a son by a former marriage. Jesse Dampier's wife was a widow when he married her."

"Just the same he's been raised a Dampier," argued Harrison.

"It makes no difference," growled Holbrook. "We aren't going to ask him to join us."

"Aw, what's all the argument about?" complained a member of the group. "If Harrison don't want to fight for his rights there are plenty of us who do. What's your plan, Holbrook? You got any notions how to go about this thing—where to start?"

"Start at the head of it," outlined the storekeeper. "Tonight we will pay Gage Dampier a visit."

"Yuh mean—"

"No. We'll give him a warning first. To protect ourselves we'll dress in range clothes and wear bandanas over our faces. We will go in full force to let Dampier know the strength of our movement.

"You mean to let him know that every last one of you is in on it," corrected Harrison. "After he knows that he can start picking you off one by one."

"He won't try that," said Holbrook confidently. "He can't get away with murder."

"There was a murder last night and I bet you he gets away with it," said Harrison.

"That's why we're forming the vigilantes—so that he won't get away with it."

"All right," shrugged the old man. "But you won't scare Dampier or any of his men. If we had them outnumbered about twenty to one we might, but we haven't. Looks to me like we need a few gunmen ourselves before we can start working successfully on Dampier's crowd."

WHILE THIS CONTROVERSY was going on, Dampier was engaged in a clash with his nephew which had been threatening for weeks. News of Matt Gould's death had sent the younger man hurrying to Gage Dampier's house. That he was thoroughly aroused showed in the way he approached the older man without the usual preliminaries.

"Well?" he rasped, confronting the big cattleman. "What do you intend to do about Matt Gould's murder?"

Gage Dampier favored him with a long, meditative look.

"That's something for the law to handle, isn't it?" he said after a time.

"What law is there in this town outside of Dampier law?" retorted Cole.

"Why, Abe Hazen represents the law in Twin Peaks," drawled Dampier.

Cole's eyes flashed angrily, then his lip curled. "Let's be honest with each other, Gage," he said. "There's no law here except Dampier law. At least that is what I was brought up to believe. I kept my mouth shut and didn't question you when a lot of funny things went on around here, but now I'm having my say!"

He broke off, glared at the older man as if expecting a rebuke. None came. Dampier merely waited expectantly, his eyes on the flushed features of the younger man. This surprising attitude angered the younger Dampier still more.

"Well," he snapped. "Say something."

"You're having your say," reminded Gage.

"It's little enough what I have to say," barked Cole. "But I'm going to start doing things. This morning a man was found murdered. Maybe you're going to sit here in the sanctuary of your own home and do nothing, but I'm not. Blalock and his gang have run this town to suit themselves long enough. Now they're going."

"Are they?"

"I'm telling you they are," cried Cole, not liking the words or tone of voice. "I aim to *run* them out!"

Dampier nodded sagely. "In my younger days I was hot-headed like you, Cole," he said in a soft, modulated voice that was tinged with bitterness. "So was your father. We did things impulsively without taking into consideration the consequences. I've since learned that it isn't a good method to follow. What you sow you are bound to reap, and the harvest is often bitter."

Cole stared at him a long time, "I don't *sabe* you," he said at length, shaking his head. "I used to respect you even above my father, but the last couple months have changed all that. You're surly, moody, and you've take to drinking too heavy. Besides that I don't like the company you keep."

"Meaning who?" responded Dampier.

"You know well enough. Haze Blalock, Monte Malott and that crowd down in the Golden Eagle. What's the connection between you and that gang of outlaws?"

A flash of fire glinted in Dampier's eyes. "Well, Cole, I never considered it necessary to invite you to take charge of my personal affairs," he drawled softly, but there was a bite to his words. "I'll admit I'm an old man, but I'm still sane and capable enough."

"I'm beginning to doubt that," Cole fired back at him. "You spoke the truth when you said you're an old man. You've aged ten years in the last two months. But that's no excuse for trying to guzzle all the whiskey in Twin Peaks. It likewise isn't an excuse for a lot of other things you've done or haven't done lately. For a man who's supposed to have the pride in his family that you have, it strikes me peculiar that you're so willing to put up with conditions that are an open insult to both your wife and daughter. I'm talking about the Golden Eagle and the crowd of riff raff that hangs out there."

"Go on," said Dampier softly when Cole paused.

"There's been a lot of criticism of you around town," resumed Cole. "Most folks figured that you are being paid by Malott and his crowd to keep your hands off the Golden Eagle. But I know it isn't that. I've checked your bank account to make sure. It's something else and I aim to find out what."

"I SEE," SAID Dampier, a hunted look coming into his eyes. "It's got so you meddle in my money affairs, too, has it?" he bent forward in his chair, leveled a forefinger at the younger man. "Now you listen to me, Cole. Your father and I formed a partnership many years ago which lasted until he died without trouble originating on either side. Perhaps the answer for that lies in the fact that we made a ruling at the start which was never broken, mainly that all personal matters and habits were our own. He made no attempt to tell me how to live my life and I did no dictating to him. So far as money went, all profits and expenses were split, but beyond that our financial affairs were kept separate and private. Since two men cannot be at the head of an organization, I was installed as overseer and my decisions were never questioned. When Jesse died his half of the partnership was handed down to yourself and your mother and I expect you to abide by the same rulings."

Cole's ears turned a flaming red, his eyes shot sparks.

"That's putting it straight enough," he said. "Now I'll tell you a few things. I've never questioned your authority, nor have I tried to unseat you from your imaginary throne. Also, I did no delving into your private affairs or money matters until the banker told me that your deal with Haze Blalock looked strange to him." He paused for a second while his eyes bored into the older man's face. "You never sold that land to Blalock, Gage. You GAVE it to him. Not one cent of money changed hands on that deal."

Looking into those angry, accusing eyes Dampier knew that there was no use denying the charge.

"Suppose no money did change hands," he evaded. "It can still be a sale."

"Then why tell me it was a cash deal and draw five thousand dollars from your own account to put into mine?" accused Cole.

"It's possible I paid you outright rather than have you wait with me until the money was forthcoming," lied Dampier out of desperation as a man does who is being crowded into a corner.

"That's possible," admitted Cole grudgingly. "But not probable." He shook his head stubbornly. "The whole thing stinks to me. There's something rotten about it somewhere. You were acquainted with Haze Blalock before he came here. You can't deny that because your first meeting was witnessed by the bartender and several others in the old Golden Eagle."

"Have I denied it?" retorted the harried cowman.

"Then what's behind all this dirty work?" demanded Cole. "You've stalled the others, but I figure I've got a right to know. So have your wife and Rita. They're both curious and worried. They understand you no better than I do."

"But, unlike you, they still think I'm man enough to handle my own affairs," retorted Dampier.

"If it was just your affairs you could take them and be damned," barked Cole. "But the whole country is mixed up in this thing. It concerns everybody including your own family. Do you think it's been pleasant for Rita and her mother to see you slip from a respected cowman into a spineless old whiskey sot who is left garnering the hate of every man in town? They can't help but hear the stories that have been going around!"

"What stories?" questioned Dampier, his troubled features pulling into a frown.

"Don't stall with me, Gage," warned Cole. "You know what stories as well as I do. They say you are backing the Blalock crowd up in their move to bleed every decent man in town out of his earnings."

"That's the talk of fools," grated Dampier.

"Then why don't you put a stop to it?" countered Cole.

Dampier could only stare at him.

"What's the answer?" rasped Cole. "Has Blalock got you hog-tied? Has he got something on you? If he has, say so and the boys and I will gun Blalock and his gang clean out of the country!"

Dampier brightened for a second, then slumped back in

his chair like a drowning man who has grasped at a piece of flotsam and missed.

"You and the boys will do nothing of the kind," he stated firmly. "That's an order, not a suggestion. I know what I'm doing. I'll handle this thing in my own way and I'll handle it without you and the crew."

THE YOUNGER DAMPIER stared at him suspiciously. "Has Blalock got something on you?" he again demanded.

"No!" snapped the cowman.

Cole nodded slowly. "Then maybe it's true, what they've been saying," he muttered. "Maybe you did import Blalock and his gang of gunmen to molest the town people and help you get control of the whole valley. Is that right?"

Dampier met his accusing eyes squarely and said: "You're old enough to form your own opinions, Cole."

"They're forming fast," grated Cole. "If that is right, then, damn you, I'll help pull on the rope that strings you up, Gage."

"You've said plenty, Cole," warned the other.

"I know it and I'm through talking," declared Cole. "This is the split, Gage. From now on you go your way and I'll go mine, but the crew goes with me and the first thing we intend to do is run Blalock and his gang out of town. If you're in with them you better stay out of the way or you're liable to stop lead along with the rest of them."

"You young idiot!" cried Dampier, shooting up from his chair. "What chance do you suppose you'd have against that crowd down in the Golden Eagle?"

"None in daylight, maybe, but in the dark it might be a different story. At night is when we aim to strike and we aren't fools enough to walk right in and start shooting it out with them. We'll get at them in a different way. We'll whittle them down one at a time."

"I won't sanction anything like that," protested Dampier.

"Nobody's asking you to," retorted Cole. "Fact is you haven't got a damned thing to do with this, Gage. You've had your chance and you fell down on it. Now I'm going at things in my own way."

"A fool's way," snorted Dampier.

"A bloody way," corrected Cole. "But a sure one. Think that over."

He gave Dampier one long, puzzled stare and turning strode out of the room. Dampier slumped back into his chair. The fingers of one hand drummed nervously on top of his desk. The muscles in his face twitched and his eyes were troubled, unveiling the fear that was clutching at his heart. A myriad of thoughts paraded before his eyes bringing visions of Matt Gould's mutilated body which led the procession of others—his nephew, members of his crew.

A lump rose up in his throat and he coughed to clear it. A mental picture of his wife and daughter struggling to bear up under grief and disgrace brought a muffled groan to his lips. In desperation he pulled himself from his chair, made his way to a cabinet and got out bottle and glass which he carried back to the desk and again slumped into his chair.

The black-cloaked figure which had been hovering beneath the side window of Dampier's room that looked out on the wooded hillside, straightened, shot a quick glance in through the opening and in one quick, deft movement, stuck a leg over the sill. Hearing a faint noise Dampier stiffened in his chair, rolled his head sideways and as his eyes darted toward the side window they suddenly widened and his lips formed a low exclamation.

"The Masked Rider!"

"Your eyesight is good if your nerve isn't," drawled the muffled voice of the hooded man as he moved silently across the floor closer to the startled cowman.

When within five feet of the cowman he paused, seemed to be scrutinizing the pale face before him. Dampier continued to stare at the black figure as though trying to pierce the black hood and see the face behind it. When he saw that both of the masked man's hands were in sight and that neither contained a gun, he regained some of his composure.

"What are you doing in here?" he demanded.

"Looking over the wreck of a man who was once a pretty big noise in these parts," drawled The Masked Rider. He raised an arm to point a finger toward the bottle of whiskey. "That's a poor place to look for help, Dampier. When a man resorts to whiskey to stiffen his nerve he's either yellow or weak—maybe both."

COLOR STAINED DAMPIER'S cheeks. A flare of quick temper showed from his eyes, but he held it in check and with a movement that was meant to be careless he pushed the bottle and glass to one side.

"I don't know what's behind this visit but you're taking an awful chance being here in broad daylight," he said.

"I'm used to taking chances," replied the masked man. "I happened to overhear your conversation with your nephew."

"Eavesdropping is a nasty business," growled Dampier.

"Not nearly as bad as what you're mixed up in," retorted the other.

Dampier's gaze raked the masked face, then shifted.

"What do you want here?" he questioned sharply.

"I'm here to talk with you."

"I've got nothing to talk to you about."

"That's what you think. I'm thinking different. You know, Dampier, there are things about your town that interest me. A lot of things are kind of puzzling, including you."

"Me!"

"Un-hunh. I can't *sabe* why you're hell-bent on cutting your own throat."

"I don't believe I understand—"

"I think you do. Fact is I heard enough of what was said between you and your nephew to *know* that you do."

"How does anything my nephew said concern you?" flashed Dampier.

"Maybe it concerns me a lot."

"Well, it doesn't," declared Dampier, showing some of his old fire. "Now get out the same way you came in and keep going. If you don't I'll—"

"Sit right here and listen to what I've got to say," finished The Masked Rider. "A man in your boots shouldn't be so all-fired anxious to get rid of a man who might help you. Without appearing to brag I'm probably the one man who can help you, Dampier."

"What makes you think I need help?"

"I don't think it, I know it. It stands to reason that you're in some kind of a jam. No man with full control of all his faculties would do the things you've done unless he were in a tight spot. No man would work so blamed hard to cut his own throat unless there was some destructive force behind him pushing him on."

"I don't know a thing you're talking about," denied Dampier.

"Then listen close," the masked man's voice grew sharp as he lost patience. "When I came into town about three o'clock this morning I found a man down in the stable who had been murdered. Since then I've learned why he was murdered and a lot of other things about this town which have a mighty big bearing on you personally. Right now you're between the devil and the deep blue sea and you're afraid to jump either way. That's why you were fixing to blot out the picture with the whiskey in the bottle. But a thing like that is only temporary, Dampier. When you come out of it you find your troubles are still with you and have probably grown worse while you groveled around in the dregs of a quart of rotgut whiskey."

"You sound like a preacher," growled the cowman. "What in hell is it you want? Say it and then get out."

"All right," agreed the hooded man. "The decent element in Twin Peaks—men who were once your friends—are holding you responsible for Matt Gould's murder. They're going to do something about that, Dampier. They'll come to you and make demands. That's one side of it. Here's the other. Your nephew left here figuring like a lot of others that you imported Blalock and his gang to help you hog control of this whole valley. That's what he thinks. It's what most of the others think. They believe that is why Blalock, Jim Barr, Monte Malott and the rest of that crowd are here. Well, I don't."

"Indeed?" said Dampier with heavy sarcasm. "Well, I'm not interested in what you think."

"It might pay you to be interested, Dampier. You see, being an outlaw myself, I know who Blalock, Shine Tremaine, Jim Barr and the rest of them really are. They aren't just a gang of hard cases whose guns are for hire. They're bandits, Dampier. Train robbers, stick-up men. That's their business instead of hiring out their guns in a penny ante land grab. You didn't hire them to come here, they came of their own accord. At first I thought you were in with them hand and fist, but after hearing things and seeing things in this town I've decided that you're in with them because you're being *forced* in. Am I right?"

DAMPIER'S CHEEKS HAD paled under the revelation of the masked man's words.

"How do you know so much about Blalock and the others!" he questioned, scowling heavily.

"I get around," said The Rider and Dampier thought he detected a low chuckle behind the mask. "That crowd has got something on you, Dampier. What it is, I don't know, but it can't be big enough to make you sacrifice your standing in the community, the respect of your family and your own self respect. Nothing should make a man overlook those last two items. It likewise shouldn't be big enough to make you stand for cold-blooded murder and that's what the killing of Matt Gould amounts to. You've got a good idea who did that job and you know how to stop more killings. That isn't the question. It's a question whether you've got nerve enough—whether you're man enough to find yourself again and uphold the faith and respect folks hereabouts, including your family—once had in you."

The hard, candid words left Dampier shaken. The muscles of his face twitched nervously as emotions surged through him and when he spoke his voice was husky.

"That's funny talk coming from you—an outlaw," he said. "You should have been a preacher."

"I might have found life a heap easier," admitted the outlaw, "But I wouldn't have seen as much of it. I like you, Dampier. That's why I want to help you, but if you don't want help—"

"Is that why you came here—to help me?"

"No. I came here on the trail of a man—a cold-blooded killer of women and children. That's the sort of gang you've got here in Twin Peaks. That's the kind of coyotes you've chosen to throw in with against men who trusted you as a friend. In trying to save your neck from something you've only shoved it further into a noose. Your friends have turned against you and when the others decide that they've used you all they can they'll get rid of you." He paused a second to let his words sink in, then said: "Do you know that Blalock is dead?"

"Dead!" exclaimed Dampier.

"Plenty. I watched two men bury him last night. Could have stopped them, I guess, but I didn't know who they were or what they were doing until it was too late."

These words had a stunning effect on the cowman. He sat slumped in his chair, staring off into space. He failed to hear the door of the room open and see the figure of his daughter appear there, but the Masked Rider saw her and before the exclamation of surprise that formed on her lips could burst into sound he had stepped out through the window and faded in amongst the trees of the slope. When the girl, with a startled cry falling from her lips, ran to the window and peered out he was gone.

CHAPTER VI

DAMPIER BARGAINS

PETE COLBY REENTERED town from the direction of Gage Dampier's house, turned into the Golden Eagle and after a glance around climbed the stairs to the rooms above. Monte Malott opened the door to his knock and Pete Colby entered the room, an odd expression on his coarse features. Malott squinted at him.

"What's biting you?" he queried. "You look like you'd seen a ghost."

"I have," muttered Pete. "Only this one was black."

Malott's face pulled into a frown. "What are you talkin' about?"

"Ghosts," grunted Pete. "Jim around?"

"He an' the rest went out to the ranch. They aim to get things cleaned up out there. From now on we're all goin' to live in town up here above the Golden Eagle. How are things around town? Finding Gould kinda got 'em stirred up, didn't it?"

"Plenty," said Pete. "Lots of growlin' goin' on. That killin' ain't goin' to do us no good in this town."

"What's the odds?" shrugged Malott. "Talk is all it'll amount to."

"I ain't so sure. They're plenty stirred up an' might make trouble."

"Nothin' we can't handle," said Malott confidently.

"That's easy enough said," grunted Pete. "But if this gang around here ever did get together they'd have us outnumbered pretty bad an' might make it tough for us."

"Who's talkin' it up mostly? Holbrook?"

"Seems to be."

"Guess the lesson we gave him is wearin' off. I'll speak to Jim about it an' maybe we can give him another one tonight that will last. Take their leader away an' the rest will mill around like a band of sheep."

"It ain't these town dads I was thinkin' about so much."

"Who, then?"

"That Cole Dampier. He's fightin' the bit an' it wouldn't surprise me none if him an' old Gage had a split this mornin'. I seen him comin' down from Dampier's house an' he had a set to his jaw that was plumb determined. The look he gave me was plumb poisonous an' kinda give me the hunch that he's nursin' some ideas about gettin' his crew behind him an' comin' after us."

"Reckon old Gage will plug that move," said Malott. "Anyway, I'd hate like hell to think we couldn't handle a half dozen cowpokes."

"I've seen some that was pretty salty."

"Regular old crape hanger, ain'tcha," grinned Malott. "Any more calamity to spill before we go down an' have a drink?"

"Yeah," said Pete. "I seen somethin' up by Dampier's house that's got me thinkin'. After I seen Cole come down from there I figured to go up an' have a look around, just kinda out of curiosity. Worked around the slope an' come up from the back way an' what do yuh think I saw comin' out of a window?"

"Depends on what you've been drinkin'," grinned Malott.

"I'm plumb serious," Pete assured him. "I seen a feller dressed all in black step out through the winder an' take to the timber. Only got a glance at him 'fore he disappeared but it looked like he had a black hood or somethin' pulled over his head."

Malott laughed. Then suddenly he sobered, directed a hard look at the other man.

"A hood did you say!" he ejaculated. "What kind of clothes! Did he have a cape on that fell down around the feller's shoulders an' dropped about down to his knees."

"Yeah, that's it," nodded Pete. "Funny lookin' rig to see a man wearin' in broad daylight. I struck off through the timber figurin' to head him off, but I missed him."

"It's probably lucky for you yuh did," muttered Malott, a sickish pallor coming over his face. "Any idea who that feller was, Pete?"

"Told you I couldn't see his face."

"You thick-headed fool," cried the saloon man. "You never will see his face. That hooded man you seen was The Masked Rider."

PETE COLBY'S MOUTH sagged open. "Yuh mean the outlaw that—"

"Call him outlaw if yuh want," snapped Malott, his teeth grinding together. "But he's put the crimp in more gangs like ours than any half dozen law hounds living."

"Wonder what in hell he's doin' up here?" puzzled the surprised Pete.

"That's what I'm wondering. You say you seen him coming out of Dampier's house?"

"Yeah, out through the winder."

"Look like anybody was chasin' him or—"

"Didn't see nobody exceptin' Dampier's gal who come to the winder an' let out a kinda screech."

"Did you see Dampier?"

"No."

"Wonder what the hell?" puzzled Malott, a worried frown pulling wrinkles into his forehead. "How long ago was it you were up there?"

"Just come down from there."

"Then get out on the street again and see what you can find out. If he done anything to Dampier we'll soon know about it. That girl will come down here to spread the news if her old man is hurt. Do you know where Joe is?"

"He was down below when I come up."

"Tell him what you seen an' tell him to throw the leather on his horse an' get out to the ranch an' tell Jim and the others. This don't look any too good to me."

"This whole damn' country is beginnin' to look worse to me every day," growled Pete as he started for the door.

When he had gone Malott went down to the bar, poured himself a stiff drink and stepped out through the swinging doors of the saloon to lounge against the front of the building. He stood there for some little time smoking thoughtfully. His roving eyes saw Pete Colby moving about the town, they picked up Joe Colby as he rode fast out of town headed for the outlaw ranch and finally they settled on a Yaqui Indian who rode up to the hitch rack in front of the Golden Eagle. He watched while Blue Hawk dropped to the ground, tethered his blaze-faced sorrel and without looking to right or left, strode into the saloon with his lithe, cat-like stride.

Malott gave him no further heed as he continued to

watch things along the street. He saw Cole Dampier come down the plank walk on the opposite side, draw even with Henry Holbrook's store and there pause as he was hailed by somebody inside. Dampier hesitated a second and went in. As he remained there what seemed a long time Malott became curious, wished there was some way of learning what went on inside the store. Had he known it, Cole Dampier was at that moment angrily facing Holbrook and two other men.

"You lie, Holbrook, when you say Gage Dampier imported that gang of outlaws to help him get control of this valley," he was saying, biting his words off short. "Are you forgetting that it was Gage Dampier and my step-father who gave you the opportunity to come in here in the first place?"

"I'm forgetting nothing," retorted Holbrook. "Gage Dampier used to be a white man, but something has sure happened to him to change that. If he doesn't intend to grab this valley then why did he bring Blalock and those others in here?"

"He didn't bring them in."

"Then what are they doing here?"

"I don't know any more about that than you do, but Gage Dampier had nothing to do with their coming and he's not implicated in any of the things that have been happening. That I do know."

Holbrook nodded. "I understand, Cole," he said. "It's natural you should champion him, but you can't get around facts. I'm not slandering Gage Dampier. I'm merely telling you things as they are. You can't get around it, Cole. If Gage wasn't mixed up with that gang some way he would have run them out of here long ago."

"Maybe he had reasons for not doing anything before, but he's acting now," declared Cole.

"How do you know?"

"I just came from having a talk with him. You're not the only ones who have paid for the privilege of living in this town since Blalock and his outfit came. Gage Dampier has paid—more than all of you put together!"

Holbrook's eyes opened wide. "Why should he pay?"

"Why shouldn't he?" countered Cole.

"After all, he's just a man like the rest of you and he has a wife and daughter to protect the same as you have families. You've been blind is all. You thought because Gage Dampier has shouldered your troubles and helped you all every time help was needed that he was some sort of superman. Well, he isn't. Against a gang like Blalock's he's got no more chance than the rest of you. To avoid bloodshed and trouble he paid like the rest of you and because he did you criticized him and cursed him for doing the same thing you all have been doing.

"When you thought you were being hurt you ran to him with your troubles and because he didn't immediately take them upon his own shoulders you turned against him— said he was behind all the dirty work—was reaping all the profits. Do you figure that was any way to treat a man who has given you nothing but a square deal for twenty years? You gave no thought to what troubles he might be having. All you thought about were your own ills and when he couldn't cure them right off you damned him for a man who had turned against you. Well, he was man enough to stand up under hard criticism and in the face of it he is again going to come through for you. The murder of Matt

Gould changed everything. We start warring on Blalock's crowd tonight."

It was a long speech, well delivered in spite of the fact that many of the statements were bitter in Cole Dampier's mouth. He had sacrificed what he considered truth and honesty to pull Gage Dampier's name out of the mire. For Gage he had little sympathy, but there were Rita and her mother to be considered and the Dampier name.

His words were convincing, perhaps more so than he had hoped for. Holbrook's face fired up, his whole demeanor changed.

"If we've made a mistake nobody is more willing to apologize than I am," he asserted. "If Gage is ready to move against those outlaws we're all behind him."

"Don't want you," said Cole crisply. "Too many will only be in the way. You're all men with families and you better stay out of this."

"But we're all ready," protested Holbrook. "We're organized."

"For what—a slaughter," growled Cole. "Talking of running that gang out of town and doing it is two different things, Holbrook. They're all gunmen and they'll fight. Don't ever fool yourself on that score. They'll fight till they drop and before they drop they'll make their bullets count."

"Then how do you expect to go about it?"

"Hit when and where they aren't looking for it," explained Cole. "I've got six good men behind me. That's enough. We start things rolling tonight."

"What about us?"

"Sit tight and do nothing and then you won't get hurt, and if you don't get hurt your families can't blame Gage Dampier for your deaths. We've never asked anybody to fight our battles and we aren't starting now, Holbrook. Remember that and keep out of this. I don't want your blood on my hands."

With that he whirled and stalked out of the store, leaving the men grouped there, staring after him dumbfounded.

Malott finally turned back into the Golden Eagle. His eyes roved over the barroom, fell on Blue Hawk sitting alone by a table close to the stairway leading to the rooms above. An almost empty bottle stood on the table in front of the Indian and he sat there staring off into space and perhaps seeing nothing. Malott moved up to the bar where the apron-clad dispenser of drinks gave him a wide grin, jerking his head toward Blue Hawk.

"In town on a periodical," he said. "When them Yaquis drink, they get it down fast."

Mallot nodded. "They sometimes go on the hog when they get fired up. If he starts anything chuck him out."

"Sure," grinned the other. "But I'm thinkin' when he gets loaded up he'll crawl off in a corner an' sleep it off. That's what they generally do."

THAT ENDED THE conversation and, due to other things more pressing, both men soon forgot all about the Indian who sat alone. But Blue Hawk didn't forget them. He had come here to learn things by suggestion of The Masked Rider whom he had met that morning back in the hills, and he was choosing the best way he knew to see and hear things without arousing suspicion. Except for one short drink, none of the missing contents of the bottle had gone down his throat, yet he presently assumed the role of a man who has imbibed too freely. His body sagged toward the table and his head bowed drowsily, so that his chin rested on his chest. Twice he tried to recover himself, shake the haze from his dulled senses, then finally gave up to the consuming urge of sleep. His head dropped down to his arms, which were resting atop the table, and he passed out in a drunken stupor.

Gage Dampier came down the trail leading to his house on the hill, struck the head end of the main street and started down it, looking to neither right or left. Men watched him pass, and turned to stare after him. Cole Dampier's words were still fresh in their ears and when Gage turned into the Golden Eagle, it appeared his declarations were being borne out. Gage Dampier was going into action and he was starting by bearding the outlaws in their own den.

Inside the saloon Dampier shot a glance around and strode up to the bar.

"Where's Jim Barr?" he demanded of the bartender.

"Out to the ranch," answered the man. He reached for a bottle. "Same brand?"

"No," snapped Dampier. "I'm here on business. Is Malott around?"

"Right behind yuh," said the bartender and Dampier turned to see the saloon man approaching.

A smile was on Malott's face. "How are yuh, Gage?" he greeted genially.

"I want to talk in private," said Dampier.

Malott sobered, gave him a quick look and jerked his head toward the stairway.

"Come on upstairs," he said and led the way.

Once behind the closed doors of Malott's rooms Dampier lost no time in voicing the reason for his visit.

"Who's at the head of this crowd since Blalock was put out of the way?" he demanded.

Malott stared at the blunt words. "What do yuh mean—since Blalock was put out of the way?"

"Don't bother to stall with me, Malott," retorted the cowman. "I know all about Blalock. He was killed and buried last night. All that is nothing to me. What I want to know is who's bossing his gang now?"

"Jim Barr," replied Malott readily enough after he realized that there was nothing to be gained by being evasive with the old cowman who, strangely enough, seemed suddenly to have turned belligerent.

"Thought so," nodded Dampier. "I suppose that's the reason Matt Gould was slaughtered last night. Barr always was a cold-blooded devil." His blue eyes scorched the saloon man's face. "You damn fools," he swore. "Don't you know that you can't get away with a killing like that?"

"Don't know anything about it except what I've heard," lied the other.

"Quit stalling and remember who you're talking to," snorted the cowman. "The whole town is up in arms."

"What's the odds?" shrugged Malott. "We've got arms, too, if it comes to that, but it won't. Ain't nobody in town got guts enough to organize that pack."

"The killing of Matt Gould is going to organize them," warned Dampier. "That was murder uncalled for in its rottenest sense. It marks the end of your stay in this town."

Malott's mean little eyes bored into his face. "You figurin' to kick over the traces, Dampier?" he questioned silkily.

"I am," asserted Dampier, "I won't be a party to murder. I was a fool for letting you come in here in the first place."

"Then you don't give a damn if folks hereabouts know what kind of a gent you are?"

"Not if keeping it a secret means the murder of innocent men."

"MAYBE YOU BETTER pull in your horns," suggested Malott. "You're in this too deep to start givin' orders now. There was a time maybe when folks hereabouts wouldn't have believed what Blalock or Jim Barr could tell about you, but they'd believe anything now. In case you don't know it the whole town hates your guts, Dampier. Your only chance is to stay on the side you picked in the first place."

Dampier shook his head stubbornly. "I'm through. You tell Jim Barr he can talk and be damned."

"What he can tell might sink you, Dampier."

"Then he'll sink himself along with me."

"Yeah, but he ain't got any family to worry about. It ain't just yourself you've got to think about, Dampier. You ain't been hurt—yet. Neither has your family."

The eyes of the two men clashed. Dampier's clouded and shifted from the smirking gaze of the other's. Realizing he had his man on the run Malott pushed his point. "If you're smart you'll pull in your neck an' let Jim Barr run this town to suit himself for a while."

"And how is that?"

"Peaceful as long as the natives don't get careless."

"What do you hope to gain by staying here?"

"Some easy money while we're getting lined up on another job," said Malott frankly.

"Money, eh?"

"Sure. Blalock had a lot of crazy notions in his head about stayin' here an' bein' a rancher, but the rest of us ain't bothered that way. Money is what we want."

"And you intend to get it out of the people of this town?"

"Sure, if they've got enough. If they ain't we might knock over your bank before we leave."

Dampier seemed to be struck by an amusing thought. He smiled, then actually laughed.

"I'm afraid you wouldn't gain much by blowing the bank," he lied smoothly. "People around here haven't been asleep. Except just what they've needed for running expenses they've withdrawn all of their money from this bank and shipped it down to Yucca. The bank here is doing practically no business. Its doors are open only as a blind. I doubt if you could get a thousand dollars out of it right now."

Malott made a poor attempt at covering his surprise and disappointment.

"Is that the truth?" he rasped harshly.

It was a bald-faced lie on Dampier's part, yet he lied further to confirm it without batting an eye.

"Why should I lie?" he said.

Malott stared at him and cursed feelingly.

"You see you've got nothing to gain by staying here," went on Dampier.

"Oh yes we have," contradicted the other. "We've got you. You're going to dig up some money, Dampier. Plenty of it."

"I have none here."

"Then get some," rasped the other.

"Your threats don't scare me," retorted Dampier. "My life means nothing to me any more. I'm ready to use it to rid this town of the blight that I brought down upon it."

"Yeah?" sneered Malott. "Don't forget you've got a wife and daughter we can work on."

"You wouldn't dare do that."

"There ain't anything Jim Barr won't do once he makes up his mind," retorted Malott. "You ain't dealing with Blalock now, Dampier. Either dig up some money—a lot of it—or we'll see how much you figure your daughter is worth!"

Hot, uncontrolled anger rushed to Dampier's head and burst. He forgot all about the gun under his coat, gave no thought to the danger of his surroundings. All he saw was Monte Malott's leering face and the neck below it and with clawed hands he made a lunge for that neck.

"Damn you— I'll choke the life out of you!" he cried.

So sudden was the assault that the big cowman was upon him before Malott knew what was coming. He writhed in the grasp of the other, tried desperately to get his gun out. It did clear leather, then one of Dampier's hands clamped on the smaller man's wrist. The gun dropped to the floor and was kicked to one side.

FIGHTING WITH ALL the foul tactics known to him Malott struggled against the hand that was clawing at his throat. His breath was shut off, his mouth hung open as he gasped vainly for air. Then one of his knees came up and crashed into the cowman's groin. Dampier's fingers relaxed, slipped from Malott's throat and the saloon man stepped back out of his grasp sucking great gasps of air into his tortured lungs.

Dampier was bent over, his head faint, his stomach churning from the foul blow he had received. And though his own head was reeling dizzily Malott's hand flashed up to a scabbard which nestled low on the back of his neck beneath his coat. The long blade of a knife flashed through the air and drove hard into Dampier's back.

The cowman groaned, sagged closer to the floor and as the saloon man raised the knife to slash again he heard a noise and whirled to see Blue Hawk come in through the door and lunge toward him. The Indian, under the guise of drunkenness, had slipped unseen up the stairs and had been listening at the door.

His own knife was out and as Malott whirled to attack him, Blue Hawk slipped under the saloon man's vicious swing and with an upward stroke that went true to the heart he sank home his own blade. Malott sagged, started to pitch to the floor, but was caught by Blue Hawk who lowered him gently.

The Indian's next thought was of Dampier. He moved quickly to the cowman, caught hold of him and started pulling him to his feet.

"Quick, *señor*," he said in a hoarse whisper. "We must be gone from here. Those below may have heard and will be up here upon us."

Dampier stared at him, his face wracked with pain. Blue Hawk caught hold of his coat, stripped it down his back and inspected the knife wound. It was in a bad spot and was bleeding freely. With sure, deft movements while Dampier groaned with the pain of it, Blue Hawk bunched the cowman's under-shirt and forced it into the gaping slash, when satisfied he had checked the flow of blood temporarily he helped Dampier on with his coat and again issued warning.

"You must have courage, *señor*," he said. "To be found here means death to us both. Can you walk?"

"I guess so," muttered Dampier.

"Then do it, *señor*. Go out of here and down those stairs as if nothing has happened. With care you may reach your home where you can send for a doctor to give the wound proper attention."

Dampier nodded as a man who is in a daze. "Who are you?" he muttered thickly.

"It is of no importance, *señor.* We waste time."

"How are you going to get out of here?" was Dampier's next question.

"Through the window, *señor.*"

"That's a long drop," grunted the cowman.

"I have fallen further, *señor.* Now go."

Without further questioning Dampier went into the hall and started to descend the stairs. Blue Hawk watched after him until the crown of Dampier's hat disappeared below the stair landing, then went to the back window, opened it and slid his body out. He hung by his hands from the sill a second, then dropped straight down, hitting the ground limp. A quick glance around quieted his fears that he might have been seen and with characteristic stealth he made his way back from the buildings and finally slipped unseen into the concealing growth of timber on the slope.

Still sick at the stomach, his head feeling strangely light, Gage Dampier made a successful exit from the Golden Eagle and strode with slow, uncertain stride up the street. As distance fell behind him his knees became shaky and a weariness that was almost overpowering came over him. But he kept his eyes glued to his home on the hill. Grim determination fought off his body weakness, carried him through to the house where, with strict orders to keep his plight a secret, he sent his daughter for the doctor. Then he closed his eyes wearily, and knew that the show-down had come.

CHAPTER VII

FIRST BLOOD

I T WAS DUSK when Jim Barr, Shine Tremaine, Joe Colby and the man known as Llano rode back toward their ranch headquarters. They were in good spirits for they had just sold the cattle that Gage Dampier had given them to the ranchers in the lower end of the valley.

"Seven fifty a head ain't much for critters, but it's all velvet seein' they didn't cost us nothin' in the first place," Jim Barr was saying.

"Reckon this ends our days of cow hazin'," observed Llano. "From now on we stay at the Golden Eagle along with Monte. He's been gettin' all the best of it. Kemper oughta have our stuff bunched together at the house time we get there."

"What's that!" suddenly exclaimed Jim Barr.

They had broken out in an open spot and above the tops of the trees ahead of them they saw a red glow that reflected against a column of smoke.

"Fire!" ejaculated Joe Colby. "Hell, that's where the shack is!"

"Come on," ordered Jim Barr and raked his horse with spurs.

With a thunder of hoofs, their horses weaving in and out among the trees, they ate up the intervening mile and arrived on the scene with drawn guns and startled eyes which gazed down on the smoldering ruins of what had once been their cabin. There, back from the glow, they exchanged glances.

"Wonder what the hell—"puzzled Llano.

"Wait here an'keep me covered,"ordered Jim Barr dropping off his horse and advancing closer to the glowing embers on foot.

He circled the smoking heap, disappeared from view. Then the others heard his voice ring out sharply.

"Come here!"

Circling the fire they saw him standing just inside the ring of light staring at a big black oak. They followed his gaze, blinked and stared again at the body of Buck Kemper swaying eerily from a limb of the tree. Sight of the hanged man brought on a long, heavy silence that was broken finally when Jim Barr ground out an oath.

"Damn their souls,"he grated. "It's fight they want, is it?"

"I didn't think they had the guts," grunted Shine Tremaine.

"Maybe killin' that stable feller kinda stirred them up," said Llano. "Who'd ever thought that gang of old goats in town would get up nerve enough to pull a thing like this?"

"Wasn't them," growled Jim Barr. "I'll lay ten to one it was young Dampier. I've figured right along we could look for trouble from that gent. I should have sunk a slug in him a long time ago."

He walked over to the tree, got out his knife and cut the rope that held the body of Buck Kemper suspended in mid-air. As it dropped with a thud to the ground he walked over to it and stooped for an examination.

"Ain't a bullet hole in him," he pronounced. "They just naturally strung him up. Ain't been done over a half hour."

"How many in Dampier's crew?" growled Shine Tremaine.

"Six besides young Dampier."

"Them ain't no odds. Let's go get 'em."

"An' run into an ambush," sneered Jim Barr. "If they've got nerve enough to do this they ain't goin' to be caught asleep. They'll be waitin' for us to show up."

"What's the line-up then?"

"Give 'em some of their own medicine."

"Yuh mean burn 'em out?"

"Shore. Not that this shack meant a damn thing to us, but settin' fire to that ranch will give 'em somethin' to think about an' while they're doin' it we'll start whittlin' down where it'll do the most good. You—Llano and Joe take yourselves a ride around to Dampier's spread and see how many fires you can get goin'. Work around wide so yuh strike below the buildings about a quarter mile off, where you'll find a couple stacks of hay. Fire them stacks first. That'll pull young Dampier an' the crew away from the buildings and the rest will be easy."

"EASY SAID," GRUMBLED Joe Colby. "That's wide open country around that outfit for a couple miles each way."

"Ain't over a half mile from the house to the hills an' timber," corrected Jim Barr. "Anyway, it'll be dark—plumb dark 'fore you get around there. I ain't askin' yuh to hunt a fight. Don't want that—yet. Just fire things up an' then hit a high lope for the hills an' work yore way back to town. Shine an' me will push on in with Buck's carcass an' be waitin' for yuh at the Golden Eagle. I'm kinda anxious to see what's comin' off in town."

"Somethin', probably," said Colby. "You ain't forgettin' what I told yuh about The Masked Rider bein' in the country, are yuh."

"No," rasped Jim Barr. "I figured jumpin' Dampier about that would keep till tonight. Can't figure what The Rider would be doin' in Dampier's house unless he come here huntin' the old man. Anyway, Monte will probably know all about it. If things wasn't goin' right I reckon he'd have sent Pete out here before this. I'm kinda honin' to meet up with The Rider. He was the cause of a couple friends of mine gettin' killed an' I ain't forgot. All I want is one shot at that duck."

"Yuh better make shore it's a good one," said Llano dryly. "That *hombre* is lightning. The man don't live who can blow a shot with him an' stand on his feet to tell about it."

"My bullets ain't particular how a gent like him is standin' when they hit him," growled Jim Barr. "But standin' here chewin' the rag about it ain't gettin' us nowhere. You an' Joe get goin', Llano. You, Shine, see if you can locate Buck's hoss. If yuh can't we'll have to fork mine double an' tote Buck on yores."

CHAPTER VIII

FIGHTING WITH FIRE

A LL DURING THE afternoon The Masked Rider had
been scouting the country in the vicinity of the
outlaw ranch. Through his binoculars he had watched the
movements of the outlaws. He saw them as they drove the
herd of cattle down to the lower end of the valley, there to
be peddled. He kept the glasses trained particularly long
on the swarthy, coarse face of Shine Tremaine and when
he lowered them he seemed to have reached a conclusion
that brought a narrowing around his eyes and a tension
on his lips.

He refrained from following them as they drove the
cattle straight down the valley, being content to stay
concealed within the timber on the slopes. He was still
lingering within less than a mile of the outlaw shack when
at heavy dusk he saw the first glow that told him the place
had been fired. Puzzled, he started working his way toward
the shack and by so doing ran almost squarely into Cole
Dampier and his riders who were loping away from the
scene.

He heard them coming just in time to bend his horse
off the trail into a thick cluster of brush. They went past
in single file close enough so that he could make out their
shapes yet far enough away that he could not recognize
any of them in the poor light. His curiosity aroused, he

led his horse back to the trail, swung into the saddle and fell into their wake.

Even before they led him to the Dampier ranch he had guessed their identity, but he kept following along wondering what their next move against the outlaws was to be. Arrived at the ranch he rode in a wide circle waiting to see whether they intended to put up there for the night or whether they would ride out again, possibly to Twin Peaks with the grim determination of aroused range men to further the move they had started.

BUT COLE DAMPIER intended no further moves that night. With his six men he rode into the ranch yard and after tolling off two of them to stand guard he jerked saddle, turned his horse into the corral and trooped with the other four men into the bunkhouse.

"That's one job well done," he told them when they were sprawled on bunks, cigarets going. "When Jim Barr and the others get back from running off those cows they've got a surprise in store for them. When they see Kemper's body swinging there maybe they'll decide we mean business."

"Yeah, an' maybe they'll decide to come here an' smoke us out," hazarded one of the waddies.

"They've got no way of knowing who did it," discounted Cole. "Anyway, I don't think they're ready to come here and declare open war. But if they should, we're ready. They can't take us by surprise. I told the boys to keep riding circle on the buildings."

"All I'm worryin' about now is how soon cookie can get some grub rassled together now that he knows we're back," grinned a youngish puncher. "My belly's plumb vacant."

"I'll shake him up a little," said Dampier and faded out the door to cross over to the cook house.

It was probably five minutes later when a yell split the air, followed by two hasty shots. Dampier, startled, froze to his tracks a second, then clawing for his gun bolted out the door. Outside he brought up short, shot a glance toward the barn and then a startled one past the building a quarter of a mile beyond where one of the twin haystacks belched flame and smoke as the fire took hold of it.

Others had also seen, for a voice rang out on the night air.

"My Gawd! They've fired the hay!"

There was a mad scramble for riding gear and the corral.

"Range wide and work in toward the fire," ordered Dampier, as he crowded in among the men. "That way anybody still around there will be outlined against the blaze. To hell with the hay. No chance of saving that, but take care of your skins."

In the space of a few minutes they were mounted and thundering away in the dark. Cole Dampier had covered possibly half the distance to the burning stacks when sane reasoning—reasoning that should have taken hold of him in the first place—now reached out to assert itself. As the thought struck him, he hauled in his horse, whirled him around and sent him racing back toward the buildings.

He could see it now. Firing the hay stacks was just a blind to pull the whole crew away from the buildings and it had almost succeeded. His hunch proved correct when, pounding into the ranch yard, he saw a dancing flame burst into being at one corner of the house as dry tinder responded to a lighted match. The shadowy figure of a man moved hastily back from the glow of it and Dampier brought up his gun and fired.

Hardly had the echo of the shot died away when an

answering shot came screaming at him out of the darkness. The heavy bullet struck Dampier in the shoulder, rocked him back in the saddle and the startled side jump of his horse sent him crashing to the ground. The fall stunned him for the moment. He lay there dazed, but faintly—it seemed far away—came the rolling thunder of shots.

DAMPIER CRAWLED TO a sitting posture, shook his head to clear it, then drew back as the rolling pound of fast-driving hoofs bore down upon him. It seemed for a second that they would trample him, but at the last moment they sheared off. Against the light thrown out by the fire which still burned at the corner of the house, he saw a charging black horse go thundering by, and bent forward in the saddle was a rider dressed in black whose cape billowed and strung out behind him.

"The Masked Rider." Dampier's lips formed the words.

Too dumbfounded to do anything but stare he watched as the hooded man pulled his horse to a sliding halt, dropped clear of the saddle and started stamping out the flames. It seemed only a moment that he was there before the crackling embers were scattered harmlessly about and he was mounted again.

Dampier came to life then. "Wait!" he yelled.

But his words took no effect. The Masked Rider was gone. Dampier heard the pounding hoofs fade away in the night. They were replaced by others as his men came pounding up.

"What happened!" ejaculated one of them, dropping to Dampier's side.

"I don't know," replied Dampier. "It dawned on me that firing those stacks was a trick to get us away from the house. I turned back and when I got here I saw a man starting a blaze there by the corner. I cut loose at him and he winged me. The jolt must have knocked me out of the saddle and dazed me. It seemed that I heard some more shooting and then a horse was bearing down on me. It cleared me and pulled up by the fire and there in the light I saw The Masked Rider beat out the flames. I yelled at him, but he climbed his horse and cleared out."

"Must have been doin' the shootin' then," said the cowboy. "I counted four shots. No chance of savin' the hay. When we heard the shootin' we come foggin' it back here. Figure there's any more of them around?"

"They'd probably be pouring lead into us if there were," said Dampier.

One of the men who had stepped over close to the corner of the house let out an exclamation.

"Hey, there's a dead man over here!"

"Who is it?" questioned Dampier.

"Wait a minute," he struck a match, cupped it in his hand so that the glow reflected on the dead man's face and called out: "It's Joe Colby. Couple bullet holes in him close together. Good shootin', Cole."

"Wasn't me," denied Cole. "Must have been The Masked Rider who got him."

"Wonder what that gent is doin' around here?"

"I don't know but I guess I can thank him for saving my skin," said Dampier. "Likewise the house. Another couple minutes and it would have been going up in smoke."

"How bad you hit?" queried one of them.

"Flesh wound is all but it's bleeding plenty. Guess I better get inside where one of you boys can help me plug it up. Rest of you better ride herd on the buildings for a while in case any of that gang come back."

"Except me," spoke up one. "I'll fog it into town after the doc."

CHAPTER IX

THE COYOTE'S WAIL

The Masked Rider had bent his black stallion toward Twin Peaks. He knew that one of the Blalock gang rode ahead of him for he had jumped them both there by the house and only one had been left behind.

Quick decisions were flashing through his mind. It looked as if open warfare was to be declared in this country and if such was the case better that he concluded the mission that he was here on and get out.

He was within a half mile of the town, off the road and picking his way through open country when he heard the long, lonesome wail of a coyote. He pulled up the black and listened. Minutes dragged by and then again came the call. A grin came over his face and lifting the hood he cupped his hands to his mouth and sent an echoing call wafting over the night air.

The cry was answered and a few minutes later hoofbeats told him of the approach of a horse.

" 'Tis you, *señor?*" came the low, guttural voice of Blue Hawk.

"Alive and in the flesh," was the masked man's jovial reply. "What are you doing out here?"

"Seeking you, *señor*. All afternoon I have looked. Many times I call."

"I've been covering a lot of country," said the masked man. "Right now I'm coming from the Dampier ranch where I had the good fortune to help young Dampier and keep the house from burning. What's new in Twin Peaks? Any news?"

"Yes, and I'm afraid it is bad, *señor*. I was forced to kill."

"Kill!" ejaculated the masked man, "Whom?"

"The one known as Malott."

"Malott, eh? Hm-mm. Well, I reckon he had it coming, Hawk."

"That he did, my friend," and Blue Hawk went on to tell what had taken place in town. "I had followed up the stairs and had been listening at the door," he explained, "I broke into the room just as Malott raised the knife for the finishing stroke. He saw me and turned the blade my way. I could do no other than use my own, *señor*."

"Course not," agreed The Rider. "How badly is Dampier hurt?"

"He is sore wounded, *señor*. I did what I could to stop the flow of blood and bade him go to his home."

"Did he make it?"

"That I do not know. I had my own escape to make and it was out through the rear window. It is as you thought, *señor*. Dampier has been forced against his will to do things he wouldn't have otherwise done."

"Got something on him, have they?"

"So it seems."

"You learn what it was?"

"It was not mentioned. I know only that it is something from his past life, *señor*, something that he does not want the *señora* Dampier and the *señorita* to know."

"Then what was the fight about? Was Dampier beginning to buck them?"

"The *señor* Dampier was rebelling. He told Malott that he would be under their control no longer. It was then that Malott threatened to do bodily harm to the *señorita*."

"And Dampier jumped him, eh?"

"*Sí.*"

"Hm-mm. Maybe a certain little conversation Dampier had this morning did some good then—put some fight in him."

"**BUT HE IS** in no condition to fight now, *señor. Quien sabe?* Perhaps he is dead."

"We'll be finding out about that. I hope he's still on his feet. I like that man, Hawk. He's been fighting a losing battle against long odds. It is our duty to help him, Hawk."

"Always you borrow trouble, *señor*," repeated the Indian, with a smile. "Is not the mission we came here on enough without seeking more?"

"Kind of an old fraud, aren't you?" accused the hooded man. "Nobody asked you to come to Dampier's rescue when you knifed Monte Malott. Anyway, this all dovetails together, Hawk. The man we seek is one of the Blalock gang."

"You have seen him, then?"

"Can't be sure about that, but I've seen a man who sure fits the description. When I face him I shall know. Today I had the opportunity to look a long time at his face. Likewise I was close enough to hear his name called. Shine Tremaine, I believe, is the one who kills women and children, Hawk, and the rest of that gang is no better. If it means fighting them all to get to Tremaine, then we'll fight them. They're wrecking a good man's life and they are a scourge on the whole country. Come on, Hawk. We've got business in Twin Peaks."

"We cannot go together, *señor.*"

"No. We split at the edge of town. You ride on in, tie your horse handy and keep a sharp lookout for developments."

"And you, *señor?*"

"I'll go directly to Dampier's house. Before going further in this I want to learn something and see how badly he is hurt. Come on. We waste time here."

They raked spurs and the ground faded under their fast moving mounts.

CHAPTER X

BULLETS CROSS

JIM BARR AND Shine Tremaine rode up to the rear of the Golden Eagle, dropped to the ground and untied the ropes that bound the body of Buck Kemper to Tremaine's saddle. Carrying the body between them they entered the back room of the saloon, dropped the body into a corner and pushed open the door leading into the bar-room. Except for one or two habitual drunks the barroom was strangely empty.

As they moved up to the lower end of the bar Hutch Keever, the bartender, came hurrying toward them from the front of the room.

"Did you see Pete?" he asked, excitement showing in his face.

"Pete—" repeated Jim Barr looking closely at Keever. "No. What's the stir?"

"Then you ain't heard that Monte is dead?"

Both men stared.

"Keep talkin'," said Jim Barr.

"Didn't discover it till around supper time. Soon as I did I sent Pete out to tell yuh."

"Get to the point," rasped Barr. "What happened to Monte?"

"Gage Dampier killed him," blurted Keever. "Used a knife on him."

"What happened to Dampier?"

"Nothin' far as I know. He walked outa here like nothin' had happened."

"What were you doin'? Where was Pete?"

"Pete was out roamin' the town an' I was here, but hell, how should I know Monte had been knifed? Like I said, Dampier walked outa here just like nothin' had happened."

"Go on," advised Barr. "Get it all out of yore system."

"Well, there ain't much I know exceptin' Dampier come in here an' him an' Monte went upstairs. After a while Dampier come down an' walked out just like nothin' had happened. I didn't think nothin' about it. When Monte didn't show up I thought maybe he had some figurin' to do up in his room an' let it go at that. It wasn't till Pete come in here lookin' for him that we found him dead."

"What makes you so sure Dampier done it?"

"Dampier was the only one that was up there with him that I know of. He musta done it."

"Dampier ain't a knife man," snapped Barr. "He'd have used his gun."

"Maybe he figured a gun would make too much noise," spoke up Shine Tremaine. "I *sabe* how that is. There's times when I find a knife comes in kinda handy."

"Looked to me like Monte got stuck with his own knife," said Keever. "It was layin' on the floor beside him an' it was bloody."

"Must have been a fight then," puzzled Barr. "Didn't yuh hear any noise?"

"Don't recall none."

"What did Dampier come down here for? Did he say?"

"Not to me."

"Well, get some whiskey down here," snapped Barr. "I need a drink. Somebody strung up Buck Kemper this evenin'. We fetched him in an' he's layin' in the back room now."

"Strung him up!" exclaimed Keever, his face paling.

"Yeah—by the neck," growled Barr. "What's the matter? Feel a rope around yores?"

"It looks like this place is gettin' kinda unhealthy," retorted Keever. "Now that yuh mention it I do kinda feel a rope."

"Losin' yore nerve?" sneered Tremaine.

"No more than you," fired back Keever. "But I don't see no hell of a lot of percentage in stayin' here. Yuh figure we got this town sewed' up an' what happens? First Monte gets bumped off an' then Buck. Besides that The Masked Rider is here. That *hombre* bein' here is enough to make me start lookin' around for a campin' spot one hell of a long ways from here."

"CLOSE YORE TRAP," snarled Jim Barr. "Part of what you say is maybe true enough, but we ain't goin' to let a couple killings stampede us. So far they've had it their way. Now we're goin' to start an' before we're finished we'll pay back them killings with interest."

"Where are the other boys?" questioned Keever.

"Llano an' Joe are out firing the Dampier ranch. They'll be ridin' in, soon. Reckon when Pete don't find us he'll have sense enough to come back here. With Monte an' Buck gone there's six of us left—enough to take this town apart."

"Maybe, but not enough to stand off all these natives if they once get nerve enough to start somethin'."

"They won't," growled Jim Barr. "Leastways not before we can clean up an' get out. Tonight's the night. When the boys get in, the first place we start is the bank. If we get enough out of that, we slope, pronto. If we don't we'll work over the rest of the town."

"That sounds like sense," seconded Keever.

"Then get things in shape here. While we're waitin' for the others to get here I'm goin' up to Dampier's house. I got a little somethin' to settle up with that gent."

"Need any help?" offered Tremaine.

Jim Barr eyed him coldly. "No. This is one killin' I can do myself."

He poured another drink, tossed it off and taking a hitch on his gun belt, turned and strode out of the saloon. He walked boldly up the street and turned into the path leading up to Dampier's house making no pretense at keeping his destination a secret. The orange glow of oil lamps shone from the windows of the big house, but Jim Barr made no attempt to reconnoiter the ground before striding boldly up on the front porch and pounding on the door. His was a cold determination and his mind was made up.

Footsteps approached the door from the inside and Rita Dampier opened it to peer out at the tall outlaw. Recognition crossed her features, but with it no pleasure at seeing him there.

"Yore father here?" questioned Jim Barr.

"Yes, but he is very sick," the girl told him. "The doctor said that he is not to be bothered."

"What's the matter with him?" growled Barr.

She shook her head. "I don't know. He got hurt some-way."

"That's too bad," muttered Barr. "Then I reckon I better see him."

"But you can't," protested Rita Dampier.

"It's important what I've got to tell him," said Barr. "He'll want to see me all right. Fact is this little visit of mine is going to make a big change in Gage Dampier."

The frown left her face, her eyes lighted hopefully.

"Does it concern what has been worrying him lately?" she asked.

"I reckon it does," replied Barr callously. "He won't have no more worries when I get done talkin' to him."

"Oh, I wish I could believe that," she cried. Then she frowned again. "But I don't know whether I should let you see him or not. He's awfully sick."

"I won't be long," promised Barr.

With this assurance she finally relented, asked him into the house and led the way to Gage Dampier's bedroom which lay just off the den. As she ushered him into the room she would have lingered, but Barr took hold of the door knob, moved his bulk toward her and gently crowded her out into the hallway.

"This is kinda private," he told her softly. "I'm kinda sure yore dad would want it that way."

SHE PAUSED THERE a moment skeptically, then as the door closed she retreated down the hallway. Dampier's face had been turned away from the door when Jim Barr entered. Now, sensing that someone was in the room with him, he turned his head slowly to face the door. His eyes widened, a low exclamation fell from his lips.

"You!" he said. "What are you doing here, Barr?"

"You should know that," said the outlaw moving closer

to the bed. He paused to gaze down into Dampier's white, drawn face. "I hear you had a run-in with Monte today, Gage. By the looks of things he must have stuck you before you turned the knife on him."

"Can't you even let a man die in peace?" groaned the cowman weakly.

"Don't tell me yo're dyin'," the outlaw feigned surprise.

Dampier moistened his lips with his tongue, wiped them with a handkerchief and held up the red stain for Barr to see.

"Blood," he murmured. "What I didn't lose getting here is going into my right lung. Stopped now, but it'll start again. What do you want?"

Barr's eyes hardened. "I came here to kill you, Dampier—wipe you off this earth, but hell, there ain't no enjoyment in killin' a man that's half dead already."

"Damned inconsiderate of me to die on you, isn't it?" said Dampier bitterly. "You might find it tough sledding here after I'm gone."

"Don't reckon we will. Yuh see we aim to pull outa here tonight."

"Too bad you didn't do that before I got in this fix," retorted Dampier. A faint smile formed on his lips. "Well, anyway, I can die knowing that you gambled on me and lost."

"Not entirely," contradicted Barr. "We aim to get paid well for our stay here before we leave an' likewise I aim to let folks know what kinda gent had 'em fooled for twenty years. Killin' yuh wouldn't give me no satisfaction, now, but tellin' what I know will, Dampier."

Dampier's teeth clicked together. A new fire came into his eyes.

"I'm dying, Barr," he cried. "Isn't that enough to satisfy your rotten, devilish mind?"

"It ain't," retorted Barr coldly. "Monte Malott is dead, Dampier. You killed him."

"Then isn't my going enough to satisfy your code of an eye for an eye?"

"No," snapped the outlaw. "I ain't forgot how you run out on me an' Blalock after them two jobs twenty years ago. You an' yore brother sloped leavin' me an' Blalock to hold the sack."

"That's a lie," said Dampier. "It was everybody for himself after that second train hold-up. You and Blalock were hell-bent for holing up in the hills close around there and Jess an' I wanted to put some distance behind us. You made your own choice."

"I reckon you figure it was our choice to lay in the pen five long years till they got around to deciding that they never had evidence enough to convict us in the first place an' paroled us," snarled Barr. "I ain't forgot them five years, Dampier. While me an' Haze were doin' time you an' yore brother were up here in this valley livin' easy on money you got from stickin' up a train. Quite a name you built up for yoreself around here. Wonder what folks will say when they find out you got yore start by stickin' up a couple trains! Wonder what they'll say when they find out there's a couple killings hangin' over yore head?"

"They're not on my head," cried Dampier with such force that a crimson foam bubbled on his lips. "You killed both of those men, Barr. You killed them needlessly. My regret is that I wasn't able to give them back their lives. I paid back every cent of the money we took—not only Jesse's and my share but also yours and Blalock's. Fifteen years we worked for that money, Barr. Then I took it down and expressed it from a small town in Arizona."

"SUPPOSE YUH FIGURED that squared yuh up with the express company, eh?" sneered Barr.

"They probably wouldn't look at it that way, but at least it helped clear up my conscience," replied Dampier.

"But yo're still scared to let folks know about it."

"For my part, no. You can't hurt me in the least by telling what you know, Barr. A dead man has no feeling. All you would do is hurt my wife and daughter and I don't believe even you are low enough to wreak vengeance on them for something they had no part in."

"No, I've got nothing against them, Dampier," the outlaw assured him. "But it's through them that I can get at you. You ain't dead yet an' before yuh go you're goin' to have a chance to lay here an' sweat blood knowin' that yore wife an' kid know they've got an outlaw in the family. An' they're goin' to know it. I aim to tell them. I aim to let the whole damn' town know it because I know what it'll do to that mind of yores, Dampier. It'll get yuh, Dampier. Damn' you, you'll know what agony is before yuh drop off!"

Blind rage surged to Dampier's head. All reason dropped away from him leaving only the one desperate desire—to reach Jim Barr's throat. Strength seemed to come to him, flow warmly through his veins and with a cry of rage he gathered his weakened body for the one desperate effort and bolted from the bed.

Nimble as a cat Jim Barr stepped back. His hand dropped to his gun. He waited there like a poised hawk, watching the futile efforts of his prey. Dampier struck the floor, wavered dizzily, then threw himself forward with every ounce of his failing strength. Again Jim Barr moved back. His gun cleared leather.

"Hold it, Barr!"

The voice cut the room like a knife. Barr whirled toward the window and saw framed there the figure of The Masked Rider. The half-drawn gun in Barr's hand came up, spat flame and lead. But a split second before it spoke The Masked Rider's heavy .45 belched its death-dealing missile. It struck the tall outlaw as his thumb slipped from the hammer and the shock was enough to throw the bullet wide. Instead of finding The Masked Rider's heart it ripped through his cloak under the left arm pit and went singing harmlessly on its way.

As Jim Barr sagged to the floor The Masked Rider stepped in through the window and without even glancing at the fallen outlaw stepped around to the place on the floor where Gage Dampier's final lunge had carried him. The cowman lay on his side, his eyes closed, blood trickling down from his mouth. The masked man needed but the one glance at him to know that he was fast dying in the grip of a hemorrhage.

He stooped, gathered the old man in his arms and carried him to the bed. Dampier's eyes opened, stared up at him trying hard to pierce the glaze that was already forming.

"Too—late," he gasped, his words thick with blood. "You—heard!"

The masked man nodded. "It will never go any farther than me, Dampier," he promised. "Jim is dead."

If Dampier heard he gave no sign as his eyes closed and his chin sagged low on his chest. The door of the room burst open and two startled, frightened women in night clothes came in, threw one wild glance around and dashed to the bed. Realizing that he could do nothing further here The Masked Rider faded back from them, moved quickly toward the window.

Both women were pleading with the old cowman to talk. Suddenly the older one screamed and The Rider knew that she had discovered that Gage Dampier was dead. Taking hold of Jim Barr's body The Rider boosted him out through the window and started to follow. Rita Dampier, kneeling at the bed beside her dead father, turned weakly, supporting herself with one hand on the floor. She pointed a trembling finger at the booted legs of Jim Barr, sliding out of the window.

"Did—he—" she stammered.

"No. Your father tried to get up and brought on a hemorrhage," he told her. "It was Barr and me doing the shooting."

With that he slipped outside and faded away in the dark, reloading his gun as he went. He had not come to Gage Dampier's house expecting to kill anybody yet that was the way the die had been cast and he had no regrets. It was either the outlaw or himself and he had been a fraction of a second faster. The fraction that not only meant his life or Barr's, but that kept hid the secret that allowed the advent of this horde.

CHAPTER XI

THE SILENT KNIFE

L LANO CAME RACING into town and hurried into the Golden Eagle shortly after Jim Barr had left the place.

"Where's Jim?" he inquired of Shine Tremaine.

"Gone up to Dampier's house. What's the stir?"

"Hell's poppin'," exclaimed Llano. "The Masked Rider has bought a hand in this game an'—I'm tellin' yuh straight—I'm gettin' outa here, pronto."

Tremaine's eyes narrowed. "Suppose he has," he growled. "Ain't goin' to let one man stampede yuh, are you? What come off at the ranch? Yuh look plumb scared."

"Then my looks ain't lyin'," declared Llano. "I don't mind fightin' but The Rider ain't human. Lead ain't never stopped him yet. Me an' Joe had fired the stacks an' was gettin' fixed to fire the house when Cole Dampier come up. Joe unlimbered on him an' I guess he got him. About that time The Rider bought a hand in it an' all hell busted loose. He got Joe an' was lookin' to get me when I lined out. I got a hunch he follered me to town an' is here now."

"Then I reckon we better scatter out an' get him."

"Don't be a fool," said Llano. "He ain't doin' this alone, else what was he doin' out at Dampier's ranch. I tell you old Gage Dampier hired that duck to come in here an' with The Rider leading them this whole damn town is goin' to start after us. They'll foller a feller like The Rider where they wouldn't nobody else. We ain't got a chance once they come after us."

A flicker passed across Tremaine's eyes. He turned them toward the door as Pete Colby came into the saloon.

"Where in hell did you get to?" were Pete's first words.

"Never mind that now," snapped Tremaine. "The Masked Rider just knocked off Joe. Llano thinks he's in town now. Go up to Dampier's house an' tell Jim he better get back down here."

As Pete started to open his mouth for further questions Tremaine cut him off.

"Do like I tell yuh," he barked. "You get over to the stable, Llano, an' get the best hosses over there an' fetch up behind. If we got to make a break we want somethin' we can get away fast on."

Pete left and was half way up the hill toward Dampier's house when the shooting broke out. He stopped dead in his tracks a second, then yanked his gun and started up the hill on the run, bending wide off the trail before he got to the house. He saw The Masked Rider step out of the bedroom window and start toward him on the run. Thinking that he had been seen Pete Colby cut loose with two shots, then wheeled and raced back toward the town.

The bullets missed taking effect on the masked man, but they came close enough to arouse quick ire. He unloosed a shot at the sound the blundering outlaw made and swung off in hot pursuit. The bullet only served to add momentum to Pete Colby's pace. As he turned into the main street he threw one last spiteful bullet back over his shoulder, then with legs pumping ran for his life toward the Golden Eagle.

He was only a few jumps from the saloon when the hooded man entered the street. Throwing two bullets at the fleeing figure, The Masked Rider raced down the street in his wake, determined to crowd things to a finish now that the ball had started rolling.

News of Gage Dampier's mysterious wound had started talk amongst the townspeople. They had seen him go into the Golden Eagle and come out again and they arrived at the logical conclusion that somebody inside the Golden Eagle had stabbed him. Cole Dampier had told them that Gage Dampier was going to start action against the outlaws so Holbrook and the others figured Dampier had received the wound while carrying out this action. Sentiment, which had been drawing away from the old cowman suddenly reversed itself and switched toward him. By dark the townspeople were organized and ready to back any move that Dampier chose to make.

THE SHOOTING AT Dampier's house startled them into life. The following shooting between Pete Colby and The Masked Rider brought them into the street. Colby, they recognized as one of the men they wanted to rid the town of and just as the outlaw made a final lunge for the saloon doors, a bullet from one of their rifles dropped him.

"There's another!" bellowed somebody as The Masked Rider came into view.

"The Masked Rider!" exclaimed another voice.

"He's an outlaw, ain't he?" cried the first speaker. "Let him have it!"

Running toward them the masked man heard the words and without trying to question their judgment he veered off the plank walk and made a dive for an opening between two buildings. Bullets whisked around him like angry hornets. He held his fire and bent every effort toward trying to find cover. A bullet seared his ribs, another thudded into the side of the building close to his head. Then he was lost to their view and running back toward the alleyway in the rear of the buildings.

"The Golden Eagle!" screamed a voice. "Let's wipe it out! Burn the place down! Clean it out for good!"

This new outcry turned the mob's thoughts from The Masked Rider and directed them toward the saloon. With threats and cries they boiled down the street—a raving mob gripped with the lust to kill and ruin.

The Rider bent toward the rear of the Golden Eagle as he reached the alley. He saw a man come tearing out the back door, pause uncertainly for a second, then race away in the opposite direction. What The Rider failed to see was the shadowy figure of Shine Tremaine as the short outlaw, hearing his approach, flattened himself against the side of the building standing next to the Golden Eagle.

Bent only on reaching the Golden Eagle before others could dart out the rear door The Rider came even with the building where Tremaine stood concealed and without glancing to right or left started to pass. Forsaking his noisy gun for the quieter knife, Shine Tremaine raised the blade and lunged toward the masked man's back. On the opposite side of the alley there was a flash of movement. An arm swung, cold steel cut through the air and went true to its mark in the throat of the stocky outlaw.

With a gurgling gasp, Tremaine faltered, staggered sideways and fell, one hand tearing at that knife in his throat. The Rider whirled, but before his gun could speak Blue Hawk's guttural voice cried a low warning.

"Do not shoot, *señor*. It will bring them back here and that we must avoid if we are to leave this mad town."

"Hawk!" exclaimed the masked man.

"*Si, señor*. The short one—the man we sought, señor, is no more. We go now."

"Thanks, Hawk," muttered The Rider. "Once again I owe you my life. I was acting like a blind fool."

"Then be the foolish one no longer," advised the Indian. He stooped, retrieved his knife and wiping the blade clean, sheathed it. "Where is it you left your horse, *señor?*"

"Up by Dampier's house."

"Then we go. Mine, too, is tied back in the trees. Our task here is finished. We ride."

"Yeah, I reckon we do, Hawk," agreed The Rider. "That mob out front is crazy. Before they have finished they will purge the town clean. Dampier is dead. He paid for his sins, but at least his family won't have to suffer for them."

"And the killer of women and children is no more, *señor*. Come, we ride."

Together they made their way to their horses, to take up again the trail of many pauses but no ending.